When Tatum's daydreams of murder become a reality, all fingers point to her.

In Tatum Wood's opinion, murdering her boss on a daily basis within the safety of her thoughts is better than therapy. Until he takes a swan dive off a building and all evidence points to her. Thank goodness she has Franklin Reed. Her mysterious, overprotective and drop-dead gorgeous coworker is all too eager to play hero. With two attacks in her building and her stalker with a penchant for roses, Franklin's injection into her life couldn't have come at a better time.

As Tatum and Franklin scramble to discover who's behind the murder, secrets are unearthed that question his motives...as well as his identity.

Books by Krissy Daniels

Aflame
How to Kill Your Boss - An Erotic Love Story

Published by Kensington Publishing Corporation

How to Kill Your Boss - An Erotic Love Story

Krissy Daniels

LYRICAL PRESS
Kensington Publishing Corp.
www.kensingtonbooks.com

Lyrical Press books are published by
Kensington Publishing Corp. 119 West 40th Street New York, NY 10018

All Kensington titles, imprints, and distributed lines are available at special quantity discounts for bulk purchases for sales promotion, premiums, fund-raising, and educational or institutional use.

Special book excerpts or customized printings can also be created to fit specific needs. For details, write or phone the office of the Kensington Special Sales Manager:
Kensington Publishing Corp.
119 West 40th Street
New York, NY 10018
Attn. Special Sales Department. Phone: 1-800-221-2647.

Kensington and the K logo Reg. U.S. Pat. & TM Off.
Lyrical Press and the L logo are trademarks of Kensington Publishing Corp.

First Electronic Edition: July 2014
eISBN-13: 978-1-61650-623-0
eISBN-10: 1-61650-623-7

First Print Edition: July 2014
ISBN-13: 978-1-61650-624-7
ISBN-10: 1-61650-624-5

Printed in the United States of America

For lovers, dreamers, and victims of douchebag bosses everywhere.

Acknowledgements

To Sexy Boyfriend and the babies that are too amazing to be mine, your patience was pushed well beyond the limit with this book and you all handled it like the champs you are. Thank you for being my rock every single day.

Corinne, thank you for putting up with me yet again. I have a newfound respect for nipples and their proper place in the literary world. You make me laugh even when I know you want to slap some sense into me. You are a gem.

Renee, thank you once again for a kick-ass cover and for all you do.

Thanks to Lyrical Press/Kensington and all who work their tooshies off behind the scenes.

Jen. From ant hills to paradise pond, Tubbs Hill streakers to pervs with a penchant for toes, you have been and always will be the Laverne to my Shirley, the Red and White to my Apple Blue. I could write a thousand adventures starring you.

Mom, Share-Bear, Auntie Lia. My heart is bursting with the love I have for you, the three women I admire most in this world. You're my calm in a sea of crazy.

And above all, thank you dear sweet baby Jesus for the narcissistic boss who inspired this story. His lies, greed and psychotic personality made for one hell of an exercise in patience, humility, and human decency in general. Thank you for the chain of events that led me here. I didn't understand at the time, but I'm starting to get it now.

Chapter 1

As the blade sliced through the taught flesh of his stretched neck, revenge was not first and foremost on my mind. When his skin spread wide, revealing the muscles and tendons beneath, I didn't squirm, gag, or suffer the slightest queasiness. Warm blood stained his shirt, sprayed across his desk, coated the leafy fern nestled in the sunny corner of his office, yet my thoughts were not filled with twisted delusions of hell yeah, he's getting what he deserves.

No.

Rocky road ice cream called my name.

Mmm. My stomach rumbled. The closest grocery store was what, five minutes away? What time was it? I used the back of his shirt to wipe his blood off my watch. He wouldn't mind. He was dead. Oh good, only nine-thirty. Plenty of time to get to the store before it closed.

When I released my death grip on the over-gelled, wiry hair rooted in Wallace Cruse's head, he slumped and fell with a hard thud against the hickory desk. I cringed, thinking that must hurt, then remembered he couldn't feel a thing.

Before dropping the weapon, I contemplated stabbing him in the back a few times, for dramatic effect. But time was-a-tickin' and I needed my chocolate fix.

"Tatum!" he called out to me with his whiney voice.

What? I killed him. Dead people didn't talk. Raising my arms over my head, I double-fisted the thick handle of the butcher knife, and with all my might pounded into a less-than-spectacular back. His flesh offered no resistance, and at first, I thought I'd missed.

So I did it again.

A pillow stuffed with pudding would've put up a better fight. The blade sunk with no effort right through flesh and bones. Its tip stuck in the edge of the desk.

Interesting. Apparently, his physical form was as weak as his moral character....

"Tatum. Tatum!" A whack to my backside snapped me back to reality. "Stop daydreaming. You gotta see this." Nan looped an arm around mine and guided me down the hall. Stacy, from accounting, shushed us from the opposite side of Wallace's door. Acting the love-sick teen, she wiggled her eyebrows, pointed toward his office, fanned her face, and swooned.

Whoever came to visit had to be hair-curling hot, because Stacy never behaved in such a manner. Maybe Wallace had landed a celebrity client again. Last time that happened, a fresh buzz of excitement chased the doldrums clean out of the place for weeks. We were long overdue for another shot of team spirit adrenaline.

"Tatum!" Wallace screeched with his high-pitched tenor. Thank goodness Nan still held my arm, because I jumped hard enough to hit the ceiling.

I'd yet to ascertain why, when Wallace needed me, he didn't use the phone like everyone else. Nan's office was one door down in the opposite direction, yet he'd never screamed for her. I'd stopped trying to figure him out years ago. Instead of dwelling on the three thousand reasons I hated my boss, I fantasy-killed him at least once a day.

A chill swept over me when I stepped through the threshold. The room, as always, reeked of overpriced hair and hand lotion. Only this time, a familiar scent tickled my nose. Dad's cologne. I choked back the emotion that gelled in my throat. Even though he'd been dead for three years, I still welled with sentiment every time I caught a whiff of the beloved fragrance.

Wallace wore his fake smile and sat, back straight, hands clasped atop his desk. The unnatural gesture wasn't for my benefit, but the person seated across from him.

"Ah, Miss Wood." He lifted his chin to me. "Mr. Reed is joining our team today. Would you make sure Steve's old office is stocked with the essentials?"

Miss Wood? Oh, jeez. Wallace only addressed me with the formal title when he needed to crank the schmooze dial to high for important clients—important meaning filthy, stinking rich. This guy wasn't a client, so why the show?

"Of course." I didn't add "Mr. Cruse" to my reply because I knew it'd knock him down a peg. "I'll be happy to." Although I'd known Wallace my whole life, he insisted I call him Mr. Cruse at work, a request only made after my father passed. Dad would've slapped him silly for being so high-handed with me.

"Anything else?" I asked, sugar-coating my words.

The man seated in front of me turned his head my direction, revealing what had incited the tizzy outside. Yikes! One glance and my heart pitter-pattered. Those eyes. Electric blue, so striking I took a step back. I snapped my attention to Wallace. His ugly I could handle, and it didn't make me drool.

A deep, intoxicating voice rose from the man before me. "Aren't you going to introduce us?" he asked, and turned to face Wallace once again.

My boss' eyebrows crinkled. "Of course. Miss Wood is our receptionist. Tatum, this is Franklin Reed." Wallace cleared his throat, a nervous gesture he'd developed over the years. It only happened when he lied, or as he called it, embellished the truth, to land clients. "I've hired an auditor to tighten up productivity around here."

Franklin rose, lithe and poised, from the chair. He turned toward me and offered a hand. "Pleasure to meet you, Tate."

Tate? Nobody had called me Tate except for my father and the assholes in high school. One-Date Tate. The nickname and the curse followed me like a perpetual shadow through most of my academic career.

I would've corrected him, but when his full mug came into view, my tongue curled up and shriveled. My IQ dropped thirty points. Again, I quickly averted my eyes. I had no choice. They threatened to pop out of my head. There was good looking and there was gorgeous. This man played in a league that put both of them to shame. "Pleasure meeting you," I managed to stutter. With grace comparable to a drunk college freshman, I grasped his hand and gave it one good shake. When I tried to pull away, he squeezed tighter and caressed a thumb across my knuckles.

My girlie parts twitched. No joke. I needed to leave before I left a puddle of desire on the floor between my feet. Holy cow, I'd never been affected in such a way.

"The pleasure is all mine." Franklin tilted his head as if inviting me to admire him.

Nope. No way. I would not look into those eyes again. The way my body reacted, I'd end up sprawled naked across the desk with a rose between my teeth. I reclaimed my hand and jetted through the door.

Chapter 2

"Enjoy your tea, Mr. Cruse. I added something special this time." I winked, smiled, and tucked the empty vial of Kill-Wallace-Cocktail I'd whipped up earlier that morning back into the pocket of my slacks.

He lifted the delicate cup to his lips and drew a long drink. "Delicious."

"I'm happy you like it."

"Why are you standing there? Get back to work. Receptionists are a dime a dozen. Without a college degree, you're lucky to have this job."

I leaned my shoulder against his doorframe and crossed my arms. Anticipation was half the fun.

Wallace slapped his hands on the desk. "I said, get back—" He coughed. Blood spewed down his chin.

"How ya feeling, Wallace?" I asked with mock concern. "You don't look so hot."

Mr. Cruse looked at me, confusion distorting his features. He opened and closed his mouth, unable to form a word.

I swelled with pride when the first crimson tear trickled down his cheek. I tapped my finger to the corner of my own eye. "You've got a little something there," I teased.

Wallace wiped at his face and released a garbled screamed when he spied blood on his hand.

I tapped my ear. "There, too."

He grabbed a tissue and dabbed first one lobe, then the other. He coughed again and choked on the fluid that bubbled up his throat.

I smiled. Oh, it made my spirits soar to watch him suffer....

A sharp pinch in the fleshy meat at the back of my arm jolted me from my fantasy. "Tate, where were you just now?" Franklin whispered in my ear, sending delicious tickles down my neck. "Boss-man is freaking out.

Stop daydreaming and get your ass in there. Cruse needs his daily ego stroke."

I smacked his arm. The firm muscle underneath his suit jacket didn't give in the slightest. Franklin had only been with Cruse Investigations for two months, but we were already the best of buddies. Office buds, anyway. His title? Auditor. His duties? Make the women drool, and some of the men, too, while gathering data and compiling reports to make the company more efficient, or something like that. For reasons I failed to comprehend, he spent more time in my office than his own.

He was obscenely gorgeous and smarter than sin. I didn't understand his career choice. Franklin should've been CEO of a Fortune 500 company, modeling, starring in movies, or traveling the world—anything. He didn't belong in our cozy office. He was a bright star that needed space to shine.

Not that I would dare complain.

I grabbed my bold and obnoxious, red-rimmed glasses. I loved them, partly because they made me feel like a naughty librarian, but mostly because Wallace hated them. He'd mentioned, on more than one occasion, how ridiculous I looked, so I only wore them when I knew we'd be sharing the same space. I didn't need glasses. My vision was near perfect. They were merely a fashion statement and a fun tool I used to get under the skin of a man I detested.

"Good afternoon, Mr. Cruse." I smiled, tilted my head in a sweet, shy fashion, and flashed my baby blues. Bastard didn't even look up from his desk.

"I'm leaving for New York tomorrow. Is the MacKenzie file ready? I need it ASAP, hoping to head out early today." Wallace scribbled on a piece of paper and got back to typing on one of the four desktops occupying his workspace. Who, in God's name, needed four PCs? Apparently Wallace did, as he made a point to use each of them every time I, or anybody else for that matter, visited his office. Perhaps to remind us he was king of the castle and important enough to need four computers.

I rolled my eyes, confident he wouldn't see. Wallace rarely looked me in the face. It'd been that way since I was a child. Mom used to tell me it was because kids made him nervous. What was his excuse now? I was all grown up. Did he feel guilty for the direction he'd steered my father's company? Could he feel the animosity I harbored? Perhaps it was because I'd known him my whole life and could see through his bullshit.

Wallace had recently turned the big five-o. Looked it, too, despite wasted efforts and thousands of dollars spent on beauty products for men. Everything about him, from his Italian shoes to his waxed brows, screamed mid-life crisis. The few wrinkles he owned were polished, buffed, and shined, nice and pretty. I wanted to laugh.

Girlie-man. It wasn't natural for a guy to primp the way he did.

"The file is ready. I'll grab it."

He looked up with dark, beady eyes. His gaze traveled the length of my body, starting with my red pumps. I'd been visually violated by the time his perusal rested on my breasts. When I inhaled, drawing my clingy white blouse tighter across my chest, his eyes bulged. Was I flirting? Of course not—just breathing, and hopefully torturing him a bit. He'd always acted nervous around me, especially when puberty settled in my chest and grew like a tumor—or two. When I'd hit my teens, Dad stopped bringing Wallace around as much. My father was amazing like that. My great protector.

I turned, regretting my wardrobe choice. The tight gray pencil skirt accentuated my ample derriere. I was sure I heard a moan as I walked away.

Franklin waited for me outside Wallace's door and followed me back to my office. He wore a cheesy grin that didn't match the dark shadows lurking behind his glare. When I leaned over my desk to grab the MacKenzie file, he moaned, too, mimicking Wallace.

"Knock it off," I scolded, unable to stifle a giggle.

"You are so bad." He pinched the bridge of my glasses, wiggled them up and down, and made a tisk, tisk sound.

"I know. It's so much fun, and he's so damned easy," I whispered.

Franklin turned to leave and I stole a moment, as I often did, to appreciate his spectacular physique. He was average height and solid. I'd never seen him without a suit on, but good gracious, he filled it out so well, I could only imagine what glorious surprises hid underneath. He wore his dark blond hair trim, almost shaved, and carried himself with an air of confidence few men could pull off without coming across as cocky pricks. The man, far too beautiful to be stuck in our boring, average company, didn't belong. I couldn't put my finger on it, but something about him didn't fit.

Before disappearing down the hall, he turned and gripped the doorframe. "Hey, Tate."

Ooh, that voice. Husky, deep, and exactly what you wanted to hear in the throes of passion. Powerful, commanding, *I'm gonna take you places you've never imagined.* My insides warmed in response. Delicious, naughty images swirled in my brain.

"Yeah?" I asked with an embarrassing enthusiasm.

"Have a beer with me after work."

Well, that was unexpected. He didn't ask, nor was it a command. The timbre powering his words made it sound more like a sinful temptation dangled in front of my nose.

"What's the occasion?" I asked.

"Wallace will be gone an entire week."

"That's certainly worth celebrating, isn't it? Except I can't. I've got plans already." Yes, it was a date with my television. No, I would not admit that to him. Besides, inter-office dating was strictly prohibited. As much as I would love a date with such a fine male specimen, my spirit couldn't take a rejection. The man took amazing to a whole new level, and I wasn't about to set myself up for heartbreak of that magnitude.

His throaty laugh nearly made my clothes fall off in wanton misbehavior. "Tate, have a drink with me. It's not a date, just friends hanging out. I promise, I'll have you home in time for your show."

"How did you know? Are you a secret agent or something?" I asked, half joking. How he knew my plans for curling up on the couch for some quality time with Antony Starr, I'd never know. I might have mentioned it to Franklin once during one of our many conversations. Not that I would remember. My brain matter turned into over cooked oatmeal whenever I was in touching distance of the man.

Could I handle a drink or two with the enigmatic Franklin without my panties self combusting? Probably not. It would be good to bust free of my shell. One drink couldn't hurt. Besides, he was so far out of my league, any chance of sparks between us fizzled before leaving my vivid imagination. Franklin was spectacular. Office eye candy.

Me? Well, my mother used to say, "That Tatum, she's short on stature, large on spunk, and amazingly average." Mom had it right. That was me in a nutshell.

"Sure, why not." Maybe I'd get to see a different side of the mystery man. Maybe he'd be loose-lipped after a few drinks and spill his deepest, darkest secrets.

* * * *

My cheeks burned hot as Hades. My heart pounded loud and relentless in my ears. I shut down my computer, tucked my cell into my purse and pushed my chair in. Pulled it out, brushed lint off the seat, and pushed it back. Hmm… Maybe I should dust my workspace. Hadn't done that in over a week. Trash needed to be dumped, floor could use a quick vacuum….

"Tatum, get out of here." Nan peeked her head around the corner. "You have a hot man waiting to get drunk with you. I can't believe you're still hanging around." Nan Cummings, the office manager, was by far my favorite coworker, aside from uber-sexy Franklin. The woman read me like an open book. Acted more like a beloved aunt than a coworker. Kept the employees in check and the place running smoothly. Basically, she was Wallace's bitch, did everything for him, and always with a smile on her face.

It was creepy, her knowledge of everybody's business. Like now, she knew I was meeting Franklin for a drink. I hadn't said a word to anyone. Franklin wouldn't have spilled the beans. His lips were tighter than a pair of Spanx. But she knew, and it didn't bother me. Gossip was not her style.

I smiled. "I'm going, I'm going." I straightened my skirt and inspected my blouse. "Should I go home and change first?"

"No, my dear. You're perfect." Wise eyes scrutinized me. "Why so nervous?"

I sighed and slumped my shoulders. "I don't know. It's not a date. It's just, I've never hung out with him outside of work. You should come with me. Then it would feel less date-y, you know?"

Her laugh warmed my heart and calmed my nerves. "Sorry sister, you're on your own tonight. I've got plans." She glanced towards Wallace's door then back to me. "Now, get going so I can lock up and get on with my evening."

Nan was the only other person Wallace trusted with a key, which meant she arrived before anyone in the morning and couldn't leave until each of us cleared out. Never once, in my four years at the firm, did I hear her complain about it.

With an exaggerated sigh, I threw my handbag over my shoulder, blew her a kiss and headed out for my non-date.

I managed to make the short drive, traipse across the gravel parking lot, and through the heavy wooden door of the Malted Maven in my stilettos without breaking a bone. All grace left my person the moment I spied Franklin sitting in the corner, suit jacket open, tie gone, top two buttons of his gray shirt undone. My ankles turned to wet noodles and my legs buckled under me. Thank the good Lord above there was a barstool within reach to steady myself.

He'd chosen a table in the darkest corner of the bar with a half-moon, vinyl booth seat. Legs crossed at the ankles, arms stretched across the top of the chair, GQ model if ever I'd seen one. When his eyes met mine, he wasted no time scooting from his perch to meet me where I stood clinging to the barstool like a crutch.

"There's my girl. I thought you were blowing me off. What took so long?" With the firmness I expected, he grabbed my elbow and walked me to the table.

Oh, busywork, passing time, trying to build courage to meet the sexiest man alive on this non-date. "Nan caught me on my way out. She needed to talk," I lied. "Sorry I made you wait." Not the least bit sorry he waited.

Franklin waited, hands in his pockets, urbane as a well-bred English gentleman, while I scooted into the seat, a feat not easily accomplished with the lack of give in my skirt. He slid in and didn't stop until his thigh rested against mine. Holy hot tamale, nothing but trouble rolled my way. His body heat melted the tension from mere nanoseconds before. I inhaled slow and deep and let the faint scent of lemon-lime, lavender, and orange fill my nostrils. Fresh and clean. He always smelled so damned good.

"Gendarme?" I asked.

His chuckle made my blood pump harder. "It is. How'd you know?"

"It was the only cologne my father wore. Not because it was his favorite, but because it was the only one that didn't irritate my mother's allergies." Dad was my hero. I loved everything about him, the way he smelled, dressed, every wrinkle that graced his face. He spent his life making Mom and me feel cherished.

Franklin held my gaze just to the point of uncomfortable before blinking away and gesturing to the woman behind the bar. "Dark beer, right?"

Damn. The bastard was good. "Yes. The darker the better."

The waitress bee-lined it toward our table, never taking her eyes off Franklin. Her shiny black hair bounced behind in a high pony, pulled tight, no doubt to show off her numerous ear piercings. When she reached our table, she studied me with a perplexed curiosity. Her black mascara and smudged eyeliner looked like it'd been applied by a professional, specifically to frame a set of deep jade eyes. With her skull and crossbone belt, she rocked the sexy, tough-bitch vibe.

"Hey Frankie, what'll it be?" she asked. Her perky voice didn't come close to matching the biker-chic facade.

Franklin pulled a fifty from his pocket and handed it to her. "We're going dark tonight, love. Surprise us."

Love? My cheeks warmed and my vision narrowed. Shit. Was I jealous? The barmaid was long and lean, like a yoga master. Not an ounce of fluff anywhere on her over-toned body. I shot flaming daggers at her ass as she walked away.

I turned to face the man sitting next to me. "Frankie?" No way was he a Frankie.

"Nickname. She gives one to all the regulars." His words traveled through my ears, yet I barely registered what he said. He inspected me, raking the length of my body with a hungry leer like he couldn't decide which lump to take a bite out of first.

"Oh, you come here often?" I looked around the room. Everything was dark; the wood of the tables and chairs, the carved ornate bar, wrought iron mirrors, sconces, even the paintings hung sparsely about were dismal in color and theme. I liked the ambiance. Was I out of my element? Without a doubt, but I'd stuck to the safe confines of my daily routine for too long. Change was good. Especially when it involved Franklin. "I have to say, Franklin Reed, you don't strike me as the type who'd frequent a place like this."

"Why not, Tatum Wood? Please, do tell." His smirk begged to be kissed. I licked my lips and wondered what he tasted like. Man-oh-man, I hadn't even started drinking yet. I could tell it was going to be a long night.

"That's easy. You're Mister Armani Suit, suave, professional. Not gloom and doom, emo, goth, whatever the bejeezers this place is."

Small dimples formed at the corners of his mouth. "I live upstairs, and did you just say bejeezers?"

"I did, Frankie."

Oh. He lived upstairs. Interesting. A hummingbird hatched, then grew in my belly and jetted around, desperate to be set free.

Miss Dark-and-Dangerous came back with our beers. Bubbly suds spilled over the glasses before she even set them down. Franklin made quick work of mopping up the mess. I got busy giving myself a foam mustache. Damn, that was good brew.

"Hey, wait," Franklin admonished me. "Toast, first." Fisting his mug, he raised his drink and tapped mine, halting my attempt at a second swig. "Here's to a week without the narcissistic asshole."

"Here's to a week without having to verbally stroke his cock." I raised my glass higher before returning it to my lips.

Franklin spit his drink and slammed the glass down. "Oh, my God."

In response to his smile, mixed with that deep, throaty laugh, my internal temperature spiked, melting the layers of ice that had claimed my unmentionables years ago.

I stared at him a little too long. A new growth of stubble dusted his square jaw and almost hid his understated cleft chin. Holy moly, those eyes. Deep, unnatural blue. An eye color you would see in an anime movie. Even with his playful expression, they glistened with wisdom and sincerity. I had to be careful, or if I peered into those eyes long enough, my loins would burst into flames.

His forehead held a few wrinkles, forged not by age, but the intense gaze he wore most of the time. I often caught him at his desk, lost in deep concentration. God, I hoped he didn't have a clue how many hours I wasted observing him.

He downed the brewski in three gulps and gestured for two more. "You're such a funny girl. That's what I love about you." His leg bounced incessantly against mine. Was he nervous?

Wait, what? That's what he loved about me? I was speechless, which was a rare occurrence, and pretended to study a painting on the wall.

Awkward?

Nah.

Chapter 3

Before long, it was nine, then nine-thirty. I'd demolished three beers, a plate of fries, two pieces of gum, taken four trips to the little girls' room, and I didn't want the night to end.

Franklin Reed proved as mesmerizing to talk to as he was to look at. We made fun of the goofballs in the bar and joked about the losers at work, mostly Wallace. Movies, check. Favorite music, check. There wasn't a breath of down time. Best part? The whole night, we laughed.

We got along great on the job, but who knew he'd be so easy to hang with outside the nine-to-five? At quarter to ten, "Ain't No Rest For The Wicked" bellowed from his shirt pocket. Retrieving his phone, he pushed a button, then tucked it away. With a proud smile, he winked at me, grabbed my hand, and led me out the front door.

"Come with me. Here, take your shoes off." Lowering himself to one knee, he rubbed his hand up the length of my calf and prompted me to lift my leg. Inciting goose bumps from hip to ankles, he slid the torture devices off my aching feet. Holy shit, it was sexy.

He rested his hands on my waist and stood. "I'd give you a piggy-back, but you'd have to hike that damn skirt all the way up your waist." Something dark and promising flickered in his eyes.

Behind the old brick building, a rickety set of stairs stretched to the third floor. "Where are we going?" I asked. I secretly hoped it wasn't up, but it was.

It took him a moment to dig his keys from his pocket and get the door open.

I'd never been to Franklin's apartment. Hadn't entertained the idea either, assuming it'd be spotless, like his desk, and frequented by supermodels. At the office, he kept everything neat and tidy, perfectly organized, nothing out of place, nothing personal on display. When we entered the apartment, I was dumbfounded. It was bare. No pictures or furniture, save a leather couch and a fifty-inch flat screen. Brick walls, wood floors, stainless steel appliances in the tiny kitchen tucked in the corner. Other than that, empty.

"Dude. Where's all your stuff?" I asked, surveying the small space.

He smiled and tossed his keys onto the bar-top partition that separated the dining room from the living room. He walked to the other side and carried two barstools around the corner.

"Don't need much. A place to eat, a place to watch the tube." He grabbed a remote from the counter and the television buzzed to life. "Make yourself comfortable." He gestured to the couch before disappearing. "I'll be right back."

I did as told and nestled into the buttery soft leather, tucking my legs under myself. The voice coming from the jumbo box hanging on his wall announced the *Banshee* season finale was coming up next. I laughed. Damn, the man was good.

He returned wearing faded jeans that hung low on his waist and a gray, trim-fitted Henley that opened to a deep V at the collar, revealing a sneak peak of bare chest. I wanted to jump his bones. Seriously, I did. I wasn't a slut or anything, but with the beer in my gut, the electricity in his eyes, and the shirt that clung like plastic wrap to his skin, I feared I could easily become one.

Franklin plopped his glorious ass on the cushion, leaving less than an inch between us. Tremors pulsed through my lower abdomen. What was he doing? What the hell was I doing? I should've never come to his apartment. Should've stopped at one beer and gone home. It was way too close for colleagues to sit together. Way too close.

"Franklin, I should head ho—"

He pinched my lips together with his thumb and forefinger. "Shush. It's starting. You're not allowed to talk for the next sixty minutes, got it?" He freed my lips and I started to protest until he flashed me a *don't-you-dare* scowl.

"Relax and enjoy, Tate." He leaned back, extended his legs in front of him and stretched his arms wide before clasping his hands behind his head.

I couldn't pay attention to the ex-con-turned-small-town-sheriff on the big screen. It took serious concentration to keep my breaths steady, my heart rate normal, my hands to myself. Franklin was too warm and all-consuming next to me. So close, so male. My skin tingled with the need to either jump him or get the heck out of there.

The first commercial in, on his trot to the refrigerator, Franklin blessed me with a long hard gander at his round firm rear. I'd caught a glimpse or two, or three thousand, of his ass at work. How could I not? The way he filled out his slacks was nothing short of divine, but holy freaking cow, what he did to a pair of jeans—downright illicit. I couldn't peel my eyes away. It was just—bam—there, accented by the slight curve of his small waist that spread into broad, muscled shoulders. He glanced at me before disappearing behind the wall.

Oops, busted.

I'm pretty sure he smirked, but the light was dim and I was buzzed, so I couldn't be certain.

He returned with two glasses of ice water and placed them on the floor between us. I squealed when he sat down and grabbed my legs from under me, placing them over his own.

"Were you staring at my ass, Tate?" he asked, voice huskier than normal.

Gulp. "Yes." Why lie? I couldn't find the courage to look at him.

With strong sure hands, Franklin massaged my left foot.

"Why?" he asked, leaning toward me.

Why? What did he mean, *why*? Because it was effin' perfect. Because I wanted to peel his jeans off and unwrap that derriere like a Christmas present. Rub it, hold it, leave claw marks. Gnaw on it like a piece of jerky. I found my voice again, along with the courage to meet him square in the eye. "You have a smoking hot ass, Mr. Reed. It begs to be ogled."

"You're blushing," he half whispered, half moaned.

If he'd intended to ruffle my feathers, it worked. Lucky for me, enough liquid courage remained in my belly and flowed through my veins to meet his challenge head-on.

I shifted and wiggled my toes. "As a matter of fact, Frankie, I check out your rump at least three hundred and twenty-five times a day. I'd appreciate it if you'd stop wearing your suit jacket at work. It covers that fine tush of yours, and when it's hidden, it puts me in a foul mood."

That something, dark and promising, flashed in his eyes again. A new wave of heat landed on my cheeks. He laughed and turned toward me, propping one knee on the couch. "Is that so, Miss Wood? I happen to appreciate your ass on a regular basis as well. This skirt you're wearing now is by far my favorite. Hugs those curves of yours perfectly. Made me drool on more than one occasion."

Oh, he was good. I should have stopped there. We worked together. Nothing about this conversation was appropriate for coworkers.

My unruly mouth and I continued, "If I could, I'd frame your ass and hang it on my wall."

Shut up, Tate. Shut up.

I threw a challenging smile his way but lost my gumption when his warm hands slid up my leg and rested just below my knee. No longer massaging, he trailed lazy fingers over my skin, up and down, back and forth. He held my gaze, stopping time and space with the smolder in his eyes.

"Tate." His voice deepened. "Someday, very soon, I will hang you on my wall, but not in a frame." With that, he leaned forward, straddled my legs and kissed the holy living heck out of me, shutting me up real fast.

Oh, I'd been kissed before. Not often, but that didn't matter anymore. No way in hell would I remember any previous smooches after Franklin Reed's assault on my lips. It wasn't slow and romantic. It definitely wasn't awkward or stymied by shyness. It was a full on, *you're mine, I'm gonna eat you alive* kind of kiss.

I melted. I liquefied beneath him, and with one swift move, his heavy body covered me from chest to knees. His arousal was evident, like a steel rod between us. If it weren't for the damned pencil skirt, my legs would have opened for him. They tried. Lordy, Lordy, they tried. Poor babies didn't have any room to move.

He released me for a brief moment. "You taste better than I imagined," he moaned, breathless and husky. I nearly shattered to pieces beneath him and groped the very thing that started the romp—his ass. It was every bit as glorious beneath my fingers as it was on the eyes. Rock hard, round and flexing with every roll of his hips against me.

He nuzzled my breasts and then, with agile fingers, unhooked the buttons on my blouse. Panic stole my breath when he tugged the cups of my bra and freed me from its binds. As if sensing my trepidation he slid a hand under my chin and tilted my face to meet his. "I've never seen anyone so beautiful."

His lips commanded mine, giving and taking, prompting me to move just the way he wanted. I committed to memory the sounds he produced while he trailed kisses along my neck, nipped at my chest, pulled my nipple between his teeth. When his tongue brushed across the hypersensitive flesh, I lost my bearings and grabbed his head, pulling him against my bosom. He licked, sucked, and nibbled, and I bit my bottom lip to keep from screaming. Holy shit, I'd never known such pleasure, never felt so alive. I was out of my mind already. If this went any further, if I gave in to this need, I'd fall hard and never recover.

Franklin's phone vibrated against my thigh nanoseconds before it announced a caller with "Wicked Game" by Chris Isaak. With a final flick of his tongue across my hardened nipple, he cussed and pushed himself off me, dug his phone out of his pocket, and disappeared around the corner. I righted my bra and scooted upright to button my blouse. It took several deep breaths to clear my head.

God, what was I thinking coming to his apartment? How could I face him at work? I needed to make a clean getaway. If our make-out session continued, I wouldn't have the strength to say no. How could any woman say no to that man?

I tiptoed on rubber legs across the shiny wood floor and grabbed my shoes. Whispers that sounded heated and angry carried through the hall. Praying for well-oiled door hinges, I slowly made my escape. I scuttled down the stairs and back around the corner of the building, ignoring the rocks that dug into my bare feet. It wasn't until I pulled out of the parking lot that I remembered to breathe. Through my rearview mirror, I watched him skid around the corner and rub the top of his head.

* * * *

Okay. Maybe my exit was a bit overdramatic, but I needed distance. Not mere miles, more like a state or two. Never in my wildest dreams would I have expected someone like Franklin to be attracted to me, let alone have fantasized a scene like the one we'd just acted out.

One-Date Tate.

Was it the alcohol? He seemed into me from the second I entered the bar. Or was that my imagination? The past few months, we'd teased and flirted at work. According to Nan, I was the only woman in the building he paid attention to. We'd never crossed the line, though. At least, it didn't seem that way. Then again, what did I know?

My cheeks ached by the time I pulled into my space in the parking garage, and I forced the smile from my face. I'd been ravished by Franklin Reed. Holy crap. Could I ever look him in the eye again? On Monday, I would return to work and pretend like nothing happened. Simple. In a few weeks or months, Franklin and I would laugh about our meaningless tryst.

I entered the elevator and pushed the button for the fifth floor. My neighbor, Jacob Smart, greeted me when the doors slid open and I stepped out.

"Hey, Tatum. Come here you gorgeous thing, give me a squeeze." I obliged and enjoyed the familiarity of his arms.

"How was your day, Jacob?" I kissed his cheek and brushed a piece of white hair off his forehead.

"Great day, today. I'm exhausted. Headed to bed." He patted my shoulder and turned to enter his apartment.

"Goodnight then. I'll see you tomorrow."

Jacob and I had shared a hallway for three years now. I moved into the building shortly after my father died. Jacob bought the neighboring unit a week after I moved in. For a sixty-something retired bookstore owner and widower, the guy was as spry as a toddler on a sugar high. We had become fast friends and he'd always been there for me, like a favorite blanket or comfort food. Wise, gentle, and patient, he called me on any bullshit I might have been idiotic enough to feed him.

I became obscenely wealthy on my twenty-first birthday. Turned out my father acquired quite a fortune after his great aunt died and kept it a secret from my mother and me. Upon his death, the money came to me. My mother wanted nothing to do with it. She'd said, "Without Antonio, I wouldn't enjoy it." Although I'd never desired material things, I did splurge and buy a condo on Alki Beach, overlooking Seattle and the Puget Sound. I had invested the rest of the cash and hadn't touched it since.

It was a good feeling to know I was set for life, but I liked working. I enjoyed getting up in the morning and having a place to go. I relished the office camaraderie.

I ended up at Cruse Investigations because Wallace Cruse was a kiss-ass mooch. He grew up with Dad, harbored some weird man-crush on him, and followed him around like a lost puppy. My father started the company when I was three, got bored, and sold it to Wallace. When I debated college, Wallace offered me a job with a cushy salary. I was nowhere near qualified, and I know he hired me to satisfy his weird need to please the man he coveted. I took the job only because I still didn't know what I wanted to do when I grew up.

As the receptionist, I spent most of my day answering phones, directing calls, scheduling appointments.

The majority of our cases? Infidelity. The majority of our clients? The upper echelon of the Seattle social scene. I'd learned over the past four years that absurd wealth didn't protect people from stupidity. It just made it easier to cover up their imprudence. After Wallace took over, Cruse Investigations quickly became the place to call when someone suspected a cheating spouse or significant other. We'd become the Jerry Springer of the private investigation world.

Wallace was the king when it came to schmoozing. King of Kiss-Ass that is. Lied through his teeth most of the time to land clients, but for some crazy reason, it worked, and he'd built himself a mini empire with my father's company.

I didn't love my job. Just didn't hate it enough to move on. Dad's aura permeated the walls. Some days, it seemed he was right there working alongside me. Did that make me crazy? Perhaps. It also gave me reason to stay. As much as I despised Wallace, I could deal with his insane personality, less than honorable business practices, and flamboyant lifestyle. He'd been part of my family for as long as I could remember. I'd never known him to be anything other than the putz he was. Didn't mean I was obligated to like him, though.

Chapter 4

The gray Seattle sky I'd come to love gave way to black, thunderous promises of a torrential downpour. I wiped salty water from my face and waved to Jacob Smart, who passed on the sidewalk just beyond the short stretch of beach. Wallace thrashed and struggled in vain to dislodge the hand that held his face below the surface of the water.

Seaweed tangled around his neck. With eyes bulged and glossy, he screamed, silent and ineffective.

I laughed. "No one will help you." I looked up to the gathering crowd on the shoreline. Some applauded. Some guffawed along with me.

"This is what happens when you make practice of screwing with people, Mr. Cruse."

His thrashing ceased. My audience cheered with whoops and hollers. I released his throat and watched the lifeless, bloated body bob away in the darkening water.

I awoke refreshed and spunkier than my norm. Did I feel guilty for killing Wallace on a regular basis, be it in daydreams or real dreams? Not a chance. Maybe it was my body's way of purging the pent-up repulsion towards him.

Despite what it seemed, violence wasn't my nature. I could barely stand to kill a spider. There was something about the man that drew morbid fantasies out of my psyche. Perhaps I needed to see a shrink. Perhaps not. Dreams were cheaper than therapy.

Warm sunshine blanketed my living room. I stood at the window and watched the early morning walkers, bikers and rollerbladers. Some moved along with purpose, but most seemed to delight in a casual stroll and revel in the rare, early spring sun.

An elderly couple caught my eye. The man, although walking with a cane, steadied his wife with his free arm. Their movements were unhurried. They smiled, laughed, greeted people as they passed. That's what I wanted. That, to me, was true love. Two people who have weathered the storms of life and stuck together. I pictured a similar future for myself. Just had to ditch the curse first.

They traveled at a tedious pace, but I couldn't tear my eyes away. That couple was far more beautiful than the beach, the mountains in the distance, or the Seattle skyline. Their love story, in my imagination, was rarer than the April sunshine and blue sky, far more fascinating than the man with the bright orange running shorts and tie-dyed muscle shirt who roller-danced with a boom box perched on his shoulder.

They passed a lamppost and my gaze rested on a man wearing black boots, dark denim, and a dark gray sweatshirt. He leaned against the massive pole, legs crossed at the ankle, hands tucked in the front pockets of his jeans. Casual, yet arrogant. His hood was pulled low, revealing nothing of his face but a pair of aviator sunglasses. Even through the dark lenses, the weight of his glare crushed me.

Something in my stomach twitched. I placed a hand on the window and leaned against the glass, hoping to get a better look. He was too far away to know for sure, but I think he smiled at me. Not a friendly *hi, how are you* kind of smile. It was more an *I got you, you're a dead bitch* kind of leer. I would have been frightened if I weren't across a busy street, in a secure building, five stories up. I was mesmerized by this stranger. From my viewpoint, I couldn't accurately gauge his height, but underneath his loose attire, the solid, formidable form was unmistakable.

Standing straight, he pulled his hood down farther and strutted away, carrying himself with fierce confidence. Badass-motherfucker came to mind. I imagined a gun tucked in the back of his jeans, a knife or two hidden strategically in the sleeves of his shirt. Apparently, I wasn't the only one affected by his stranger-danger vibe. Each and every passerby gave him a wide berth as he strode away.

What a way to start my morning. Someday, my vivid imagination was going to get me into a heap of trouble.

* * * *

I wrapped up my Saturday morning ritual of coffee and muffins with Jacob. In typical Jacob style, he inquired about the status of my love life. I scrunched my face and told him boys grossed me out. That always made him smile.

I loved Jacob like an uncle, but there were some things a girl shouldn't talk about. My romp on Franklin's couch would be one of them. I sent him on his way with a plate full of leftover muffins, kissed his cheek, and watched him shuffle across the hall to his door.

I was about to shut myself in when I heard the elevator ding. Being the curious bloke I was, I peeked through the crack of my door to see who was coming. I nearly fell on my ass when the hooded stranger from outside stepped into the corridor. Without hesitation, I slammed the door shut and secured both locks.

Heart racing, I peered through the peephole. Eons passed before a dark form blocked my view. I jumped back and covered my mouth to stifle my panicked gasps. Shit. Did he hold a finger against the hole? What the hell? Frozen in place, I waited for a knock that didn't come. My heart hammered painful blows against my chest, pumping heated blood through my ears and skull. I jumped when I heard muffled voices and a loud slam. It had to be Jacob's door. We were the only apartments sharing this floor.

I listened, then listened some more. Excruciating minutes passed before I was able to trigger the nerves that connected my brain to my legs. This was insane. Jacob had a visitor. So what? Why was I getting so worked up? Maybe my overactive imagination needed a long vacation.

I threw on my sweatshirt and grabbed my sunglasses. A walk on the beach would do me some good. Sunshine, blue sky, and salty air. I peeked again before leaving to be sure no hooded creeps lingered in the hall. The coast was clear so I made my escape.

I only needed to cross the street to reach my destination. There was a walking and bike path, a patch of grass, and then the beach. Despite the sunshine, it was way too chilly to park it in the sand and enjoy the view, so I headed west. Merging onto the walking path took an insane amount of gumption, much like I-5 during rush hour. Somehow I managed and even dodged a cyclist with an impressive amount of grace.

Instead of clearing my head, I filled it with dizzying thoughts and questions about my non-date with Franklin. What would happen on Monday? How could I face him after running like I did? Oh crap. What if I'd stayed? Would I have woken in his bed this morning instead of my own? Hmm. He must be yummy in the morning all sleepy and…oh, no. I couldn't let my mind go there.

I made the decision to call him. At least it would make things less uncomfortable on Monday. Except I didn't have his number. We'd never exchanged digits, never had reason to. Maybe Nan could help me. Would that be creepy? Make me a stalker? Clearly, if he'd wanted to give me his phone number, he would have, right? Except, I hadn't given him a chance. I was the one who bolted after all.

Okay. Enough was enough. I'd call Nan as soon as I got home and get his contact info. She'd have it on file. The woman practically ran the damned company, for crying out loud.

I was less than a block away from my building and lost in reflection when a bulldozer wearing a gray hoodie knocked me off my feet and flat on my back. I lay on the sidewalk for a moment, stunned but unhurt as far as I could tell. From the corner of my eye, I watched him sprint away and duck around the corner of a building.

"Asshole!" I shouted. Not that it did any good. A jogger stopped to help me to my feet.

"You okay?" she asked, panting. Her face turned ten shades of pale. She looked wide-eyed, down the length of my body. "Oh, my God. Let me call an ambulance."

"What? No. I'm fine." I reassured her.

"But you're bleeding." She gestured to my stomach.

Yup. There was blood smeared across the front of my clothes. I frantically searched for a wound. No pain. I pulled up my shirt. Nothing. Not a scratch. I inspected my hands. They were bloody, but only from touching my soiled garment.

It must have come from hoodie man. My throat closed tight and I grabbed the jogger to steady myself. "Oh no, oh no, oh no."

I sprinted the short distance home. The elevator took at least three hours and twenty-five minutes to reach my floor. As I approached Jacob's door, my heart stopped beating, the hallway narrowed and lengthened, and I fell to my knees. It was wide open. I pulled myself up, gripped the wall for support, and peeped in the doorway on shaky legs.

* * * *

Detective Leland Waters jotted one more note in his little black book, handed me a card, and patted me on the shoulder. "Miss Wood. Here's my number. Please call if you think of anything else."

I nodded because I hadn't a damned word left to say. I'd told him everything I could remember about the man who'd haunted my day, from the moment I'd spied him out the window until I found Jacob, bloody and clinging to life on his newly tiled floor.

Was this a dream? Only a few short hours ago, Jacob and I laughed over coffee. Now, the muffins I'd baked, as I did every weekend for him, sat in a pretty basket atop his counter, soiled with gore.

"I'll be in touch, Miss Wood." He handed the bag containing my bloody clothes to another officer. The familiar ding of the elevator resonated through the hall. When Franklin stepped through the doors, escorted by a bald, stalky officer, my shield of numb lifted and like I'd been tossed in a tub of icy water, a brisk dose of reality drowned me in emotion that somehow, until that point, I'd held at bay.

The men around me blurred, all but Franklin. After a brief word with Detective Waters, he pushed through the field of blue and stormed toward me. I couldn't peel my eyes from him. I could hear nothing but my own heartbeat, see nothing but Franklin Reed. Then, he whisked me into my home, the door slammed behind me, and rock solid arms wrapped around my middle.

"Tate. Are you okay? Shit. I was going insane downstairs. Police, ambulances." He stopped talking and held me tighter.

It was then that I started to shake and allowed tears to fall. I dropped to my knees and let the dam burst. Franklin followed me to the floor and cradled me. I don't know how long we sat there or if he spoke. I did know, with Franklin Reed holding the pieces of me together, I could survive anything.

I woke hours later on my couch, wrapped in the afghan my grandmother crocheted for me the year before she died. Franklin rested on the floor, back against the sofa, watching television with the volume on mute. I ached to reach out and touch him, but I didn't have that right. He wasn't mine.

"Thank you," I whispered.

He turned, piercing me deep with a blazing gaze. Concern, but not pity, etched the lines of his face. "I couldn't leave until I knew you were okay."

My heart lurched at the sentiment in his voice. It was the most desirable sound in the world. He held up a sandwich and a beer. "Helped myself. Hope you don't mind." Placing the food back on the coffee table, he turned and grabbed my hand.

"How did you know where I live?" I pushed into the sitting position. He didn't release my hand. Just held it, sure and steady. I trembled under the power in his simple, comforting gesture. Not from fear, but the raw masculine force that came from his touch.

His smile soothed my jagged emotions. "Stalking 101. I took a class. It's opened a whole new world to me."

I forced a grin. He reached over to cup my face. "I was worried I did something wrong last night. You ran out so fast. I needed to make sure we were good." Caressing my cheek with his thumb, he studied my lips, then my eyes, then my lips again. Did he want to kiss me? I wanted him to, more than I'd ever wanted anything. Something held him back.

"I'm sorry," I whispered. "I'm sorry I freaked and bolted. It's just that—" I stopped. What was I supposed to say? *Sorry, bub, if you want to get with this, I need a ring on my finger? I don't do casual sex?* Sheesh. Was there any girl my age in Seattle who didn't do casual sex?

More likely than not, a man as fine as Mr. Reed collected a plethora of over eager ho-bags. All of whom would eagerly spread their legs for the chance to be touched by the glory that was Franklin.

I sighed. "I need commitment. I need to know I'm more to a man than just a place to stick his dick. Call me crazy." I was probably the only girl in the universe who would run away from a man as delicious as Franklin, but I wasn't about to say that out loud.

"Tatum Wood. What makes you think I wanted to stick my dick in you?" He pretended to be offended.

"Well, Mr. Reed. It could have been the fact that your dick was harder than a diamond dildo and desperate to shred the fabric of my skirt." Oh God, did I just say that? I needed to tighten the reins on my loose tongue.

He must have read the horror on my face. His jaw dropped, then closed, then the wrinkles in his forehead deepened.

"Tell me what happened today. Every detail." His tone, no longer playful, was a dead-on impersonation of my father.

Okay… Subject changed.

I told him about hoodie man and how it seemed he'd been watching me. Franklin grilled me harder than Detective Waters. He pulled information from me I didn't realize I'd retained, like he'd done it a million times before. I found it odd that he failed to query me about the stranger.

He asked about my relationship with Jacob. How did we meet? What did I know about him? How often did we talk? Was he ever in my apartment? How many times? Did he have a key? Every detail. No stone left unturned.

"Why so many questions about Jacob? He's the victim, remember?" Swelling tears blurred my vision. "What does my relationship with him have to do with the poor man being gutted like a pig?"

Franklin stood and paced the length of my living room. "I'm sorry. I feel like we're missing something." He rubbed his finger up and down the cleft of his chin. "Wicked Game" blared from his ass, drawing my attention to the tantalizing part of him that got me in trouble the night before. Cussing under his breath, he pulled the cell from his back pocket, opened my balcony door, and disappeared into the darkness.

Whomever that ringtone belonged to, Franklin didn't like talking to him and apparently needed privacy every time he did.

Chapter 5

I watched, breathless, as the sexiest man alive blazed an angry trail back and forth across my deck. I couldn't hear the conversation but his body language spoke volumes. Clenched fist, angry pacing, shoulders taut. Silhouetted against city lights in the distant background, his physique consumed my attention, drowning out the street noise, blinding me to the surrounding landscape. Oh, to hold such power. Franklin carried himself in the same manner hoodie man had: formidable. Difference was, Franklin wore it with a sexual confidence that drew people in, unlike hoodie man's menacing cloak.

I hadn't realized how intently I stared until he stopped and faced me, phone to ear, other hand rubbing his temple. His chest rose and fell. I heard a mumbled "fuck," then he tucked the cell away. When he opened the glass slider, the rush of cool air reminded me to breathe.

My voice packed its bags and headed for Fiji. "Everything ok?" I asked with a squeak. "Do you need to go? I'll be fine if you need to go."

He strode toward me with such purpose, my guts clenched. His eyes burned with radiant authority. "No. I'm not going anywhere." He bent, flanked my shoulders with fisted hands and braced me against the back of my couch. His lips brushed my ear, his breath heating my skin and every cell in my body. "There's no way in hell I'd leave you alone tonight."

A wave of sweet relief washed over me. As much as I hated to be a burden or play the helpless girl, I was not keen on the idea of spending the evening alone in my big apartment.

Pushing himself away, he snatched his keys and headed out. "I need to grab some things from my car. Lock the door behind me."

I nodded. Sheesh, overprotective much? It wasn't like someone would break into my apartment in the few minutes it took him to get to his car and back. Besides, the police were still present and busy right outside.

Seven minutes and forty-eight seconds later, I buzzed Franklin back into the building. He stepped through the door with a large gym bag slung over his shoulder. "Where should I put this?" he asked, moving through the room like a man on a mission.

"Oh. You're staying the night. Like the whole night?" To say I was shocked would be an understatement. Ecstatic glee took over my insides, head to toe.

"I told you. Not leaving you alone. I'm fine on the couch or the floor."

I bit back a snicker. Yeah right, Franklin on the floor? There had to be a law against such an atrocity. "No need. I have a guest room." I led him down the hallway to my extra bedroom. The jaunt was short, but seemed an eternity with his presence looming behind me, protective and overwhelming.

Before turning the knob, I turned to face him. "So, you are my first official overnight guest." I swung the door open with dramatic flair and swept my arm wide to present the room. "Please be gentle with her. The shower is in there." I pointed to the bathroom.

He set the bag down on the bed but didn't take his eyes off me for a blink. The furnace burning slow and steady in my belly cranked to high.

"Do you always come prepared for sleepovers?" I smirked at him.

"Something like that," he chuckled.

I was sure he did the sleepover thing often. A revolving supply of bags were probably stashed in his car, one for every night of the week. It would certainly explain the barren state of his apartment.

"Thank you," I blurted, pressing my hand to my chest. "I didn't want to be alone."

He cupped my shoulders and shook me playfully. "Come on, now. The Tate I know wouldn't be afraid of some silly, gruesome assault, would she?"

I laughed and hugged him. I couldn't help it. My cheek pressed against his warm, hard chest when he squeezed me back. His breath tickled the top of my head before he landed a soft kiss. I inhaled deep and slow. I wanted to smell him. Skin, sweat, anything. What I got was a big whiff of freshly laundered cotton.

He held me tight. My body responded, every nerve vibrating in anticipation.

Oh crap.

Franklin shifted and pulled away, only enough to look down. "There's something you need to know about me."

No. I knew it. The illusion was too perfect to be real. The bomb was about to drop.

Reluctantly, I slipped from his embrace and sat on the edge of the queen-sized bed. I gripped the tall bedpost and held on for dear life. "Let's hear it." The quiver in my voice betrayed the veneer of confidence I'd built.

With a deep intake of breath, he sat next to me, pressing shoulder and thigh, warm and solid, against my trembling body.

"I was married. It was a long time ago and it didn't end on a pretty note."

Okay. That wasn't too bad. So what? Divorcee'. No big deal, and not a shock. The man was beautiful. Why wouldn't he have been married?

I managed a nod. He wasn't finished.

"She's the only woman I've ever been with." That was a bit of a shock. A bit unbelievable, too.

"Okay." Why was he telling me this?

Franklin slid his hand across my thigh and laced his fingers through my own. "I want you in every way possible. It's not only physical. I know we work together. I know everything about this is wrong, but fuck, I can't get you out of my head. The way you taste." His tongue traced his lower lip and his gaze traveled to my mouth. "The way our bodies fit together, the way you make me laugh. Holy shit. I haven't laughed so much in years." He held me captive with his words, the expression he wore, the heat burning me alive from the inside out.

So, he didn't just want a place to stick his dick. Suddenly, I wanted to be that place anyway. I wanted to be the only place he ever stuck it again. Would I get hurt? Most likely. It'd be worth the cost of the ride, of that I was certain. Would we get fired if anyone found out? Sure. But who would ever know?

Oh, to hell with workplace ethics.

"I've been patient—" He started to speak again, but I shut him up when I bit his lower lip and sucked. He didn't fight me off when I straddled his thighs and pushed him flat across the bed. It took him about a tenth of a second to claim my mouth and kiss me hard enough to steal my breath.

His duffel hit the floor with a thud. Then he slid strong, hot fingers underneath my yoga pants, cupped my ass with a hard squeeze, and groaned. Man alive—that set my blood on fire.

* * * *

Sex should have been the last thing on my mind. Franklin Reed should not have been in my home, especially not on my bed. Maybe I needed some excitement to wipe the gruesome images of Jacob from my head. Maybe, being this near to Franklin was sensory overload, and I was like every other warm-blooded female on the planet and completely at the mercy of raw, male sex appeal.

In that moment, I didn't care why I was unable to form the simple combination of two letters, N and O.

He kissed me. Claimed me. Assaulted my mouth with such seductive ambition, I'd need an oxygen mask when he finished.

The force he used to knead my butt bordered on painful, but with every movement of his strong hands, a fire surged through my skin. His kiss, desperate and hurried, deepened as did the strength he used to smash me against a growing erection.

I pulled away, desperate for precious oxygen. Holy shit. Franklin stared up at me with hungry, tortured eyes. Lust-filled. Ravenous. Fervent. He devoured me with a contemplation I'd never experienced. Paralyzed me with the intimacy of his gaze, chest thumping against mine.

I memorized his eyes, every fleck and shimmer of color, the curve of his lashes, each fine wrinkle carved around his lids. I couldn't blink or look away, afraid that if I did, I'd lose him, even if this were only for one night.

"There's so much I need to say to you," he whispered, voice thick with emotion.

Oh God, I was going to lose him.

I shook my head no. "Please, right now I just want to feel you." I pressed my lips to his, hoping to silence the inevitable rejection. He slid his hands to the small of my back, then higher. I shifted to pull my weight off him. With a sharp inhale, he wrapped his arms around me and flipped so I was pinned beneath him.

Caged like a wild animal.

With hands fisted on either side of my shoulders, he straddled my thighs. His long sleeved T-shirt did nothing to conceal the sculptured male muscle underneath. I couldn't wait to see what the damned clothing hid. In fact, I couldn't wait to help him get out of it.

I grabbed his shirt hem and tugged upward. A playful smile stretched across his face, and he lifted his arms, allowing me to peel the cotton from his taught skin. He sat back on his heels, hands to knees, and studied me as if deciding which part of my body to ravish first. Perfect, because it gave me time to examine him.

Okay. It was ridiculous. I'd seen plenty of shirtless men. None of them up close and personal, but hey, I watched movies, skimmed through magazines, browsed the internet. Sexy bodies were everywhere, but never, ever, had I seen a man so innately, well, male. One hundred percent, grade-A certified beefcake, pure sex, born to procreate—or at least make women want to procreate.

His skin stretched so tight across his chest and abs, I could trace every muscle, every vein. Under clothing, his narrow waist gave the illusion of slightness. In the buff—pure power. It veed to an obscenely cut pack of abs and swelled to pecs that could have been chiseled from the finest granite, buffed then polished to perfection.

"Oh my God," I gasped. Unworthy? Yep. I was a whole bunch of soft and squishy. The man straddling me? Blindingly beautiful. Greek God, gladiator, sexy fireman, supermodel… I could go on all day.

I laughed. Couldn't help it.

The way he cocked his head to the side made him even more scrumptious. "What's so funny?"

"Look at you. What, do you work out like sixteen hours a day? I mean, seriously?" I tried to sit up. Franklin slapped a palm to the center of my bosom and held me down.

I pinched at various points on his body, hoping to find flabby skin or an ounce of fat somewhere.

Perfection. Head to toe.

How could I get naked next to him?

"No fat anywhere? Come on."

Before I could grunt in frustration, he clasped my hands over my head and with warm, moist lips, nibbled my earlobe. "Your turn to strip."

Oh, my. This *was* happening. With graceful ease, he freed my arms and removed my shirt and bra. Had I the inclination to stop him, it was too late. We'd passed the point of no return.

My nipples took on a life of their own, begging for attention. "Holy shit, baby. Look at you." He gazed upon them with feral hunger, but didn't tend to my breasts right away. Instead, he smoothed his hand over my stomach and ran a finger under the waistband of my yoga pants. He slid down the length of my legs, trailing kisses across my abdomen, paying special attention to the soft area around my navel. I quivered under his strokes, an embarrassing display of unbridled lust. He looked up at me. I turned away. I would shatter if I got lost under that intense scrutiny again.

I closed my eyes and focused on the heated trails his lips and tongue blazed across my skin. When he snagged the sides of my waistband and peeled my pants down my hips, my insides exploded with cruel bursts of fear and self-doubt.

One-Date Tate.

I wouldn't let the ugly in. Not tonight. I wanted him, whether it led to something more or not.

I clasped his wrists. "Stop."

Stop. I regretted the word before it left my lips. Franklin's shoulders slumped, his chest rose and fell, forcing a puff of frustrated air across my abdomen. He looked at me without lifting his head and tugged my pants back to my waist.

"Franklin, wait." I sat up, meeting him face to face. "I don't want you to stop. It's just…" Oh, crap. Never, in the two months that I'd known him, did I expect to have this conversation with Franklin. "I don't have any condoms. I've no use for them. Don't date very often." More like, don't date ever. I'd been on birth control for years to regulate my periods, but that was TMI for this situation. Heated bursts of blood hit my cheeks and he reached up to cup the side of my face.

"I don't either." He dotted my nose and forehead with soft kisses and sat up, gracing me with a playful grin. "I'm not ready to stop. We can still have fun."

With panther-like grace, he pushed himself off the bed and stood over me, chest heaving, eyes burning. Holding me captive with his hypnotic stare, he slid his hands to the waistband of his jeans and worked the first clasp with slow, guarded movement. The bulge behind the fabric filled me with prickles of anticipation. The sweet torture amplified when I noticed the flex of muscle in his forearms as he maneuvered each button with rugged hands. I couldn't wait until those fingers touched my most sacred of places, and somehow I knew they would know exactly where to go and what to do.

I licked my lips and watched the show, eager yet terrified of what was to come. Thank God, I'd showered and reacquainted myself with Lady Bic.

Much to my disappointment, Franklin unfastened three buttons and stopped. He zeroed in on my waistband once again. There was no slow-and-gentle this time. In one swift move, my pants disappeared, leaving me bare.

I wished I had a camera to capture the expression on his face. "No panties? You are so fucking sexy." He continued removing his jeans.

"Let me." I sat up and scooted toward the edge of the bed. I needed to touch him, to feel his naked flesh under my palm. His erection jerked against my fingers. I undid his last two buttons and peeled his jeans down his thighs, leaving him in nothing but black boxer briefs. He kicked the denim to the side and bent to kiss me, blocking my attempt at removing his last article of clothing. "Not yet. Tonight is for you."

Franklin Reed knelt before me, maneuvered his body between my thighs and lifted a heavy, aching breast to his mouth. A strange noise rose from my throat. Holy cow, did I whimper? He pulled deep on my nipple and sucked. Currents of ecstasy pulsed through me, and I gripped the edge of the mattress to anchor myself.

His tongue brushed over the sensitive flesh. Driven by instinct, I grabbed his head and pulled him harder against my swollen D-cups. Franklin moved from one breast to the other and mumbled something about soft and sweet. I couldn't respond. I could barely form a coherent thought. My insides burned. Every flick of his tongue, every brush of his lips, made me quiver and crave more.

Then his fingers found my sex. I ached down there. An ache that pulsed in sync with the flow of blood pounding in my ears. When his thumb grazed the surface of my sensitive tissue, I moaned. I'd never moaned before. Not with desire, anyway. I couldn't take much more. Certainly I'd be reduced to ash if he continued. Franklin spread my thighs wider and lowered his head.

Oh. My. I'd never seen anything more sensual than Franklin's head between my legs and dreamy blue eyes promising me pleasure beyond reason. "I've waited too long to taste you," he whispered before plunging his tongue between my wet folds.

The way he'd worked my mouth with kisses was child's play compared to what he did down there. With each stroke, each suck, nibble, plunge…I convulsed in wanton pleasure. I fisted the bedding, ground my hips against his face. My legs, reacting to his unspoken commands, wrapped around his neck. I squeezed my thighs together to speed things up or slow them down. Hell, I hadn't a clue what I needed or wanted, except more.

I'd never been consumed so completely—mind, body and spirit. I needed him inside me, controlling, possessing. He gave everything. I wanted more.

A tempest brewed within me. I tried to slow him down. I was so sensitive, wound so tight, there was no way I'd survive the release. When he plunged two fingers inside me, I threw myself back on the bed and bucked my hips in a shameful display. The violent orgasm nearly shattered me on its own, but Franklin latched on and sucked hard, drawing my release farther. The mixture of pain and pleasure was so intense, so exhausting, I couldn't muster strength to open my eyes when he crawled on top of me and pressed his erection against my belly.

His lips found mine and I grabbed his ass when he pumped himself between our flesh. Weary as I was, I met his thrusts and opened my eyes when he growled my name, his semen spilling onto my skin. He trembled and collapsed at my side, resting a heavy, muscled thigh across my hips.

Much to my surprise and shame, I started to cry.

* * * *

"What the hell?" I mumbled through garbled sobs, too wrung out to turn away from him.

"Fuck, baby." Franklin leaned over me and pulled my chin to face him. "What is it? What's wrong?"

"Nothing's wrong." I wiped pesky tears from my eyes. "That was… Wow. I've never been, you know, not like that. It's never been so intense." A white lie. I'd never been kissed down there, let alone brought to the brink of death and back. The very idea of oral pleasure had always seemed taboo, despite being, in my opinion, more intimate than intercourse. I'd feared I would be too self conscious or bashful to enjoy it. I wasn't, not with Franklin. Sexy. Wanton. Uninhibited. Anything but shy.

The wrinkles on his forehead deepened. "You're not telling me something."

Seriously, how did he know? "Okay, smart guy. I've never done the oral sex thing. I've never orgasmed with a man. I've suffered through exactly two sexual experiences, both with fumbling boys who didn't have a clue what they were doing. Neither did I for that matter."

An arrogant smile lit up his face, and he rose from the bed. Smug bastard. "I'm gonna get you cleaned off. Don't move." He strutted to the bathroom. Naked. Badass. Franklin moved with fierce confidence. When he returned with a warm, wet washcloth and a towel, I struggled to keep my eyes above his waistline, but his erection stood proud and…

"Holy cow, you're huge!" I slapped my hand over my mouth. The words had escaped. No reeling them in. How could a man be hard so soon after ejaculating? He smirked and wiped his semen from my heated skin. He was tender and thorough and didn't seem to mind that I stared at his hard-on or that I trembled every time he touched me. I think he enjoyed it.

When I was clean and dry, he disposed of the towels and pulled on a pair of black sweat pants he'd retrieved from his duffel bag. I scooted under the blankets and held them open for him to slide in. I hoped like hell he wouldn't turn me down.

He didn't.

As if we'd been lovers for years, he pulled me against his chest and snuggled right in.

"I'm sorry about your friend," he whispered.

"Thank you." An elephant made a lounge chair of my chest. Worry seeped through the sex haze invading my brain. I didn't know if Jacob had any family nearby. Was anyone with him at the hospital? We talked almost daily, but I knew little about his personal life. Our conversations had centered around me, and he had always changed the subject when I did any digging.

Shit. Did I know anything other than he was a widower and retired bookstore owner? I rarely entered his apartment. When I did, it was only to wait inside the front door.

"I have to see how Jacob is. What hospital did they take him to?" I asked, ashamed that I'd been so wrapped up in my own selfish bliss that I hadn't checked on him.

Franklin sighed. "He's in good hands. We'll call first thing in the morning, okay?"

I lay down and Franklin pulled me back into his safe embrace. How had I ever slept without the comfort of his arms?

"What are we doing, Franklin?" I asked, hoping to hide my insecurity.

"Spooning."

I laughed. That word did not belong in his vocabulary. It was too fluffy for his deep voice and daunting physical form.

"Come on, I'm trying to be serious," I huffed. "This isn't me. I don't do hook-ups. I don't do one night stands."

He squeezed me tight. "I know, Tate. I know that's not who you are. Do you feel safe right now?"

"Yes." I did, physically and emotionally.

"Then that's what we're doing. Tonight, I'm keeping you safe."

That was good enough for me.

Chapter 6

Wallace cackled and flashed his five-hundred-dollar shade-of-white smile at the waitress. Miss Bleach Blonde bent to whisper something in his ear and nearly spilled her saline-stuffed double-D's over his shoulder in the process.

I watched from my perch across the street. He slid a hand up the back of her thigh and rested it below her left butt cheek. He thought no one would notice, but I did. I also witnessed the dark blush spread across her face.

Poor little fool.

I wiped sweat from my brow, aimed, and pulled the trigger. "Eat lead, asshole," I whispered.

Dead on.

The bullet entered above his right eyebrow and embedded itself in the cement column directly behind him. The waitress screamed and dove to the ground. I stood, held the muzzle to my lips, and blew the smoke away.

"Good shootin', sugar." A hearty gentleman patted me on the back as he passed.

"Thanks. I've been practicing." I smiled and twirled the small pistol around my index finger before tucking it back into the holster strapped to my right hip.

Morning came too soon. I rubbed my eyes open, took in the unfamiliar surroundings and wrestled a surge of panic. My bearings took a few minutes to catch up with me. Mr. Reed was nowhere to be found, and empty frigidness hovered where his body should've been. Was last night a dream?

I gathered my clothes and made the walk of shame to my bedroom. I needed a long hot soak in the tub.

No. Coffee, then a good scrub.

Uh-uh. Shower first. There might be a super sexy stud waiting for me. I'd rather jump out the window than greet him with morning hair or breath. How could I face him at all? How could I share an office space with him after last night?

I took my time. Let the hot water soothe aching muscles, tense from the stress of finding Jacob nearly dead and sore from the exertion of the mind-blowing orgasm. Jeez, I'd never have to work out if I kept Franklin around.

I was about to turn off the water when the shower door slid open, then closed. A heavy hand splayed across my abdomen, yanking my rear against an erection that begged for attention. A sharp nip on my ear and hot breath on my neck set my skin ablaze.

"Fuck, I can't keep my hands off you," he groaned, and pulled me tighter against him, roping one arm around my waist and the other across my breasts. Instinctively I arched, savoring the weight of his arm on my chest and the evidence of his arousal on my backside.

"Then don't," I managed to utter.

Franklin trailed kisses across my jaw, down my neck, and across my shoulder. With adept hands, he massaged my breasts, rolled the peaks between his fingers, rubbed his hardened sex across the slickness of my butt.

"Last night was torture," he mumbled through gritted teeth. I turned to find him staring down at me, his desire radiant through heavy lids. "All I could think about was ravishing you." His tongue rolled across his bottom lip and a crooked smile, full of hellfire, made an appearance just before he crushed his mouth to mine.

It dangled on the verge of painful, the way he claimed me, stole my breath, crushed our bodies together. My blood, my skin burned. I kissed him back. Hard. Hungry. Greedy. I was a lucky girl. For one more moment, this beautiful creature was mine. This beast of a man could eat me alive, and I would let him. No more worrying about tomorrow. I wanted more of him. However I could get it.

He kissed me until my lips ached, then moved to my chest and worshipped my breasts with fervent discipline. I moaned when he drew a nipple into his mouth and sucked. He groaned in response.

Blood pounded through my body with a thunderous intensity. My insides throbbed, clenched, begged for mercy. As if attuned to my need, he plunged two fingers deep between my legs, found my entrance and penetrated me. He pulled them out, massaged between my legs, and slid them back in.

"You're so tight. So fucking perfect."

Franklin knelt, guided my leg over his shoulder, and with master skill, worked me into a carnal frenzy. With his fingers deep inside me, Franklin Reed did things with his mouth I didn't know were possible. I came with such intense shudders, my leg collapsed beneath me.

Solid arms held me steady until my brain and muscles reconnected. He helped me stand and pinned me to the wall, clasping my hands above my head. I was sure he could read the shock on my face when he pushed his erection between my legs, grazing the sensitive tissue he'd just ravished.

Lips lowered to mine, he asked, "Trust me?"

Like I had a choice. No way was I strong enough to fight him off if I didn't. No way did I want him to stop whatever he had planned. I was no longer in my own head. My body and brain had disconnected. I was a puppet and Franklin pulled the strings.

He kissed the corner of my mouth, then moved to whisper in my ear. "I can't wait to bury myself in you. Claim every bit of that sweet pussy and make it mine. Fill you until there's absolutely nothing between us." He forced his erection deeper between my legs. I ground my pubic bone against the thickness. I couldn't stop myself. The friction triggered ripples of pleasure and I wanted more.

Letting go of my arms, he clenched my hips and thrust hard, over and over. Each time, grinding against me. He was fucking me. Fucking the fleshy meat between my thighs. It was so damned erotic, another orgasm already threatened to tear me apart. When he came, when his semen dripped down my legs, I bit my lip and buried my face in his chest, to keep from screaming out with the force of my own release.

* * * *

I was left alone to finish my shower. The man rocked my world, then strutted away, naked, wet, and oozing confidence. He returned moments later wearing jeans, beads of water across his chest, and a daunting glare.

"I've got something to take care of. I grabbed your keys. I'll lock the door behind me." He paused and raked my body from top to bottom with a sharp, haunted perusal. It chilled me, even under the hot water.

"I won't be gone long. Promise me, you won't go anywhere or open the door for anyone." His forearm rippled as he tightened his grip on the shower door. God, the muscles that man sported. What a freakin' turn-on.

"Um, ok." I made a face. "Bossy, much?"

Franklin didn't appreciate my snarky remark. His Adam's apple protruded, jaw tightened, brows pinched.

"Tatum. Promise me."

"No problem." Nothing to worry about. Jacob was the only one who ever knocked on my door. Him and the pizza delivery guy. Pretty sure neither of them would come by for a Sunday morning chit-chat.

He turned to leave, paused at the door, shook his head, then disappeared around the corner.

I wasn't sure what to make of his mood shift. Reminded me of my father. Dad was the most loving, mild-mannered guy I'd ever known. But when it came to my safety, the gentle giant could crank up the protective dial to raging beast mode.

I emerged from the shower, wrinkled and rubber-legged. I threw on some mascara and lip gloss, fluffed my dark blond hair, and dug my favorite jeans from the dryer.

A hot pot of coffee awaited me on the kitchen counter next to a half finished cup. Black. It was darker than what I was used to but smelled divine. I paused before pouring cream into my mug and pictured Franklin in all his naked glory. No room for half-n-half in a body that physically fit—that void of fat.

I grabbed an apple and headed for the balcony. A cool breeze greeted me when I stepped outside. The sun made an honorable attempt to emerge from the fluffy billows of gray hanging in the sky. The usual hustle and bustle of Alki Beach on a Sunday morning was well underway, street and foot traffic already thick. A few brave, hardcore beach lovers stretched on oversized towels on the sand.

I loved my home. My view. Safety had never been a concern.

Until my neighbor and dear friend was brutally attacked.

Life could turn on a dime. My happy-go-lucky outlook? Yeah, that changed too. I used to study people in awe and wonderment. Now, I scrutinized each character. Sized them up. Judged by appearances which ones were most likely to commit heinous crimes. It sucked. It sucked bad.

I didn't want to people-watch anymore.

I was about to go back inside when a figure caught my eye. Dark gray hoodie, dark sweats, aviator glasses.

Holy shit.

The man jogged along the footpath, stopped to tie his shoe, lifted his head, and looked directly at me. Was it my imagination again? He stared for a long time, then raised his hand and waved.

I froze, teeth half sunken in my fruit.

His wave morphed into a pointed finger. Then a fake pistol. He shot his fake pistol. At me.

Blood drained from my head and congealed in my feet. I couldn't move.

He stood, then jogged away in the direction he'd come.

I screamed like a horror movie victim when something squeezed my shoulder.

Driven by pure adrenaline, acting on impulse, I whirled around and rammed my apple between Franklin's baby blues.

Faster than I could process what'd happened, I was on the floor. Franklin had straddled me and I'd been completely decommissioned. Again, I found myself unable to move. Pinned to the floor, wrists bound, legs immobilized, lungs emptied.

"Fuck, Tate. What the hell?" He wiped apple mush from his face. He wasn't out of breath, yet I couldn't find mine.

"Hoodie man." I pushed the words out between gasps for precious oxygen. "He was outside."

Franklin was on his feet and peering over the balcony in a heartbeat. "Where? Which way?" He turned to look at me but I still couldn't breathe.

As quick as he'd sent me to the floor, he pulled me to my feet. Damn, the man moved fast.

Blood managed to find its way back to my head. Thoughts cleared.

I punched hard at his chest. "Are you a damn ninja? Jeez, Franklin. You can't sneak up on people like that!"

"I'm sorry, didn't you hear me come in?" He shot me a stupefied glance.

"What was that?" I gestured to the floor. "You could've killed me." I patted myself from chest to buttocks, in search of injury. Found nothing.

"Are you hurt?" he asked, irritated and snappy.

"No," I grunted. "So not the point."

"Exactly the point. You weren't hurt."

Bastard. Where did he learn to move like that? "I think it was him. He looked right at me, then pointed his finger like a gun."

"Shit. Are you sure?" Hands fisting and stretching at his sides, he strode to the kitchen. I followed.

"No." Shoulders slumped, I shook my head. "Maybe it was my imagination." Or the fact that he'd fried my brain beyond repair with his fine tongue skills earlier.

"Come here," I ordered. I wet a towel and wiped the sticky mess from his handsome face. "I'm sorry. Just jumpy I guess." With a shrug, I tossed the cloth into the sink and brushed a finger across the wrinkles between his brows.

"Think it's gonna bruise?" His sensual drawl coated my ears, soothed my raw nerves. "Killer reflexes you got there."

I nodded. "I'm sorry." A purple bump already marred his face. Not big, just enough to be a reminder of the skirmish. "How you gonna explain this at work?"

I gasped when his lips hovered above mine and his arm encircled my waist.

"I'll tell them my girlfriend is abusive, but the sex is so hot, I can't bring myself to leave her."

Girlfriend? Why did that word, coming from his mouth, make me want to put on a princess dress and twirl around the kitchen?

* * * *

By noon, my doors sported brand new, state-of-the-art hardware, and three bulky men, dressed in light blue poplin shirts with Rogue Security logos, invaded every square inch of my home to perform last minute adjustments on the surveillance cameras they'd installed. Not one of them spoke more than two words to me. Franklin barked commands and they obeyed—all business, all stealth. Barely shot me a glance when they finally left. What kind of pull did Franklin carry to get these men to work on a Sunday?

"So that's where you went? Shopping? This is a bit over the top, don't you think?" I passed him a turkey sandwich and a bowl of fruit salad. "You should've asked me first. I don't need a security system. There are cameras throughout the building, a doorman, and a secured entryway."

Franklin rubbed his eyes with the palms of his hands, shook his head, and rolled his shoulders. "The program this building uses is a joke. A moron could get through or bypass it altogether. A woman living alone in this city can never be too careful."

"I'm not helpless."

"Didn't say you were." His smirk, although devilishly sexy, got under my skin. Something was off with him. "Just said you can never be too careful. This is the same one I use at my place."

"I didn't see any cameras in your apartment." Why would he need security? He lived in the Georgetown neighborhood. Not the safest place to be, but it was mostly industrial, not considered a high crime area. Who'd break in? The apartment was barren aside from his flat screen.

"You won't see any here when I'm finished." He pulled turkey from between the white bread and popped it in his mouth.

"How do you know this stuff?" I asked. Why did he feel the need to force it down my throat?

He didn't look at me, but his jaw clenched and he swallowed hard. "The shit I know would blow your mind." The wrinkles in his forehead deepened.

"I don't know anything about you, Mr. Reed. Besides the fact you are obscenely gorgeous and way too smart to work for Wallace Cruse. Seriously. What's your deal?" I was half joking.

He wasn't.

He responded with an icy glare. He wasn't going to answer me, but he contemplated the idea. I could see it on his face. Damn, his eyes cut through me like swords. Distracting as hell.

"Where's your computer? I need to connect you to the system. Your cell, too, so you can keep tabs from anywhere."

He changed the subject again. I wanted to bang my fist on the table and demand his life story. Instead, I crossed my arms and slouched in my seat. "Is this necessary?" Had the spirit of my overprotective, overbearing, dead father possessed Franklin's body?

A loud buzz came from his left butt cheek. With a grunt, he grabbed his phone from his pocket, headed towards the balcony, stopped short, then stomped out the front door.

Feeling ten levels of irritated, I tossed his half-eaten lunch in the trash and headed for the guest bedroom. I tried to make myself useful while Mr. Moody Pants took care of yet another call meant for nobody's ears but his. Unleashing my frustrations on the bedding, I tossed pillows on the floor and stripped the mattress with dramatic flair.

The private calls were beginning to unnerve me. What was he hiding? What was I not supposed to hear? It wasn't any of my business. I held no rights to him or his private life. We'd spent the last twenty-four hours together, and he disappeared every time his phone buzzed.

I wasn't getting the warm and fuzzies I'd expected after doing the things we did in my shower. On my bed. His couch.

Oh crap. Just thinking about it made me weak in the knees.

I bundled up the sheets and comforter and tripped over Franklin's duffel. My foot got caught in the damned handle, and I crashed to the floor with a loud thud. My knees took the brunt of the fall. The bedding protected my face from some serious carpet burn. Thank goodness, no one was around to witness my lack of grace. I untangled my foot from his duffel strap and crammed the spilled contents back into the bag. Thank the sweet heavens above, he wasn't there to witness my shameful act of rummaging through his private property.

What did I hope to find? Hadn't a clue. The opportunity presented itself. Who was I to deny fate, even if it was a result of my own clumsiness?

I found nothing out of the ordinary. Toiletries, bottle of Gendarme, few changes of clothes. It smelled of him. Warm, fresh, and all male. I was about to shove the bag back under the bed when something caught my eye, laying in the corner of the room next to the jeans I'd tried to rip off him last night. A wallet-sized picture of me and Jacob. The black-and-white image was fuzzy, like it'd been taken from a considerable distance. I was laughing in the photo. He'd probably told me one of his goofy jokes. We were in the cafe down the street, enjoying a cup of coffee.

My heart raced. Shit. The last time Jacob and I had visited the cafe was at least three weeks ago. Alarms blared in my head. This weekend needed to be over. I folded the jeans and placed them on the bed.

The picture? Oh, I would keep that for a while.

* * * *

The longer I waited for him to come back, the higher the red bar on my anger meter rose. His muffled voice rose and fell outside, his footsteps tracked up and down the hallway. At one point, I peeked through the peephole to find him standing in front of Jacob's door, phone to his ear, shoulders taut, his free hand clenched at his side. Judging by his stance, the phone convo was not a happy one.

Why would he take a picture of me and Jacob? Why the concern with my safety? Who was this whirlwind who'd stormed into my life and decimated the wall I'd lived behind?

Crap.

I'd let this near stranger into my home. Had let him violate me in torturous, pleasurable ways. Had trusted him completely. What a naive dumbass. My father must be doing flip-flops in his grave.

No time like the present to right a wrong. I stomped to the extra bedroom, grabbed his duffel and jeans, and headed for the front door.

I took one last whiff of his dreamy scent, then tossed his shit into the hall.

"I've got things to take care of," I shouted. "Thanks for a lovely weekend." I slammed the door, flipped both bolts and the chain lock.

Almost immediately, he pounded. I ignored it. Soon, my phone rang. I ignored it as well.

One more knock. Softer this time. I swallowed down the clumps of sand in my throat, then marched away from the temptation that lingered only inches away to finish making the guest bed.

I was pleasantly surprised by the amount of cleaning I could get done when pissed. I vacuumed, dusted, rearranged a closet, cleaned both bathrooms, washed windows. Not the front windows. I didn't want to look toward the beach, didn't want to see or be seen. By dinnertime, my arms ached and exhaustion set in, but my house looked like I'd won the Merry Maids lottery.

Franklin hadn't attempted to contact me. Thank goodness. I wouldn't have known what to say to him anyway. Monday morning would pose a challenge. I wasn't one to call in sick for no good reason, but Lordy was I tempted. I contemplated it for a moment, then shrugged the thought away. I couldn't let my indiscretion with a coworker alter my work ethic any more than it already had.

I wasn't hungry, but I grabbed my pint of Rocky Road, plopped my tired butt on the couch, and channel surfed my way to zombie land.

Sometime later, I woke with a pint of melted ice cream in my lap and a kink in my neck. I heard voices outside my door and tiptoed over to spy. Before I had a chance to peek, a sharp knock made me squeal and nearly empty my bladder where I stood.

Another knock. "Miss Wood. It's Detective Waters."

Knees weak, I drew a deep breath and unlatched my three new locks. "Hi. What's going on?"

Over his shoulder, several uniformed men huddled in a tight circle. Jacob's door was ajar and the police tape drifted across the floor like a drunk snake.

"May I have a word?" His large smile put me at ease until he snickered.

"Of course, come in." I moved aside and gestured for him to enter.

He pulled a handkerchief from his pocket and wiped at my chin. His gaze darted to the drippy container on my coffee table, then back to me. "Rocky Road. It was my wife's favorite." A deep dimple formed on the left side of his face. He returned the hanky to the breast pocket of his shirt.

My cheeks burned hotter than a freshly toasted marshmallow.

Wise brown eyes scrutinized me. "Are you alone, Miss Wood?"

"Um, yes." Gulp.

"I'm afraid we have a situation next door." As he spoke, he studied the living room. Searched. Took inventory.

"Why? What happened? Is it Jacob?" For the third time that day, my hair stood on end. For the first time in three years, I contemplated moving.

"Miss Wood. I'm afraid I'm not at liberty to say. If you don't mind, could I ask you a few more questions?"

"Of course."

Not at liberty to say, huh? Too bad. I was done with secrets for the day. I pushed passed the six-foot-something, burly policeman and bolted across the hallway towards Jacob's apartment. Another officer tried to swing me in the opposite direction. Two blinks too late. He tried to block my view, but I caught a glimpse of what had everyone's panties in a bunch.

A man, wearing a dark gray hoodie and dark sweats, hung, suspended by ropes, in Jacob's foyer, just beyond his door. Arms and legs sprawled, head fallen forward. Like a giant X. Blood pooled thick and shiny below him. So much blood.

My knees and ankles gave out. The floor came at me like a speeding bullet. I was suspended in the air by a solid arm, then set upright. I looked up into the warm eyes of Detective Waters.

"Shit. Miss Wood. I'm so sorry. You weren't supposed to see that." He scooted me back into my apartment. "Stiles. Shut that fucking door," he shouted.

My own door slammed behind me.

"I—I saw him." Thoughts spun in a nauseating cycle. "He. Jogging. I saw."

The detective braced me with a steady arm. A musky pine scent filled my senses. Warm. Soothing. "My deepest apologies. Those jackasses are being demoted first thing in the morning."

"No. You don't understand…" I shook my head and backed away. "I saw that man outside. This morning." Head spinning, my vision narrowed.

Detective Waters guided me to the couch and forced me into the cushions. He strode to the kitchen, searched my cupboards for a glass, and brought me some tap water. "Tell me what happened."

I took a small sip of the warm, chlorine-flavored aqua, then replayed the morning's events for him, minus the sexy stranger who'd outfitted my apartment in super spyware. I should've told him about Franklin.

I didn't.

I was pissed. I wanted an explanation from mysterious Mr. Reed before the police got a crack at him.

"Have you been home all day?" The beefy cop sat next to me.

"Yes." His weight sunk the cushion and I fell against his shoulder. He didn't seem to mind. His breath smelled of mint and coffee. I scooted over and turned toward him.

"Did you hear or see anything?" He flipped through the pages of his notebook.

"No. Nothing. I did have my music louder than it should've been. I was cleaning for most of the day." How I didn't hear or see anything so brutal happening right next door was beyond my comprehension.

"Miss Wood. I'm going to show you a picture. It's graphic. I'm sorry, but I need to know if you recognize him."

My gut clenched. More gore? No, thank you. Visions of Jacob's mangled body flashed before my eyes. Bile rose in my throat. I choked it down with more warm water.

Detective Waters handed over his cell. A close-up of the dead man's face filled the screen. Tattoos covered his shaved head. They also stretched up his neck and rose just above a square jawline. His cheeks were bloody. One eye was swollen shut. His lip, split wide open, revealed two bloody teeth.

"I'm sorry. I don't know this man." Not that I would've recognized his bruised and bloodied mug. The tattoos? I would've remembered meeting someone wearing that ink.

"Miss Wood. Do you have somewhere you can stay tonight?" I bounced when he rose to stand.

"I don't have anywhere to go." Mom was in Florida. No siblings.

"No family, friends?"

I shook my head. "No. Not really." Sure, I had a few close friends, but none I would burden with my troubles.

"Do I need to go?"

"You're not required to leave. Wouldn't you feel safer staying with someone? What about your boyfriend, the man who was here yesterday?"

I almost laughed. Bit hard on my lip instead. "Oh, he's not my boyfriend."

The handsome detective's eyes grew wide. "Could've fooled me. I noticed the way he looked at you." He winked as if he'd given me top-secret, valuable information. Wow. The gruff detective was a romantic at heart. How sweet.

"Not to worry. We'll be working through the night, I suspect. There will be officers stationed outside as well. Please don't be offended when they insist on escorting you in and out as you go."

"Thank you." I attempted a smile. "Where did they take Jacob? I called the three major hospitals earlier and nobody had record of him being admitted."

The detective's face hardened. "As soon as I hear how he's doing, I'll let you know." He paused as if debating whether or not to say more, then huffed. "You have my number. Call me any time. Day or night." He winked, then closed the door behind him.

Chapter 7

The black leather bodysuit squeaked as I prowled the unlit alley. I should've broken it in before carrying out my mission. Thank goodness the city noise hid the swoosh, swoosh of my thighs rubbing together. The mile-high spike heels made it difficult to navigate the cobblestone street, but damn they looked hot, and they were the main attraction for the evening's events.

I pulled the black mask into place, covering my face from nose to forehead. I didn't have a mirror to check myself, but who wouldn't look sexy and mysterious in a get-up like this?

I flattened myself against the wall and waited for my prey. Footsteps grew louder, bounced off the old brick buildings. One set. Good, he was alone. Made my job so much easier.

My heart raced with nervous excitement as he drew closer. I took one last deep breath, squatted, and performed a swinging, side-sweep kick as he passed. Caught him an inch above his ankles. He fell face-first at my side with a grunt.

The heel of my boot found a nice little resting spot at the base of his neck.

"Good evening, Mr. Cruse." I'd lowered my voice to make it sound dangerous and sultry.

He tried to rise. I held him in place with my stiletto spike.

"What are you doing?" He struggled to speak and fought to keep his open mouth away from the dirty ground.

"Tell me, Mr. Cruse. Are you even the slightest bit sorry for the terrible things you've done?"

Wallace squirmed underneath the weight of my foot. I pressed harder. He grunted and blew a puff of air.

"Do you suffer any remorse for the lives you've ruined on your journey to the top?"

Shrill laughter rose from the ground. "Never."

"I was hoping you'd say that." His flesh strained under the pressure of my heel. I angled my foot. Pushed harder. His skin popped, breaking under the strain.

"Is that Italian leather?" he asked with a whimper.

"Oh yes, Mr. Cruse. I knew you'd appreciate the outfit. Paid an arm and a leg for these boots. They're worth every penny though. Wanna know why?"

Wallace blinked and nodded.

With a slight twist, the spring-loaded blade in the heel of my thigh-highs pierced his neck and made a soft ding when it dug into the stone beneath him.

"Who are you?" Blood spurted between his lips, dribbled down his chin.

"I'm payback and I'm a bitch."

Morning hung over me like a layer of oily fog, heavy and suffocating.

I struggled to rise and haul myself to the shower. Barely mustered the energy to wash my hair. Getting dressed posed a challenge. Each article of clothing I tried on rubbed my skin like a scouring pad. The AM hours were usually my favorite time of day. That was no longer the case.

Franklin Reed and his damn panty-melting smile, his unexpected, yet timely injection into my life, had the gears in my brain grinding off kilter. Made it difficult to accomplish the smallest of tasks. I gave up hope of kick-starting my day with coffee when I'd brewed a whole pot of nothing but hot water.

I wasn't nervous about facing him at the office. Maybe I was too angry. Confused. In shock? Couldn't be certain. I was damn sure, though, I didn't want to sit in my house the entire day and sulk or worry over the horrors of the past forty-eight hours. Work was a much needed distraction. I could ignore Franklin if need be. Like I could ignore a toothpick jammed under my fingernail.

A young police officer, obviously new gauging by the spring in his step and the cock in his voice, escorted me to my car. By some miracle, I managed to make it to the office ten minutes early. I'd even taken a detour to pick up a venti caramel macchiato. Breakfast of champions.

I fought the urge to buy a morning drink for my new, now ex, sex buddy. A thank-you for rocking my world, for giving me crippling orgasms. On a normal day, I would've. Bastard wasn't getting any nicey-nice from me.

Not until he explained why there was a picture of me in his pants, and why every conversation via cell was treated as top secret.

I greeted Nan with a fake smile as I passed. The gesture wasn't returned, which was out of character for her. In her defense, she was on the phone, and held a cup of tea to her lips. Seemed to be chin-deep in an intense exchange by the glower she wore.

When I rounded the corner to my office, I wobbled in my platform pumps. The space reeked of male heat. Warm, spicy. Oh, so sexy.

Damn him.

A white to-go cup of something steamy sat on my desk, right next to a single red rose.

Just my luck, he'd beaten me to work.

Thank goodness Wallace was out of town. No way could I juggle his narcissistic ways as well as Franklin's overwhelming presence. Not after the weekend I'd managed to escape.

I swallowed the last drip of sugary heaven from my cup and moved aside the mystery drink. I pondered, but didn't touch the rose. Wasn't ready to process that yet. Bold move on his part. Office policy prohibited dating co-workers. How would I explain this if anyone asked? Why would he risk our jobs? We weren't even dating. Just fornicating. I walked to the window to open the shades, lingering to enjoy the view.

"Are you trying to make me jealous?" Heated breath tickled the back of my head. The funk of anger and male testosterone wafted off him.

Startled, I swung around and knocked a file folder from Franklin's hand. He didn't look down. Didn't bend to pick it up. His chest rose and fell. Piercing blue eyes narrowed.

My ticker danced a jig behind my ribcage. Even angry, he took my breath away. I skirted him and shuffled to my desk, biding time. He followed, hot on my heels.

"I wouldn't have touched you if I'd known there was somebody else. I don't play games, Tate." He leaned past me and the silk of his shirt brushed my cheek. He grabbed the rose then twirled it in front of my nose. The venom I'd been eager to unleash on him melted when disappointment, or maybe sadness, flashed in his eyes.

Wait. What? Somebody else? I snatched the flower from him. A thorn pricked my thumb. "Ouch." I cussed under my breath, tossed the rose on my keyboard, and snagged a tissue to dab the blood. "That's not from you?" I turned and gripped the edge of my desk for support. This was not the discussion I'd anticipated.

With a quick glance at the door, Franklin brought our bodies flush, suffocated me in his heat and lowered his lips to tickle my cheek. "I don't do roses. Too cliché." He straightened and took a step back. "If I did, I wouldn't be careless enough to give you one here and risk your job. Why would you think that was from me?" He looked honestly perplexed.

Which only pissed me off.

"Hmm, let's see. For starters, to apologize, maybe?" I couldn't loosen my death grip.

His gaze raked my body. Up, then down, then up again. "What exactly would I be apologizing for? You kicked me out, remember?"

Was he serious?

"What for? What *for*? Are you dense? For fooling me into trusting you. Getting me naked. Keeping secrets." I turned to dig the evidence from my purse and shoved the photo into the palm of his hand. "For spying on me. God, how could I be so careless? How long exactly has this been going on, Mr. Reed? Don't lie to me. I can't take any more bullshit."

When I should've run for the door, I slumped into my chair, crossed my arms and legs simultaneously, and waited. I needed to hear his explanation.

Franklin backed away, propped his shoulder against the wall and studied the pictures. "Is this why you threw me out?"

"Yes." I held my head high. "And the secret phone calls."

His gaze hardened. So did the knot in my gut. I wasn't about to let him intimidate me. "Explain the photo please."

"This isn't mine. I found it."

"Where?"

"Next to your car, in the parking garage." He shoved it into his pocket. "You're right about one thing. Someone is spying on you. It sure as hell isn't me. You can be damned sure I'll find out who it is."

The angry heat that fueled my morning left my body in one swift gust, only to be replaced with ice cold panic.

With a quick glance to the hallway, he came closer and lowered his voice. He paused and rubbed his eyes with the palms of his hands. "Maybe not you. Maybe your neighbor. It makes more sense, considering the brutality of his attack."

It dawned on me that he hadn't heard the latest breaking news. "Franklin, they found hoodie man in Jacob's apartment yesterday. Someone strung him up in the entryway. It was awful…" I cringed and shook my head as if the motion would clear the images from my brain. "The blood—"

"You saw him?" He cut me off, scolding through gritted teeth. "Why the fuck didn't you call me?" A crimson glow coated his face. I'm pretty sure I witnessed a new wrinkle carving itself into his forehead.

"I didn't call you because I'm not your problem. This isn't your problem. We fucked, Franklin. Nothing more. It doesn't give us any claim over one another."

"For Christ's sake, lower you voice." With another glance over his shoulder, he leaned toward me, pulled my chair closer to him then pressed his lips to my ear.

My muscles turned to warm butter.

"You shouldn't use that word. Your mouth is too pretty. Let's get one thing straight." His whispered breaths were flames licking my skin. "We didn't fuck. What I did to you was merely foreplay. Understand?"

His palm rested on my thigh. Fingers dug in. Demanded I listen and listen good.

"When I take you, and I hope it'll be soon, there will be no question in that clever little mind of yours that you've been thoroughly…" He bit my ear, slid his hand up my thigh and squeezed harder. "Well, you know."

His free hand slid around my neck, under my hair, gripped hard at the base of my skull. Sparks shot through my abdomen. Our eyes met only for a brief moment before he forced our mouths together and kissed me hard. As fast as he attacked, he released me, pushed my chair away and strode across the room to look out the window.

"Morning all!" Nan's cheerful smile drooped the moment she laid eyes on me, slumped, heaving, disheveled in my chair.

I raised a palm. "Happy Monday Nan. Have a good weekend?" I impressed myself with the ability to speak after the kiss. Although, by the look on her face, I hadn't fooled her.

Franklin kept his back turned. Grunted a "good morning" to her. She glanced at me, eyebrows raised, and flashed me an *oh, we're so going to talk* smile.

I lowered my gaze. Busted. The woman had superhuman mind-reading abilities.

"Even from out of state, Mr. Cruse is sucking in more clients. We're going to have a busy week. Seems there aren't any couples left in Seattle who aren't cheating on each other." Nan glanced at the single flower on my desk then back to me. "Shall we disappear for lunch later?"

I nodded, squeezing my thighs together.

She handed me a stack of file folders, winked, then made her exit with a playful spring in her step. Thank God, she wasn't the nosey type, otherwise lunch would be torture.

When the coast was clear, I prodded the formidable man devouring the space we shared. "Why didn't you tell me about the picture until now?"

He didn't turn to face me, but did grant me a great view of his profile. Square, strong jawbone, thick lashes, scruffier-than-usual stubble.

"You'd been through enough. I was waiting for the right time. It's why I pushed on the extra security." His shoulders bunched and his head tilted to the side. "You honestly don't know who the rose is from?"

"No. I assumed it was you." Like an idiot.

"I'll take care of it." He ripped the obtrusion from my desk and tossed it in the trash. I was glad to see it go. I wasn't glad to see Franklin button his suit jacket and storm down the hall.

What just happened? I came to work hell-bent on getting answers and there I sat with bruised lips, a female version of a woody and more questions. Grrr. And I hadn't even fired up my computer yet.

Mondays sucked.

* * * *

Lunch was torture. Nan suddenly took an unusual interest in my love life. I only went so far as telling her Franklin and I enjoyed our time at the bar. The events that happened afterward were for me alone. She pried. I lied. Nan didn't buy it and prodded more.

When finally sick of the twenty questions, I attempted to change the subject. "Did you hear about the murder?"

Eyes wide, she shook her head and drew a long drink of iced tea through her straw.

Unusual. Nan was my own personal news network. I never had to watch. Nan kept me updated. Twitter, internet, radio. It hit her from a hundred directions. How did she not hear about the murder? Two horrific attacks in the same home. How did that not make headlines?

I briefly told her about Jacob's attack and the man found dead. I left out the part about me finding him, or the fact he was near and dear to me. I couldn't handle any sympathy.

"Strange it wasn't broadcast." She pulled out her tablet and started to search. "Nothing. There is absolutely nothing here about any murder. That's odd." She sucked her bottom lip between her teeth and tapped her straw against the edge of her glass. I could almost see the gears grinding behind her soft brown eyes. "What do you know about the guy?" she asked, cocking her head to the side.

"Not much," I lied and shrugged my shoulders. "I'd only bumped into him a few times on the elevator."

Why did I feel the need to omit the truth? Not sure. Self-preservation, maybe? Didn't want to have an emotional breakdown? Perhaps. Part of me was perturbed that Nan, notorious for minding her own business even though she somehow knew everyone's affairs, was suddenly nosier than a bloodhound.

Agitated by the fact that Jacob's attack was on the hush-hush, my paranoia spiked dangerously fast. Maybe Franklin was right: whoever took the pictures was actually spying on Jacob, not me.

I needed lunch to be over so I could get to my office and Google Jacob Smart. "Well, Nan. It's the start of a busy week. Let's get to it." I left a five and some change on the table and we headed out.

When I returned to my desk, hell-bent on digging up some Jacob dirt, Franklin was still MIA. I hadn't a clue where he'd ghosted off to, but whatever. Gave me time to spy.

For three hours, I ignored my work and researched Jacob. I even dug deep into our under-the-radar and barely legal police and government searches. Came up with nada. Zip. The Jacob Smart I knew seemingly didn't exist. The bookstore he'd supposedly owned? Big, fat, in-your-face fib. The man wasn't even listed as the owner of his condo.

Once again, my hunt for answers only filled my noggin with more questions. Franklin's words spun in my head. *The shit I know would blow your mind.*

Who was Franklin Reed? I glanced at the door, then typed his name in the search bar. There were close to a gazillion results. I scrolled through the first few pages and gave up. It didn't feel right checking up on him, especially when he could sneak in any second.

Without Franklin sharing my personal space, the room seemed void and cold. I hadn't realized how comfortable he'd become or how much I relied on his company to get me through the daily drudgery of our jobs. Did that mean I missed him? Crapola, but it did. I missed the secretive, ninja stealth sexpot that'd given me the best romp of my life. Goosebumps tickled me from scalp to toes.

Stupid, girlie libido.

I pushed to my feet and headed towards Nan's office. "Hey, have you heard from Franklin?"

She didn't take her eyes off her computer screen. "Yes. He went home sick. Told me not to expect him for a few days."

Sick? What was he up to?

Nan's fingers danced atop her keyboard. "I've been watching the news all afternoon. There's nothing about your murder." Frustration thick in her voice, she shook her head. "Creepy, isn't it? Such a brutal murder in our city not mentioned anywhere?"

"Yeah. Weird." She had no idea. I wasn't about to enlighten her.

Nan pushed her chair back, stood, and grabbed my shoulders. "Why don't you come and stay with me for a few days? You must be terrified to go home."

Yes, any sane person would've been all over that offer of safe haven. Apparently, Franklin non-fucked the sanity clean out of my horny little brain. "Thanks, Nan. I appreciate the offer. I'm staying with a friend," I fibbed. I didn't want to, but I also didn't feel like explaining to her the many reasons I wanted to stay at my place, each of them beginning and ending with Franklin. As much as I loved the woman, getting to know her in that personal of a capacity held no appeal to me.

"Oh. Okay. That's good." Her expression sagged and she went back to typing on her computer. "What did you say his name was?" she asked, staring blankly at her screen.

"Jacob Smart." I shouldn't have given his full name, if that even was his name, but it didn't hurt to have someone else on the hunt for answers.

I ambled back to my desk and plugged my way through three of the new case files. How Wallace was able to schmooze these high profile clients was beyond me. And why did rich people even bother getting married? According to our records, every marriage in Seattle with a household income above the seven-digit mark suffered from dick-in-the-wrong-woman disease. The job did little to foster my faith in the human spirit.

Was Franklin the faithful type? No clue. By the way he reacted to finding the rose on my desk, it seemed he was. I hoped so, anyway. Not that we were a couple or anything.

I plopped the finished documents on Nan's desk, waved a goodbye, and headed out the door. The underground garage was well lit and monitored by our own security team, but when I stepped off the elevator, ice cold dread smacked me right between the eyes. My parking space was two slots away from the door, and I'd never been afraid to walk to my car alone. I glanced around. John from IT was pulling out of the lot in his new Prius. He smiled and nodded. I waved goodbye.

I turned to unlock my car and froze when I noticed a single red rose tucked under my windshield wiper.

I stood still and debated whether or not to touch the evil flower. The elevator ding echoed through the underground cavern. The door slid open and out walked Stacy and Pete, our two accountants. They shouted goodbyes to me and headed to their cars.

I pretended to dig for my keys instead of standing around like a dumbass. When they were out of view, I picked up the rose and tossed it on the ground. Then I stomped on the stupid, creepy thing and kicked it under the car parked next to mine.

My hands trembled, making it impossible to push the unlock button on my key fob. Sheesh. I needed to put this day far, far behind me. Already on edge, my bladder nearly burst when a deep voice called out to me. I turned and came face to chest with Detective Waters.

"Holy shit! Are you trying to give me a heart attack?" I slammed my palms against his pecs.

"Miss Wood." He fought back a smile. "I didn't mean to scare you. I wanted to get in touch before you headed home."

"Well, here I am. Touch away." Oh, shit. Did I say that? "I mean. Crap. What's up?"

His face crinkled, as if it hurt to witness my lack of verbal grace. "I called your cell and left a few messages. I wanted to talk to you in person, so I took a chance and swung by. I'm glad I caught you."

I rested my butt against my car door and crossed my arms. My cell, huh? Shoot. Must've forgotten to turn it on. I was so preoccupied I hadn't noticed my phone didn't buzz, not even once.

"I'm sorry, detective. My phone's been turned off all day."

"Please, call me Leland." He rocked back on his heels and crossed his arms over his chest. "I'm no longer on the case so there's no need for the formalities."

"No longer on the case?" I asked, unnerved by the look of vexation on his face. "What's happened? Did you solve the murder?"

"No, Miss Wood. That's why I need to speak with you."

I held my palm up to stop him. "I call you Leland, you call me Tatum. Deal?"

"Deal," he grunted, scanning the parking lot corner to corner.

He sure was handsome for a man his age. Especially when his dimples appeared and the wrinkles around his eyes crinkled together.

"So. The SPD has been relieved of the case. It seems this neighbor of yours was involved in some deeply guarded government shit." He raised an eyebrow. "Please don't ask me to elaborate. I've crossed the line already by coming here." Leland leaned against the car, his hip and shoulder pressing against mine. Not in an inappropriate way, but more an overprotective, big brother sort of way.

I turned and lifted my chin to meet him eye to eye. "What does this have to do with me?"

"Before they took over, I found this." He pulled a photo from his chest pocket. I stared at it. Held it closer to my face. Then my knees wobbled. The photo looked to be at least thirty years old, but there was no denying two of the subjects. My dad and Jacob seated in what appeared to be a bar, flanked by two scantily clad women. Glasses raised. Smiles wide.

"That's your father," he stated.

I rubbed my finger across the image of dad's face. He seemed so happy. "How did you know it was my dad?"

"I knew your father. Wood is a common name so I didn't put two and two together until I found the photo. Antonio Wood. Tatum Wood. You have his eyes."

"How did you know him?"

"I can't discuss the nature of our relationship. You have to trust me. I don't think it's a coincidence that Jacob Smart bought the condo next door to you. I didn't share the photo with the suits." He turned to face me. "They are going to question you again. Tell them exactly what you already told us, nothing more. This conversation never happened. If you need anything, call me on this number." He shoved a folded piece of paper into my hand. "Not the number I gave you before. They'll be tracing my calls."

My hands shook as I tried to decipher the handwritten digits. "I don't…what…should I be…" God. My mind reeled. Dad? How was this possible? "What's going on, Leland? Should I be worried?"

He released a frustrated gust of air. "I'm not sure what's going on. I need to dig deeper. I want you to know, I've got your back."

I held up a hand to stop him from speaking. "Is this why the attacks weren't on any news feeds? I mean, it's strange, right? They should've at least made the local news."

Leland closed his eyes and shook his head. "I can't tell you any more than I already have. Just know I'm here for you."

"Why?"

His shoulders slumped and he backed away. "I owe your father. Keep the photo. I made a copy." He turned and stormed through the exit doors.

I jumped into my car, turned the locks, and powered up my cell. Yup, there were three missed calls from the same unknown number.

I didn't bother to listen. I just wanted to get home and put Monday behind me.

Chapter 8

The rest of the week passed without incident. Jacob's apartment was a hotbed of men in dark suits, shiny shoes, and shinier hair when I returned home on Monday evening and, following Leland's advice, I told them exactly what I'd already told the police. Nothing more, nothing less.

I had managed to coerce one of them into telling me that Jacob was recovering well and that I needn't worry about him. They remained tight-lipped when I asked where he was, but they did promise to keep me updated on his health.

Mysterious Mr. Reed was a no-show at the office. Wallace landed more clients, which doubled my workload. That was a good thing. I dug in and kept my thoughts on other people's problems. There wasn't time to think about murders or non-dates or mind-blowing orgasms.

I hadn't heard from Franklin, either. I did check my phone at least a hundred times a day in case he'd texted. But he didn't, and that stung more than I'd expected it to. Emptiness consumed me. My house, my bed, my gut. Nothing but a dark void. I'd only spent a weekend with him. Not even an entire weekend. Already, a Franklin-sized hole occupied most of my heart.

On Friday, a few minutes after five, I packed up my things and headed out. A large-breasted, Botox-injected, bleach-blonde stepped off the elevator and headed straight for me. "Nan Cummings?" she asked, her bottom lip barely moving.

My face scrunched in an embarrassing display of morbid curiosity. I couldn't take my eyes off her plump lips. "She's in her office. Down the hall, first door on the right." I pointed her in the right direction.

She smiled. At least I think it was a smile. Her eyes seemed happier anyway. "Thank you, dear." She turned to go and tripped. I threw out an arm to catch her. Somehow, her hand tangled in my hair. When she pulled away, strands of my blond locks went with her, snagged by her gaudy rings.

"Ouch." I winced and pressed a hand to the back of my head to soothe the sting.

"Oh. Oh, I'm so sorry. Are you okay?" She righted herself. "I'm such a klutz."

"I'm okay. Killer heels, huh?" I joked.

"You'd think I would've learned to walk in them by now," she muttered, then pivoted and swayed down the hall, her designer shoes clacking against the hardwood. I recognized her as Dahlia Montgomery, one of the cheating spouses Cruse Investigations had been hired to expose. The proof we provided of her torrid affair saved her husband millions on the divorce settlement, and Wallace received a hefty bonus. A large sum, which he did not share with the people whom actually dug up the dirt. One of the many reasons I despised Wallace Cruse.

What business could Dahlia possibly have with Nan? Were we even allowed to meet with her? Part of me wanted to tiptoe down the hall and eavesdrop, but most of me needed to crawl into bed. Nan was a big girl. If anyone could handle a sticky situation, it was her.

I reached my car, slid into the seat, and kicked off my shoes. Ah, I loved the time of day when I could take off my pumps, almost as much as I loved chucking my bra the minute I got home. I twisted around to grab my flip-flops off the backseat and screamed out loud when I found a dozen red roses lying in their place.

"Holy shit." My heart raced, my hands trembled. "Sick bastard!" I jumped out of the car, ripped the back door open, and threw the wretched flowers on the ground. I'd never peeled out of the parking garage before, but I couldn't shake the feeling I was being watched and wanted to get the hell out of there. I needed Franklin. Craved the safety of his arms. I knew it was crazy. He was a stranger. An extraordinary, arcane man who made my heart swoon and my brain turn to mush.

I started on my usual route, but the ache in my gut turned to a sharp stab and the only person with the ability to unknot my intestines lived the opposite direction. I swerved across three lanes to make the exit and managed the fifteen minute trek to Franklin's apartment without breaking any traffic laws.

I took the stairs two by two and banged on his door, huffing and puffing to catch my breath. No answer. I pounded louder. Nothing. Shoot. I couldn't go home. I didn't want to offer a fake smile to another federal agent or police officer, or whoever the hell they were.

I ended up in the Malted Maven, in the same seat I sat in for my first and last non-date, only one week ago. The same waitress waved at me from behind the counter, poured a drink from the tap, and sashayed my way.

"Hey, you're Frankie's girl," she announced, her voice warmer than I recalled. "Dark beer, right?" She placed the foamy mug in front of me.

I smiled, not exactly feeling the emotion behind the action. "Franklin's friend. Just friends. Have you seen him?" I asked.

"Not today, but he's here every night. I bet he'll be in soon." She wiped down my table, flaunting her perfect boobs and toned arms. "Is he meeting you?"

I shook my head. "No. I was hoping to run into him. He's not upstairs. What's your name?" I asked.

Her smile grew. "Lizzie. You're Tate, right?"

Franklin and Dad were the only people who called me Tate. But this girl remembered my drink order from a week ago—and had called me Frankie's girl. She earned the right to use my nickname. "Yeah, Tate." I offered my hand to her. "It's nice to officially make your acquaintance."

Lizzie shook my hand, told me she'd be back soon, and headed toward a table of depressed looking twenty-somethings dressed in plaid shirts, each sporting an overgrown beard and thick rimmed glasses. I was sure if I looked under the table, they'd be wearing the same grungy loafers in different shades of brown. I didn't get the whole thick beard fad. I mean, seriously, who would want to kiss that?

I checked the time on my phone. Five forty-five. Where was he? If he were sick, which I highly doubted, why wasn't he in bed? Why hadn't he called? Mister *I'm so concerned about you I'm going to stay the night at your house and install a new security system and boss you around* left me high and dry and hornier than a bored housewife. How could he barrel into my life that way and then disappear?

Try as I might, I couldn't hold on to the anger. It was my life story, after all—One-Date Tate. He'd hung around longer than the others.

Lizzie plopped a plate of fries in front of me. "Mind if I join you? Taking a break, I'm famished. You should eat, too. Beer and an empty stomach don't mix." She scooted next to me and adjusted her ponytail.

"You're an angel. I'm starving." I wasn't shy. I dug in.

With a mouthful of greasy potato, she asked, "How do you know Frankie?"

I swallowed my bite and washed it down with a sip of beer. "We work together." Shared a bed once, too. And a shower. An apple. Couple of amazing orgasms. Oh, yeah.

"And you're dating? How the hell do you make that work?" She hoisted my mug and helped herself to a swig.

I shook my head and instantly regretted it. Head shaking, after two beers, wasn't a wise move. I teetered in my seat. "Oh, we're not dating."

She snorted, then laughed out loud. "Yeah, right. Tell Frankie that. You're all he talks about, when he talks. Do you know how many times he gets hit on in a night? He blows the bitches off before they even get started. Tells everyone he has a girlfriend."

Girlfriend? I'm sure my eyes popped out of my head. Not only from surprise, but because she sounded irked.

"He won't even look at another woman. I mean, seriously. He's got pussy flying at him from ninety different directions." She paused and looked me square in the eye. "Just so you know, I'm crushing on your man big time, but we've never hooked up. Not for lack of trying on my part. I gave up after the first six months of rejections."

It was my turn to snort. "Only six months? He's not my man, but thanks for being up front. I wanted to ask, but was afraid you'd kick my ass."

Lizzie threw her arm around my shoulder and pulled me close. "He is your man. I know this because you're the only girl I've seen him bring in here. And FYI, I could kick your ass if I wanted to. I like you, so you're safe."

Perhaps it was the beer, or that my emotions were all over the place, but I kissed her cheek and gave her a squeeze. "How long has Franklin lived here?" I asked, hoping she liked me enough to spill some beans.

"About three years now." She scanned the crowd of people. "I'm surprised he hasn't shown his face. He hasn't missed a night this week."

Ha! I knew it. He wasn't sick. Bastard. My spirits sank to my toes. He'd been avoiding me all week. "I should head home. It's getting late. If I stay, I'll keep drinking, then I'll need to call a taxi. I hate taxis."

Lizzie pursed her lips in a pout. "You can't leave. You're the only cool person here tonight. Stay, please? If you get wasted, you can sleep on my couch. I live a block away."

I didn't want to spend the evening alone. Hanging out in a bar all night held little appeal, but it was better than the alternative. "I think I love you." I raised my glass to her. "Now, get me another beer, bitch."

Lizzie threw a fry at my chest, scooted out of our booth and reached for my empty glass. "Bitch is right, and this bitch is making sure you have fun tonight."

I did need to have fun. I'd survived a hellacious week, dammit. If I couldn't burn off steam via Body de la Franklin, then I would do it the old fashioned way—alcohol, loud music and some dancing. The bar didn't have a dance floor, but who cared? Life was what you made of it. I drank, ordered more fries, and resorted to dancing in my seat.

Lizzie came to my table smiling like she'd won the lottery and placed another drink in front of me. "This beer is courtesy of the hot dude perched in the dark corner." She nodded over her shoulder toward the door.

Biting my lip to stifle a laugh, I leaned in my seat to see around her. A large man wearing a black leather jacket, dark jeans and square-framed Oakleys gave me a salute and slipped out the door. He looked familiar, but he disappeared so fast, I was unable to steal a good look.

"He sends a message." Clearing her throat, she cupped her hands over her chest. "The roses bleed, as does my heart."

Roses? Oh, shit. I jumped out from behind the table and grabbed Lizzie's arm. "Him? The guy who just walked out the door?"

"Yes. What's wrong?"

"Do you know who he is?" I shook her. "Has he been here before?"

"No." Lizzie peeled my hands from her shoulders. "He's been sitting there for about an hour."

"Did you see his face? Get a name?" I asked, keenly aware of the tremble in my voice.

"No."

"Did he use a credit card?"

"No. Cash. Why?" Her jade eyes darkened with worry.

Shit! I scooped up my purse and keys, slipped my flip flops back on and sprinted for the door.

"Tate!" Lizzie shouted. "What the hell?"

I stood on the sidewalk, looked left then right. A motorcycle revved to life around the other side of the building. I ran that direction, but wasn't fast enough. The perp disappeared down a dark alley.

I made a mad dash to my car. The same roses I smashed in the parking garage earlier in the day lay across the hood, held together by a black ribbon.

"Are you freaking kidding me?" I screamed.

Lizzie patted my arm. "What was that about?" She spied the flowers and picked them up. "The roses bleed," she whispered, then gasped. "Do you have a stalker, Tate?" Knowing eyes glared at me.

I nodded, fighting a wave of tears. "Apparently, I do."

Once again, the bouquet hit the ground in a violent fashion. "I'm so sorry. I didn't know. I wouldn't have—"

I interrupted. "It's not your fault. I wish I could've gotten a look at the piece of shit."

"Have you reported it?"

I shook my head. "Not yet. Don't worry, I will."

"Don't fuck with this shit, Tate. I know a guy, if you need help."

I knew a guy, too. And damn, I needed the comfort his arms provided. I also carried Detective Waters' private number in my purse. "I've got a detective on speed dial." I hooked my arm through her elbow and walked back toward the front entrance.

We stopped dead in our tracks when Franklin stumbled around the corner wearing his lady-killer jeans and a tall brunette on his arm. He kissed her cheek, stuffed a wad of money into her hand and slapped her leather-clad ass before she slid into a black town car that waited on the street.

He watched the car drive away. It had given me time to turn and run, but I couldn't move. Lizzie released an impressive combination of cuss words. Franklin turned. His eyes widened in shock, then narrowed to a dangerous glare.

"What are you doing here?" he asked, taking long, calculated strides my way.

Lizzie stepped into my line of vision. "I'm right inside if you need me." She squeezed my hand, then pointed at Franklin. "Jackass," she grunted before heading into the bar.

"Was that a whore?" Oops. There went my mouth again. I wanted to curl into myself, tuck my tail, and retreat. Instead, I lifted my chin and forced my shoulders to the upright position.

Franklin's cheeks reddened. His fingers stretched, then fisted. "Why are you here?" he asked after drawing a deep breath.

I turned and stormed toward my car. His footsteps crunched in the gravel behind me. Dangerously close behind me. I shouted over my shoulder. "Because I'm the world's biggest idiot."

I kicked the crumpled roses out of my way and fumbled for my keys. Hard muscle pressed against my back. Tingles flittered across my chest.

"You're not leaving." Franklin gripped my hipbones, digging deep, and pulled my rear snug against his erection. Breath that reeked of sweet liquor warmed my cheek.

Anger welled, a shit storm of frustration and fury whirled through me. I jerked his hands off my hips and dropped my keys in the process. "Do you think I'm that pathetic? You just screwed a whore, you piece of shit." I bent to retrieve my keys and got a handful of rose petal instead.

I threw them in the air and collapsed in the dirt, a heaving mess of drunken, scared, heartbroken female.

* * * *

Once again, on a Friday night, I curled up on Franklin's couch, tipsy, with a too-tight skirt and bare feet. This time, however, I couldn't appreciate his sculpted form, tight ass, or brilliant eyes. Heck, I couldn't see a thing through the salty liquid flowing from my eyes.

He disappeared down the hall and returned with a roll of toilet paper. Grabbing a wad, I buried my face in my hands, and with hitched breaths, told Mr. Reed that I hated his guts. He squatted in front of me and laid his palms on my knees, sending unwelcome, delicious prickles through my flesh.

"You don't hate me," he said with that deep gravel that made me want to dip him in hot fudge sauce, roll him in a pan of crushed nuts, then clean him with my tongue.

"I do, I really, really do."

He leaned closer. "You don't hate me."

Of course I didn't. I wanted to. "I hate what you do to me."

"What is it I do?" he asked, sliding his hands further up my thighs.

My legs wanted to fall open and welcome him in. I squeezed my knees together. "You know, and I'm not saying it out loud."

"She wasn't a whore." His tone darkened and his fingers tightened around my flesh.

I dropped my hands from my face and rested them on top of his. "I saw you give her money and touch her ass and kiss...." I couldn't finish the sentence. It hurt too much to say the words. The green-eyed monster struck with a vengeance—and that made me pathetic, didn't it?

"I pay her for services that I can't discuss with you. She's a good friend. I've known her for years."

"No sex?" I asked with a hoarse whisper.

"She doesn't like men."

"You didn't answer my question."

"Damn, Tate. No. I didn't have sex with her. Is that what this is about? You assumed I was sleeping around?"

I leaned back against the cushions. "I haven't heard from you all week. Jacob Smart isn't Jacob Smart, and he knew my father and…shit. Someone keeps leaving me roses. He was at the bar. I think he's stalking me."

"At the bar? Tonight?" Franklin stood and stumbled backwards. "Why in the hell didn't you call me?"

"It just happened. I don't have your number."

He yanked my handbag from the floor and rifled through it until he found my cell. "I gave you my contact info on Sunday. You're the only person I know who's not permanently attached to her phone." He held the screen toward me. "See? I'm number one on your speed dial."

Yanking the phone from his hand, I snapped at him, "You didn't tell me. I'm not a damn mind reader."

"You kicked me out before I could show you anything." He plopped his fine ass right next to mine, leaving zero wiggle room. "You should also know, I haven't been sick. I had another case—" He shook his head. "I mean job. I had another job to finish up." Leaning sideways, he pulled a key out of his pocket. "I made myself a set for your place and finished setting your security system today."

"The feds didn't harass you?" They knew I lived alone. How did he slip past?

He paused before answering. His jaw twitched. "No."

"Wait a minute." I sat up, curling my legs underneath me. "You're keeping something from me."

Franklin stood and picked up where he left off with the pacing, stretching and clenching his fists in rhythm with his steps. He did that fist exercise whenever he needed to calm down. He stopped, cocked his head, raised a hand. Paced some more. Then knelt before me again.

"Tatum."

Tatum? He never called me Tatum. And, he sounded exactly like my Dad used to when giving me a speech or a tongue-lashing.

"There are things I can't tell you. I need you to trust me." He tilted his head to catch my gaze, which wandered unwittingly to his yummy lips. "Look at me. I need to know you're hearing me."

I found his baby blues.

"Everything I'm doing is for you. I can't tell you any more than that. I know it doesn't make sense. I'm asking. I'm begging you to please trust me."

"What's going on?" I asked. Was he drunk?

"Baby, listen. I can't say another word. Just. Fuck. You just have to do what I say. Please."

Scared? Yeah. I was scared. Because I knew he spoke the truth even though it didn't make a lick of sense. I could see it in his eyes. Feel it in my bones. What was he protecting me from? Who died and made him my guardian angel?

His pleading expression turned my insides to a gooey mess, and I leaned forward to steal a nibble of his soft lips.

Franklin groaned, pulled away from me, and squeezed his eyes closed. "What are you doing to me?" Before I could react, he pinned me against the back of the couch and devoured my mouth.

This man. This powerhouse of male flesh didn't just kiss. He staked his claim. It wasn't an endearing gesture. It was an assertion. *You're mine.* It was a command. *Give me all of you.* It was a promise. *I'll be your shelter.*

He kissed me sober. Kissed me witless. When he stopped, I was warm putty, molded into the cushions. His lips hovered over mine. "I missed you so goddamned much."

He missed me? "You're doing it again," I whispered.

Pressing his forehead to mine, he groaned. "Doing what again?"

"Making me hate you."

Franklin slid my skirt up my hips, forced my legs around his waist and rolled until he was seated and I straddled him. His strong hands pulled me against his groin, grinding me against an impressive erection.

"What did I do?" He asked, staring at my lips and dragging his tongue across his own.

"You say you missed me, but you didn't call once this week. You kiss me until I'm crazy. You make me want you more than I've ever wanted anything. I don't know what this is between us. I don't know anything about you. I hate it. I hate that I'm a brainless bimbo when it comes to you."

Franklin laughed. It vibrated my chest, squeezed air from my lungs and sent warm tingles to my female parts. Snaking his arms around my middle, he crushed me against him. I nuzzled the crook of his neck, pressed my ear to his chest and listened to the life force pump and flow through his body. His heartbeat slowed, breaths deepened, and within minutes, Franklin Reed was fast asleep beneath me.

Not for one second did his hold on me falter. I never would have imagined another man's embrace feeling safer than Dad's.

Chapter 9

"Breathtaking, isn't it?" I pressed my thighs against the barrier and stretched my neck to get a better look over the edge. The cliff shot straight down into a ravine lined with jagged rocks and hungry scavengers.

I turned my head toward the man bound at wrists and ankles by my side. "I asked you a question."

Beady peepers blinked at me and he nodded a "yes."

"Do you like the suit?" I asked.

He mumbled through the gag in his mouth.

"I'm happy you like it." I turned to him, straightened his tie, and brushed lint from his collar. "It's a good suit to die in."

Wallace bounced up and down on his toes, a pathetic scramble for freedom. The poor bastard didn't have an athletic bone in his body and fell hard to his knees.

I sighed and squatted to help him up when, from behind, someone grabbed my shoulder and stopped me.

"Let me do the honors." Franklin stepped around me, yanked Wallace to his feet by the lapels and hoisted him to the edge of the cliff. He turned to me, nodded, and stepped back. "He's all yours, darling."

"Why thank you, you handsome devil." I pinched Franklin's cheek and sauntered to Walter's side, threw out my hip and bumped him over the edge. I regretted not pulling the gag from his mouth first. It would've been much more satisfying if I could have heard his screams.

I wiped the hangover haze from my eyes and yawned. Now I'd drawn Franklin into my morbid dreams. Poor guy. I pressed my nose into the soft pillow. It carried a hint of Gendarme and a whole lot of Franklin's male sexual spiciness. Cocooned in a heavy comforter, I struggled to sit up. A tall glass of water and a bottle of ibuprofen sat within reach on the floor, along with a note.

I snatched up the yellow piece of paper. The handwriting was barely legible, but I got the gist of it. Franklin had shit to take care of—top secret, no doubt. He ordered me to drink the water and help myself to a shower and breakfast. He left a key on the kitchen counter for me to lock up when I left and said he'd meet me at my house later in the afternoon. In caps, he ordered me to check my phone throughout the day. That was it. No signature. No *I can't wait to see you* or *have a good day.*

I tossed the blanket over the back of the couch and smiled when I looked down at myself. In place of my skirt and blouse were a pair of navy sweats and a faded Pearl Jam T-shirt. I had no recollection of changing clothes, or being put to bed. Although, I wasn't technically in bed. If he went to such trouble to make me comfortable, why leave me on the couch?

I padded to the kitchen. The clock read ten thirty-four AM. Wow. I hadn't slept that late in years. A note was taped to the coffee pot instructing me to push the start button. I did, and within seconds, the aroma of dark roasted bliss filled the small space. He'd thoughtfully placed a red mug next to the machine.

I headed down the hall to find the little girls' room. There were three closed doors for me to choose from. Door number one was a large closet. Door number two, locked. Number three opened to a quaint bathroom with hardly enough room for the pedestal sink, commode, and glass-encased shower. It was clean. I didn't expect a bachelor's washroom to be so fresh and shiny. Of course, I snooped through his medicine cabinet. It was as empty as the rest of his apartment. Toothbrush, toothpaste, deodorant, bottle of pain reliever and shaving tools. Nothing snoop-worthy. Except for his smell permeating the air, the place didn't feel lived in.

I rested my hip against the sink and in my half-alert state attempted to unravel the mystery that was Franklin. Something was off. I strolled back into the kitchen and finished half a cup of kickass java before I figured out what it was. Franklin's apartment was void of any personal items. There were no photos of family or friends, no mail, no music or video collection to give me a clue to who this man was.

Then it dawned on me the locked door must be his bedroom. Why lock me out of his room? What was he hiding? He wanted me to trust him, but it was clear he didn't trust me.

I finished another cup of joe and started to fold the comforter when I heard the roar of a motorcycle engine outside. My skin prickled, and I tiptoed to the one small window in the living room. I peeked through the heavy blinds, careful not to wiggle them. Parked next to my car was the man from the bar, sitting on a shiny black Harley. He wasn't wearing a helmet, but his face was covered by the hood of his sweatshirt and dark sunglasses. He tilted his head to look around. I could make out a square jawline dusted with stubble, but not much else. He pulled a black rose from inside his jacket and laid it across my windshield.

"Son of a bitch," I spewed. I wanted to jump out the window and pounce the asshole, but I was three stories up, so that wouldn't have ended well for me.

Lucky for him.

Instead, I grabbed my cell and texted Franklin, like any good little girlfriend would do.

stalker creep is outside your apartment

I paced and chewed my lip. In less than thirty seconds my phone vibrated.

lock door bolt, don't leave coming home.

I sprinted to the front door and slid the lock into place, certain my heartbeat could be heard miles away. I slunk back to the window for another peek. The ass-wad leaned against my car and tapped at his cell.

I peed myself a little when my phone vibrated with a text from an unknown caller.

u didn't drive home last night slut
didn't think u were that kind of girl
playing hide n seek?

Blood sluiced ice cold through my veins, my extremities numbed, and I barely found the courage to lift my eyes from the screen. When I did, man and motorcycle were halfway down the alley. Again, I failed to get one digit off his license plate. And I worked for a detective agency? Perhaps it was time to consider a new career path.

Eighteen minutes and thirty-two seconds later, Franklin pounded on his door. "It's me, Tate. Open up."

I unbolted the lock and threw myself into his arms. Over-dramatic? Probably. Didn't care. He hugged me so tight I think a rib cracked, but I didn't complain. I was ecstatic it wasn't a one-sided gesture. He held me for a long moment, then stepped back and eyed me up and down.

"Did you get a good look? License plate, description, anything?" he asked, anger evident in his tone.

I hung my head in shame. "No."

"How about a picture with your phone?"

Shit. "No." Obviously, my brain ceased to function under pressure.

I slapped my cell into his palm. "He has my number. The asshole has my number. He sent me a text."

"Son of a bitch." Franklin read the message, then proceeded to smash my cell against his brick wall. It didn't survive the assault. Pieces of it came close to hitting my face. "When I find out who the fucker is, he's dead." He stomped back and forth the small distance between me and the wall.

"Like my phone? What the hell?" I squatted and picked up the larger pieces. "You didn't have to kill my phone. I just got this one."

He mumbled something that sounded like "He'll beg for mercy."

"What did you say?" I asked.

His brows pinched, the wrinkles in his forehead deeper than I'd ever seen. I wanted to kiss them away, but he didn't look in the kissing mood.

He offered a hand to help me up. "Nothing. Never mind. I'm sorry about your phone. I lost my temper. Shouldn't have done that in front of you."

I stood and he took the broken pieces from my hand, avoiding eye contact. He walked to the kitchen and dropped them on the table.

I huffed. "It's time to get the police involved. It's not just roses anymore."

"He sent you a text, which means we have his number." Franklin's glare traveled the length of my body, rested on my breasts, then met my gaze. "I should be taking care of this, not the SPD. But fuck, you're the worst kind of distraction. I'm off my game."

"What is that supposed to mean?"

"What you do to that shirt is downright sinful." Stepping into my personal space, he tugged on the hem, then slid his hands under the worn cotton to grip my waist.

He didn't answer my question, but I was unable to voice my objection. He rubbed his thumbs in soft strokes up and down, then slid his hands around my back, down to my ass and squeezed. "You fill these out well." He kissed me, pulled the waistband of the sweats and let it snap. "No greater ass in the world than yours."

"I can think of one." Uh, huh. His rock-hard gluteus maximus was as perfect as they came. I knew because I'd seen him in the buff. Even though I could count the real live naked rears I'd viewed in my lifetime on one finger, I couldn't imagine anything more splendid than his. I massaged his keister, or tried anyway. It was impossible to administer a good squeeze to something that had no give.

Franklin groaned. It came from low in his chest. The sound touched somewhere deep in my bosom. He nibbled my earlobe and whispered, "I want nothing more than to fuck you crazy right now. But we have to go."

Huh. What? Prickles of disappointment jetted across my flesh. "Go?" I asked.

"I'm getting you out of here. Away from the crazy shit." He kicked a piece of my cell across the floor. "We'll get you a new phone on the way. I'll be right back." He jogged down the hall and I heard the rattle of keys as he unlocked a door.

It took every bit of self-restraint not to run after him and get a look-see into his top secret lair. I was a good girl. Besides, I was still stunned by his announcement. Where could he be taking me?

He came out seconds later with a duffel slung over his shoulder and scooted me toward the door.

"Wait. I don't have shoes. I'm not dressed."

"Don't worry. I've got you covered." Franklin squatted, grabbed me below my hips and tossed me over his shoulder like I weighed little more than a sack of potatoes. It was uncomfortable and totally unsexy, but I let him carry me down the stairs and stuff me into his SUV.

"I haven't even brushed my teeth," I protested.

He chuckled, slammed my door, and tossed his bag in the seat behind me.

My insides warmed when he slid into the vehicle and grabbed the steering wheel with his masculine hands. There was something so arousing about a pair of strong, thickly-veined male hands. My heart skipped a beat when his leg shifted to press the brake and his thigh muscle bulged underneath the tight denim of his jeans.

I lost my breath when he turned to me, eyes blazing, and ordered me to buckle up. God, what he did to me. It was unnatural, unbelievable, unfair. If I were *that kind of girl*, which I wasn't, I would've torn off my clothes right there in the parking lot and begged him to ravish me.

I needed a distraction. "Franklin Reed. I demand to know where you're taking me." I pretended to pout.

He pretended to smile. It was fake, because the corners of his eyes crinkled when he smiled for real. There wasn't so much as a crease. "Top secret." Franklin paid more attention to the rearview mirror than the road ahead of him.

"Are we being followed?" I teased and turned to look behind me.

"I don't think so. I'm circling around a few times, just to be sure."

Oh. He *was* worried about a tail. My stalker, no doubt. A pang of guilt squeezed my chest. I sunk into my seat and tried to stay upbeat.

"Seriously, I've got no shoes. Where are we going?" I asked, wiggling my toes.

"A place where no one can touch us. You won't need shoes. I'm going to spend the rest of my weekend memorizing every nook and cranny of that delectable body of yours."

A furnace lit behind my cheeks. My brain voided itself of any witty retorts or sassy comebacks.

Franklin laughed. A real laugh with a genuine smile. "Holy shit. This is a first. Tatum Wood silenced. I never thought I'd see the day."

I laughed, too, on the outside.

On the inside, well, I was a hot mess of raging hormones and giddy schoolgirl.

* * * *

We headed south for an hour, east for a short trot, then deep into the mountains for another thirty minutes. The paved highway morphed into a winding, pothole-littered, narrow roadway that resembled a walking path. It grew steeper as we trudged forward, and sunlight dissipated through the thick of trees.

The farther from civilization we traveled, the more Franklin's facial features softened. We reached a modest cabin, and he parked right next to the front stoop.

A blast of cold, clean air hit me as soon as he opened the door. It burned my lungs like winter wind. He scooped me up and carried me to the worn wood porch.

"It's open. I'll grab our bags." Planting a kiss on my forehead, he set me down on the first step.

He pulled a suitcase from the back of his Toyota with a cocky grin on his face. He shook his head and mumbled something to himself that sounded like, "I'm going to burn in hell for this." That made no sense. I was sure I heard wrong.

I entered the cabin. For being in the middle of nowhere, its modern amenities and decor surprised me. Stainless steel appliances, an oversized, deep-seated leather couch, matching recliner, flat screen. An ornate stairway led to an open loft that, from my vantage point, fit a queen-sized bed and not much more. There was a frosted glass door beneath the stairs I assumed led to the bathroom. It was small, cozy, and perfect.

Franklin carried our luggage up the stairs and laid it on the bed. He hopped back down and grabbed two grocery bags from outside the door.

I grabbed one of the sacks. "Is that why you left this morning, to stock up for my kidnapping?"

His proud smile made my heart drop to my gut and bounce back up again.

"You packed clothing for me?"

He set a bottle of wine on the counter. "I did. Even shoes. Not that you'll need them."

I started to unpack the groceries and nearly choked when I pulled out a box of condoms. "You know, you've already gotten into my pants, you didn't need to go to all this trouble to bag me again." Oh dear, was this finally going to happen?

He grabbed the carton of Trojans and tossed them on the couch. It bounced off the cushion and landed on the floor. "I'm going to fuck you properly. Out here, there won't be any distractions." He sauntered across the room, opened the sliding glass door, retrieved his cell from his back pocket and dropped it outside.

"Wow. You mean business, don't you? No phones, no stalkers, a year's supply of condoms. This better be one hell of a romp-fest, buddy, 'cause you've piqued my interest."

Eyebrows raised, he shot a glance at my chest, where two pesky points threatened to rip through the thin cotton. "That's not all that's peaked, is it?" He turned to close the door, then prowled my direction.

My cheeks burned hot. My pulse pounded louder than a bass drum through my ears. God, I wanted this man, needed his hands on me, longed to be smothered with his scent.

I wiggled my eyebrows at him, grabbed the hem of my shirt, well, his shirt, and pulled it over my head. I reached back, unhooked my bra and let it fall to the floor. Franklin's eyes widened and he paused, losing his confident demeanor for the briefest moment before pulling me to his chest and crushing his lips against mine. "Not wasting any time, are we?"

I slid my hands around his waist, under his shirt, and caressed his warm skin. "We've wasted too much time already."

Franklin tucked his thumbs into the waistband of my sweats and yanked me against his erection. Holy crap.

"Yeah, love, too much time," he groaned, then devoured my mouth with a kiss that left no room for doubt of his intentions, and hot damn, they were naughty. His assault on my lips reeked of desperate longing, a primal urge to assure me he was mine. He trembled, then kissed me harder while he tugged my sweats down my hips. I finished the job by wiggling and kicking them off.

Never breaking contact, he guided me to the couch and let go only long enough to get rid of his own clothing. He cupped the back of my head and nudged me down across the cold leather. With his other hand, he cupped my breast, massaged, explored, tugged my nipple then blazed a trail to my sex. He brushed his fingers softly through my tuft of hair, lingering at my opening before pushing two inside me.

"Fuck." Franklin stopped kissing me but didn't lift his mouth from mine. "So warm and wet. I'm out of my fucking mind for you right now." He lowered his head to pull a nipple into his mouth.

I bucked my hips into his hand, arched my breast against his mouth. Ripples of pleasure tore through me, forcing my eyes closed. Franklin reached down and snatched the black box off the floor. He fumbled with the packaging but eventually managed to free a condom from the pouch. My heart beat a hole through my chest as he rolled it on. To watch, while he touched himself, was almost too much for my delicate senses. Oh, God. Why was I so hot? Was the room on fire? He laid over me and pushed a thigh between my legs. His erection bobbed against my skin.

"I need to be in you. God, I've waited so fucking long," he groaned. His thick, husky voice enraptured me.

My vision blurred, pulse raced, thoughts spun. I needed him with an indescribable desperation. I needed him to fill me, dominate and claim me. In that moment, that slow-motion, foggy-brained, lust filled moment in time, nothing mattered but Franklin.

I wrapped my legs around his waist, dug my fingers into his shoulders, and begged him to take me. "Fuck me. I need you, please." Never, in a million years, would I have envisioned begging a man, especially using those words, but I did. Who was this lust-crazed beast inhabiting my body?

He lifted his head from my chest, his eyes glimmering with unshed tears, which only made me hotter for him. Then he raised his hips, guided his sex through my folds and impaled me in one slow, steady stroke. I cried his name and choked back a sob.

Franklin tensed. He buried his face in my neck and took a deep breath. It burned, the way he filled and stretched me. To be honest, it hurt like hell, and I fought the urge to push him off. Thank God, he didn't move right away. It was perfect, painful pleasure, but I needed that small space in time to catch my breath and push through the discomfort.

He studied my face, eyes dark with concern. "Am I hurting you?" he asked through labored breaths. "Fuck. You're so tight, baby."

I shook my head no, fearing if I spoke, he'd hear the pain in my voice—and I didn't want him to stop. I never wanted this to stop.

Franklin kissed me softly, then buried his face next to mine in the cushion. Moisture tickled my cheek. I wasn't sure if it was his tears or my own. He whispered in my ear, "So fucking long. Jesus. You're finally mine."

His words didn't make sense, but penetrated the most guarded parts of me. He raised his hips, withdrew nice and slow, then filled me again. I bit my lip hard to keep from crying out. How could something hurt so bad and at the same time feel so perfect, so right?

"Don't stop. I need you inside me. Fuck me, please," I pleaded.

He did. He fucked me on the leather couch in the cabin hidden from the world. He rocked his hips gently until I relaxed and started to move with him. He kissed my mouth, my neck, licked my tears. Whispered words that broke my heart over and over. "Beautiful angel. My everything. I don't deserve you. Saved me. Need you so fucking bad. Never leave. Please. I'll die without you."

His thrusts deepened and my body coiled. I dug my fingers into his ass. When he buried his face in my neck and muttered, "I've loved you for so long," I lost my bearings and exploded. The orgasm was excruciating and beautiful, and for a moment, I feared I might die from the flood of emotion swelling inside me. When my insides tightened around him, he lost it, too.

"Fuck, Tate. Fucking hell." He pumped furiously and I lifted my hips to meet his. His body tensed, arms trembled, breaths blew heated and ragged into my ear. He collapsed on top of me and murmured, "My sweet, beautiful angel."

* * * *

I woke some time later, wrapped in a layer of naked male and a heavy wool blanket. Awake, Franklin was a sight to behold, but asleep, holy heaven above, the man was downright angelic.

His full lips were slightly parted and still moist. His thick lashes fanned against his cheeks. No stress wrinkles. He appeared so much younger when he slept.

I stretched my neck and kissed him, savoring the softness of his mouth. He smiled, blinked his eyes open and sighed. "It wasn't a dream."

Was he for real?

His arm tightened around me, smashing my breasts against his chest. A whole new set of fireworks exploded in my gut.

Franklin let me go, sat up, and wrapped the blanket around me like a burrito. He turned to look at me with a smirk on his face and a smile in his eyes. "Romp-fest, huh?"

I smiled and batted my lashes.

"I'm down with that." He brushed a finger across my cheek. "Let me start a fire. Gets cold in here at night. You hungry?" He rose off the couch, pulled his jeans on, then tugged his shirt over his head.

Food? I was pretty sure I'd never have to eat again. There wasn't a thing in the world that would satisfy me the way Franklin did. "No. I'm not hungry. Can I help?"

He shook his head no.

I studied the fine male specimen moving about like a caveman, gathering wood, making fire, grunting from time to time. I could've watched him forever. Oh my, his form, his expressions, the way he dominated the room was more than a girl could handle.

"Is this your cabin?" I asked.

He poked at a log then glanced over his shoulder at me. "It's mine. Do you like it?"

I sat up and pulled the blanket tight around my body. "I do. It reminds me of my dad. He loved to get lost in the mountains. At least twice a year, he'd sneak away to his hunting cabin for a week or so. I was never allowed to go with him. He said hunting wasn't for girls."

Franklin turned back toward the fire. He sighed and his shoulders slumped. "You miss your father?"

"Every day," I whispered. I wanted to tell him how much he reminded me of Dad, but I didn't.

"You two were close, weren't you?" With a loud crackle, the fire roared, outlining Franklin's body with a warm orange glow.

"He was a freakin' superhero in my eyes. Overprotective as hell, but I wouldn't have had it any other way. How about you? Were you close with your father?" Since we were getting personal and stuff, it seemed a good time to dig.

"No. My dad disappeared when I was young."

I tried to picture Franklin as a child, but failed. I could only see the virile, protective man who'd stolen my heart. "I'm sorry. Was it hard not having a father?" I cringed after asking the question. There was personal, and there was too damn personal. I feared I'd crossed the line.

Franklin remained silent while he stoked the flames, then rose and came to sit by me. "My mom struggled, didn't date after my father left. Except for one man. I still remember the first time she brought him home. I was eight, I think. The guy was huge, and I didn't know how to act around him. But, you know what? He squatted down to my level, made eye contact, held out his hand, and introduced himself. Showed me respect. We were the best of buds after that. He and my mom didn't work out because she never got over the loss of my dad, but the guy stepped up and took me under his wing, mentored me. I've never met a better man." Franklin's eyes twinkled with unshed tears. Most men would be ashamed to cry. Franklin held my gaze until the emotion faded.

"I'd like to meet him someday." I leaned my head on his shoulder.

"He passed away a few years ago."

"I'm sorry."

So Franklin and I had something in common. We'd both lost the most important man in our lives. He was lucky. Not many men would step in to help a single mother raise her son, especially an ex-girlfriend.

Franklin's chest rose and fell. Then he turned, lifted me onto his lap, and pulled the blanket off my naked body. "Let's get back to that romp-fest, shall we?"

I laughed. "Can we try the bed this time?" I pried myself from his grip, stood, and offered a hand to pull him up.

He traced my body with a hungry gaze, his eyes resting between my thighs for an uncomfortable spell before finding my face. "You're bleeding."

Horrified, I looked down. It wasn't time for my period.

A heated blush spread from my cheeks to my toes. "I told you, I haven't been with anyone."

This time, his face reddened. "Haven't been with anyone *in a long time,* or haven't *been* with anyone?" he asked, clasping his hands over the top of his head. "You told me you've had two sexual experiences."

Oh crap. We were gonna have *that* conversation. I suppose I should've been more honest with him the first time. "What I said was, two sexual experiences with fumbling idiots who didn't know what they were doing."

"Meaning?" he asked with an irritated bite to his tone.

"Meaning, I didn't actually have intercourse, per se." I'd never felt more exposed in my life. Standing naked in the middle of Amish country with an *I'm no longer a virgin* neon sign flashing over my head would've been more bearable.

The cabin was dark, save the glow from the fire. Heat radiated against my backside but didn't repel the cold. Franklin's icy glare raked my body again and again. My muscles ached with the restraint it took to keep from running away. What did I do wrong? My sexual past, or lack thereof, should have absolutely no bearing on Franklin's feelings for me. Right? Shit.

I held my palms up and shrugged my shoulders. "Look who's speechless now."

Unblinking, he shook his head.

The firelight danced in his retinas. I snapped my fingers in his face. "You okay?" I asked.

Franklin huffed, pushed himself off the couch, and scooped me over his shoulder as he stood.

"Are you a freaking barbarian? For crying out loud. Put me down."

He smacked my bare ass. "Let's shower."

We squeezed through the tiny bathroom door and he plopped me on the cold tile floor. He shed his clothing and reached around me to turn on the water. I shuddered, not from cold, but the sight of his back as he stretched, the roll of his muscles as he moved. Yum. Yum. Yum.

"Does this place run on a generator?" I asked, realization dawning on me a little too late. I'd turned into a horror movie cliché—naive girl, dark woods, middle of nowhere, a man too good to be true. If that wasn't a set up for a B-movie murder scene, I didn't know what was.

He pulled me into the small space and chuckled. "We're not that far from civilization. It just seems like it because it's so well hidden. We have electricity."

Franklin lathered the soap. As if he'd done it a thousand times before, he pressed his hands to my skin and washed me. It was more an exotic massage in a steamy, tiny, tiled room than a shower. He left no part of me untouched, unexplored. When it came time to wash between my legs, the place he saved for last, he knelt, paused for a deep breath, then lightly brushed a finger up and down my labia.

"Did I hurt you?" he whispered, raising his eyes, but not his face to me. "And don't lie. Don't ever lie to me again."

Gulp.

"It hurt. But it was a good hurt, if that makes sense."

He continued to stroke me with tender caresses. I slapped my hand against the wall to brace myself. His touch alone nearly brought me to my knees.

"You should have told me. I wouldn't have…" He shook his head. "I can't take care of you, or protect you if you're lying or telling me half truths."

I rubbed my free hand over the top of his head. He closed his eyes and leaned into my palm.

"I'm sorry," I whispered. "It happened so fast, I didn't have a second to think about it. And to be fair, this is your fault."

My knees buckled when he slid a finger inside me.

"My fault?" He grinned.

"If you weren't so damned overwhelming, I might be able to think straight once in a while."

He retreated, then pushed inside me again, rubbing and teasing with his gentle touch. Every part of me down there was tender. Franklin never stroked too hard. He worked with such precision, my body prepared for another joining with his. Then his lips latched on to my clit. Franklin didn't mess around with foreplay. He sucked hard on my nub and curved his finger inside me. My body coiled then exploded in waves of excruciating pleasure. My muscles turned to mush, my bones to wet noodles. My legs trembled and threatened to buckle. Franklin removed his hand from between my thighs and gripped my hip to support me. His lips remained where they were, sucking, pulling, drawing every last quiver from my body.

I grabbed his head. "Stop. Please, stop. It's too sensitive."

He let go, kissed my belly on the soft spot above my patch of hair, and stood. With one arm around my shoulders and the other my waist, he pulled me against his slick body and pressed his erection between us.

I lifted my chin to taste his mouth. He kissed me soft and tender, not with the territorial ferocity I'd come to enjoy. Cupping my cheeks with both hands, he held me still and explored my lips, my tongue, my chin, then my nose. He cherished me with kisses that reflected love, not just lust.

I could feel his desire before, but now there was something more. The kind of something that led to a frilly white dress, a little yellow house with a white picket fence, and a party riddled with pastel baby decorations. For the first time in my life, I believed I could be one-half of a ninety-year-old couple helping each other along the sidewalk in super slow motion. I'd have the walker, and Franklin would carry the cane.

I relaxed into him, inhaled his breath, reveled in the flavor and scent that was so innately masculine and powerful.

Then Franklin shocked the shit out of me. He wrapped his arms around my head and neck, pressed my face into his chest and cried. At first, I'd mistaken his spasms for laughter. But no, he sobbed.

I coiled my arms around his waist and tried to breathe. It wasn't easy with my face smashed between a solid pec and an iron hard forearm. Somehow, I managed to draw oxygen into my lungs. I'd never seen a man cry, nor imagined myself trapped in the arms of a naked man while he wept. But there I was, completely clueless. What was the proper etiquette for such a situation? I squeezed his middle, stroked his back, and waited for the convulsions to stop.

His words from earlier bounced to and fro in my head like a game of Ping-Pong.

God, I've waited so fucking long... You're finally mine... I'll die without you...

Had he actually said those things? Or had I been so sex crazed that his words jumbled in my head?

The things I know would blow your mind.

I didn't know this man at all, did I? He could have brought me deep into the mountains to slice me into pieces and roast me with potatoes and a sprig or two of rosemary. Not a single being on earth knew where I was or whom I was with.

Not even me.

Silent and aloof, Franklin turned off the water, dried me, then himself, and led me to bed.

"Are we going to talk about what just happened?" I asked, irked by the unnerving quiet.

"I want to. Just need to find the right words, okay love?"

Love? That was the third time he'd referred to me as "love." It pissed me off to no end that it made me feel soft and fuzzy every time—and I'd kept a tally.

I laid my head on his shoulder and twisted my fingers through the tuft of hair on his chest. The silence in the remote location, the place I would likely become a main course to a one-man meal, gnawed at my nerves and fueled my over-stimulated imagination. I concentrated on the loudest noise I could distinguish—Franklin's heartbeat thumping into my brain, soothing and seductive.

I counted the beats, focused on the rhythm, then fell asleep craving juicy steak, roasted potatoes, and red wine.

Chapter 10

Grumpaluffagus and I trekked along the riverbed, slipping and sliding on the wet rocks. Up ahead, Wallace stood knee-high in the brisk current, flicking his fishing rod back and forth above his head.

I scratched behind my buddy's ear. He nudged me with a massive shoulder and nearly knocked me on my butt.

"See that man?" I asked and pointed up the river.

Grumpy answered with a head shake and a snort.

"I do so despise him. He's done some terrible, terrible things. Wanna know what the worst part is?" I unhooked the leash from his spike-studded collar. "He thinks he can get away with it because he has money."

A string of drool dangled above my feet when he growled.

"Now he's eating your yummy fish."

Grumpy shook his head and bounced up and down on his mighty front paws, his snout curled in a snarl.

"He'll be easy to catch, and I bet he tastes every bit as good as those scaly appetizers. Plus, you'll have some bones to chew when you've finished your meal." I ruffled the fur between his ears. "Now, be a good little teddy bear and eat that bad man."

I patted the grizzly's hindquarters, turned, and headed back down the rocky shore. I smiled when I heard a shrill scream, laughed out loud when a shredded pair of waders floated past me.

"Baby?"

A heavy hand shook me back to consciousness. "What's so funny?"

Wow, that voice. What a way to wake up. I peeled my moist face from his warm skin. "Sorry. I was dreaming."

"Must've been a good one."

"It was." One of the best yet.

He trailed a finger up and down the curve of my back. "Tell me."

I buried my nose in his chest and shook my head. "You don't want to know."

"I want to know everything. Especially if it makes you laugh." How did he always know the right thing to say?

"It was about Wallace."

Franklin's body tensed.

I smacked his chest. "I'll tell you, but no judging, okay?"

"Cross my heart."

I couldn't believe I was telling somebody. "I dream about killing him. Almost every day. It usually isn't pretty."

"That's why you were laughing?" he asked with a chuckle.

I nodded. "Warped, huh?"

"Just a little, Killer."

"Killer? Ha! You're funny." I smacked his arm. "I fantasize about it at work, too. When I'm zoning out, and you have to yell to get my attention, I'm usually murdering him."

"Huh," he huffed. "Morbid, but kinda sexy." He shifted to his side and molded my breast in his hand, pinching my nipple between his thumb and forefinger. My breath caught and my hips rolled and pressed into him, seeking his skin, his heat…just him.

I pressed a finger to his lips when he leaned in for a kiss. "Nope. I spilled the beans. Now it's your turn."

He groaned and nipped the pad of my finger.

"You didn't judge. I won't either," I promised and laid my hand over his heart.

"No one has ever given me a gift aside from my mother." He pressed his forehead to mine. Tingles flittered across my skin.

"You gave me the most precious gift." His voice thickened. "One I don't deserve. I took it like a greedy son of a bitch. You can never have it back. It's mine forever. It hit me in the shower, how fucking monumental that was…" He cupped my ass and ground me against his swollen cock. "I didn't expect it. I was overwhelmed." His lips tickled my cheek. "I just wish I'd known, I would've been careful with you."

"It was perfect," I managed to mumble through the lump stuck in my throat. "And you're perfect."

"I'm not. God, I'll never be good enough for you."

That wasn't the self-confident Franklin I'd worked side by side with for the past couple of months. He wasn't the man who'd swooped down from his white cloud to cloak me with his protective shield. The Franklin, lying naked with me in the dark, seemed halfway real and for the first time…attainable.

I'd set him high on a pedestal, to worship and adore. So close, but forever out of reach. With the absence of light, when his unreal beauty couldn't blind me, I saw the man inside. I liked what was in there. I liked it so much, my chest hurt.

"Let's not waste any more time talking," I said, sliding my hand down the bumpy muscles of his torso.

He gripped my wrist and stopped me. "I don't want to hurt you. We should take it easy."

"I'm a twenty-four year old virgin. *Was* a twenty-four year old virgin. I'm a freakin' pressure cooker ready to blow. You can't lay next to me all naked and muscular and super sexy and expect me to sleep. Come on. I've got a lot of catching up to do."

Franklin laughed. I loved his laugh. I loved making him laugh.

I didn't know what hour of the night or morning it was, but by the time the sun peeked through the trees, I'd gained an intimate knowledge of my body. Franklin's, too.

The drive home that afternoon was mostly a blur. We did stop to buy a new phone. Franklin insisted I get a new number and a whole new carrier. His, actually. The sex coma I'd been in the entire day prevented me from arguing. I'd change it later if necessary, when my thoughts weren't inundated with visions of male body parts.

"Shall I stay with you tonight?" he asked when he pulled next to my car in the parking lot of his apartment. I knew it was more a statement than a question.

"Um, duh." I stuck my tongue out and crossed my eyes.

He put the suitcase in my trunk and made sure I was belted in the driver's seat before closing the door. "I'll run upstairs, grab some clean clothes. Be right down. I'll follow you home, don't leave without me."

"Okay, Dad." I gave him a two-finger salute and watched his fine ass strut across the gravel lot. I scanned my surroundings after he disappeared behind the door. It was daylight, yet the innocent parking lot reminded me of a cemetery on a foggy night during a full moon. A motorcycle passed on the street and my pulse raced. A tall man walked by and I shrunk in my seat. Shit. The stalker creep had wedged his way under my skin and stuck, hindering my ability to look at the world through rose-colored glasses.

Franklin took too damned long to come back. When he did, I released my death grip on the steering wheel. He gave me a thumbs up and pulled a baseball cap low on his forehead before hopping in his car.

He rode my ass the entire drive home.

* * * *

Who knew a zipper could be sexy? I'd never given much consideration to the sound the slider made as it bumped over metal teeth, traveling downward, freeing its captor from the binds of cotton, leather, or in my case, denim. But through the short, heavy breaths, the smack of wet lips across my collarbone, the drone of cars passing in the street below, that one sound resonated above every other. Franklin Reed pulled the zipper of my jeans down with a slow, steady, controlled motion, driving me completely out of my mind with want.

I wiggled, hoping to speed things up.

"We have all night, Killer. No need to rush." The muscles behind that zipper tightened in response to the deep rasp of his voice.

Oh, how I did need to rush. Every part of me burned and swelled with the ebb and flow of heated blood pounding through my veins. The softest touch, each whisper or slight shift of his body, amplified the vibrations of overwrought nerves. I would die. I truly would die if he didn't grant me a reprieve from the torture.

I couldn't take any more. "You're killing me," I screamed, pushing him away.

My cheeks throbbed, flushed with need. That was nothing compared to the burn behind Franklin's eyes when he watched me strip the last of my clothing away. My jeans landed somewhere near the bathroom door. My panties? Who cared?

Exhausted as I was from the zero hours of sleep granted the night before, my sole concern was to have the man, who stood in his birthday suit center stage in my bedroom, in any position other than upright. As long as any of our body parts touched, I'd be a happy, happy girl. I stepped closer, ready to pounce. Franklin took a step back, folded his arms across his chest and made a clicking noise with his tongue. "Good God, woman. That body is blazing." Holding a hand up, he spun his finger in a fast circle. "Turn around."

I wasn't oblivious to the dimples gracing my plump rear. I had natural curves, cellulite in a few places. Body image had never been an issue. I didn't need a man or a size two waist to make me feel pretty, but holy heaven above, the way his eyes narrowed and lips twisted—Sophia Loren, Marilyn Monroe, hell, even Scarlett Johansson had nothing on me. I turned slow, jetted my rear and tossed my hair over my shoulder.

Smack.

Franklin's hand stung my fanny. I squealed.

"This ass is mine." From behind, he rubbed away the bite of his slap. I reached back and guided his hands to my chest. "And these?"

He massaged my breasts, holding their weight. "These tits are mine."

A fiery spasm roared between my legs. As if sensing the heat, he slid one hand down my stomach and cupped my sex. "And this, Killer, belongs to me." He trailed wet kisses along my shoulder and up my neck. "Forever," he whispered, sliding a finger inside me.

Forever? Wow. That sounded insane. How could he talk about forever, this stranger who'd become my world? It was too soon. At least that's what common sense dictated. I wanted an eternity with him, as sure as the sun would rise in the morning.

His clever fingers rubbed and invaded, his lips moistened my skin from ear to chin. His erection pushed between my butt cheeks, settling nice and tight.

"I'm the only man who's been inside you. I get so fucking hard just thinking about it." He pushed deeper. "Promise me, love. Tell me there will never be another." His strong finger curled and white heat exploded inside me. My legs buckled and Franklin let me collapse to the floor, catching me in his lap, never retreating. I came with violent shudders around his thick, magical finger. My head fell against his shoulder, my body tensed and quivered in his arms. He held me tight, rocked with me as I writhed in wanton pleasure, fucking his hand.

When I relaxed into him, he didn't relent. He cupped my sex, circling the sensitive nub with his thumb, teased a nipple between his fingers with the other hand. "Say it, love. I want you to say it. Your words, your promise. They mean everything."

Completely out of my mind with orgasmic overload, I hadn't a clue what he wanted me to say, let alone the wherewithal to slow my breathing enough to speak.

Releasing my nipple, he squeezed my jaw and forced my face to meet his. "No other man will have you, Tate. Say it."

Holy shit.

His eyes burned, hands trembled. "Say it," he commanded through gritted teeth.

"I only want you." I forced my words through jagged breaths.

His thumb circled harder, possessive against me. "No other man. Promise me."

Pillow talk, heat-of-the-moment, lust-fueled words? Nope. Franklin pulled some Mark Wahlberg in Fear, Julian Sands in Boxing Helena shit. Was I afraid? Yes—of disappointing him or scaring him away.

I grasped his wrist and pulled his hand from between my thighs. Then I turned and wrapped my legs around his waist, my arms around his neck. "No other man. Ever. Only you."

Did I only say that to appease him?

No. I wanted him—all of him, in every way possible. I just couldn't understand why he wanted me, plain old, soft-and-squishy me. But he did, and I would've done or said anything he asked. Not because I was powerless to resist his charms. Nor was I a mindless bimbo trying to up her social status by association with a should-be super model. It was because, in Franklin, I sensed not only a kindred spirit, but a haunting desire for unconditional trust and commitment. Those were key ingredients in any successful relationship.

I had them to give in spades.

* * * *

We'd slept in because we'd kept each other awake most of the night. He'd discovered my birth control pills in the bathroom and came out wearing a shit-eating grin. He confessed that he'd always worn a condom with his ex. Since I'd never been with another man, and he'd been safe, we ditched the Magnums. After that, it was no holds barred.

After I'd dipped my toe in the pool of sexual bliss, I felt the need to cannonball into the deepest end, float the bottom and only come up for air when absolutely necessary.

We rushed to get ready for work. I threw my cell into my purse, grabbed my keys, and almost forgot to lock the door as we scurried out. Franklin, however, did not. Shooting a scornful glare, he pulled his own set of keys from his suit jacket and took care of business.

We rode the elevator to the parking garage and he escorted me, hand in hand, to my car and held the door while I situated myself.

"See you there, Killer." He kneaded my breast, kissed me hard, and waited for me to fasten my safety belt. We'd agreed at some point during the night's festivities that, considering office gossip, it'd be better to take separate cars to work.

I watched him leave through the pedestrian door, shoulders back, head held high, rockin' the hell out of his Armani suit. How could he afford Armani anything? On the salary Wallace paid his lower level employees, Suits-R-Us would better fit his budget. The sight of him, especially the backside, had my thoughts traversing a torrid path. I was tempted to forget about work and drag the man back upstairs.

A pang of fear ripped through my chest when he strutted out of sight, like it was the last gander I'd ever get of his magnificent form. I shifted the car into drive and tapped the wheel, struggling for breath and impatiently waiting for the heavy grille door to inch its way up, up, up. I tore through before it completely opened. My pulse stopped racing only after I spied Franklin leaning against his car with his cell raised to his ear. He flashed his pearly whites my direction. Air returned to my lungs.

Whew. What the hell was that mini panic attack about? Lack of sleep. Yes. Must be overtired. I waved to him and headed toward a fresh new Monday with hopes it'd be better than the last.

I checked my rearview, Franklin-style, certain Mr. Sexy Pants was hot on my tail. Disappointment misted through me when there was no sign of him. A few blocks later, I checked again. No Franklin, but there was a man on a motorcycle two cars behind—and by golly, he straddled a black Harley.

Gut clench? Yup.

Rapid heartbeat? Um, yeah. Jackrabbit speed.

I swerved into the right lane to make my exit, cutting off a not-so-friendly Audi. I ignored the middle finger waving objections and focused on the motorcycle's actions. Staying two cars behind, he slipped into my lane.

Shit.

A storm brewed in my belly. Steam rolled between my ears. I waited for the light that seemed perpetually red. Where was Franklin? Mr. Overprotective-and-Overbearing suddenly decided to leave me on my own? My usual route would've taken me left. To test my I'm-being-followed theory, I turned right. So did the motorcycle.

Another right. He swerved between my car and a parcel delivery truck to land behind me. I took a sharp left, pissing off more than a few drivers and a couple pedestrians.

Motorcycle man followed, this time riding my ass. I could've slammed on the brakes and ended things right quick. I could've driven to the police station only a few blocks away. I decided it best to get to work, where Franklin should be waiting. At least, I hoped like hell he was.

To my surprise and relief, half the SPD surrounded our building, accompanied by two fire trucks, a news crew, and a fleet of unmarked matching black Buicks. I parked behind Franklin's SUV in the middle of the street.

Motorcycle man, apparently displeased by the scene, turned his bike around with minimal squealing of tires. He disappeared before I could get a look at his license number.

My heart skipped a beat when Franklin strode toward me, but it sunk to my gut when Detective Waters appeared from behind an ambulance and interrupted his trek. They exchanged words. Franklin's wrinkles set hard, and Leland's shoulders raised at least an inch. I stayed right where I was, snug as a bug in my safe little car.

Detective Waters typed something on his cell, shook Franklin's hand, and walked away after nodding my direction.

For crying out loud, what now?

Franklin climbed into my passenger seat.

"What's going on?" I was almost afraid to ask.

Face grim, eyes dark, he muttered, "Wallace is dead."

"What?" I heard the words. They didn't make sense.

"Murdered," he mumbled, eyes glazed, jaw tight.

I shook my head. "No!"

He leaned over the console and pulled me into the safety of his arms.

"What do you mean, murdered? I don't understand." I tried to wiggle free. Franklin held me tight as if he needed the comfort more than I did.

"Someone threw him off the roof. The detective wouldn't tell me more than that."

I'd known the dick-wad my whole life. He was like the creepy uncle that nobody wanted around, yet could never get rid of. But he'd always been there. I couldn't accept he was dead. "I don't know what to say."

"I know, baby."

I looked up to see Nan coming out the front entrance tucked under the arm of a robust but gentle-looking officer. Face red and wet with tears, she looked my direction before he helped her into the back of his car.

No. This was not happening. No way did someone murder Wallace. I was the only one allowed to do that. Before Franklin could stop me, I jumped from the car and jogged toward the building. I needed to see for myself.

Bad idea? Hell yes.

I hadn't considered Wallace's body would still be on the cold pavement like a rag-doll that'd been tossed on the ground, limbs impossibly twisted, face unrecognizable. Uncovered, on display for the world to see.

Funny, the blood didn't bother me so much. Maybe because I'd seen it so many times in my dreams. What did bother me? This wasn't a dream I could wake from and shake off with a giggle. This reality wasn't amusing in any way.

A solid voice over my shoulder made me jump. "I'm sorry, ma'am, you'll need to return to your vehicle."

A hand splayed against my lower back. "Are you crazy? What the hell were you thinking?" Franklin's rebuke sliced through the fog invading my brain. He wrapped an arm around my waist and nudged me back toward the car. "We need to go. Detective Waters asked us to meet him at the police station to answer some questions."

I started to turn, but a glimpse of something green caught my eye near Wallace's foot, the one that wasn't twisted the wrong way. "Wait." I pushed Franklin's arm off to get a better look. "No. It can't be."

He leaned over my shoulder. "Fuck."

A shriveled, long stemmed, red rose lay on the ground next to Wallace, untouched by the blood.

* * * *

"Thank you for coming in. We'll be talking to each employee. I wanted to get you in and out of here as quick as possible, considering—"

"The dead bodies following me around like flies," I interrupted, unable to hold back a nervous smirk.

Leland slammed his pen on the table, rubbed his eyes, then crossed his arms. Apparently he wasn't amused by my inability to keep my mouth shut when appropriate. I wasn't trying to be funny. Two dead men and one brutal attack in two weeks? If it wasn't a cruel joke, what the hell was going on? Were there hidden cameras and a jolly host hiding behind the desk, waiting to jump out and tell me I'd been duped? The shit I'd witnessed didn't happen in the real world. Certainly not my sheltered corner of it.

"Miss Wood."

"Tatum," I reminded him. I leaned back in my chair and mimicked his posture.

"How well did you know Mr. Cruse?" he asked, raising an eyebrow.

"I've known him my whole life. He was friends with my father. He was always around."

"I see." He scribbled something on his yellow notepad. Chicken scratch from my perspective. "You don't seem upset." Leland held his pen in the writing position but lifted his eyes to mine, weariness evident by the dark half-moon shapes underneath.

"I should be, shouldn't I? Maybe I'm in shock or something."

"People who are in shock don't know they're in shock, and you don't have any symptoms," he grunted.

There went that theory. Maybe I'd seen too many corpses to be bothered by the sight of them anymore. "I won't lie. I didn't like him much. Nobody did. Any idea what happened?"

"We're putting the pieces together and I'm asking the questions, remember?"

"I just...my father started the company. He got bored and sold it to Wallace. I don't need the job, don't like it much, either. I've stayed on because I feel close to my dad in that building."

"I understand." The detective pursed his lips. "Where were you last night and this morning?"

"At home." I swallowed hard. "With Franklin."

"I see." His face lit up and a hefty dose of *I told you so* flashed in his eyes.

I needed to change the subject, and fast. "What about the rose?"

"What rose?"

"The one laying on the ground next to the body."

"You saw the body?" He slammed his pen down again.

Oops. That damn mouth of mine. Did I get somebody in trouble? "It wasn't anybody's fault. I needed to see for myself that he was dead. They tried to stop me." I proceeded to tell Leland about the roses and my stalker, leaving no detail out.

"Miss Wood, why didn't you let me know this has been going on?"

"I was going to. Things have just been crazy."

He massaged his right temple."Yeah. Crazy is right."

"Any news on Jacob Smart?" I asked, more curious about his connection with my father than anything.

Leland shot a nervous glance to the door, then the camera mounted in the corner of the room. "No, and we can't discuss that here," he whispered.

"What's going to happen to Cruse Investigations? What about our clients? When can we get back to work?"

"You'll be contacted when the place has been cleared. Shouldn't be long. And Miss Wood, as much as I like you, I'd enjoy not having to see your face again for a while. Try to steer clear of trouble, will ya?" He half smiled and shook my hand.

I stepped into the hallway. Franklin leaned against the wall opposite me, hands tucked in his pockets, tie loose, legs crossed at the ankle. My cheeks heated. If public sex were legal, I would've jumped him right there. No joke.

"How you holding up?" He stood straight and grabbed my hand.

"Better than I should be, I suppose." At least according to the good detective.

The door behind me opened with a jerk and I wheeled around, bumping against Franklin's shoulder. "Reed," Leland shouted. "Need a minute." He paused and looked at me. "A private word."

Franklin squeezed my hand. "I'll be right back. Don't go anywhere." With a kiss to my head, he left me standing alone.

I leaned against the wall and watched people go about their business. Several uniformed men passed and nodded. A round, perky woman bounced past carrying two boxes of Krispy Kremes. My stomach grumbled. The aroma of java wafted my way.

I was about to go in search of the coffee but Franklin tore through the door with a red face and a scowl that made my hackles rise. He grabbed my elbow and tugged me toward the elevator.

"What?" I shrieked, struggling to balance while keeping pace with his strides. "Ouch. Let go."

His grip tightened.

I tried to yank my arm free, which apparently pissed him off. He slammed me so hard against his chest, my teeth rattled. What in the world happened in the two minutes he was with Detective Waters?

The elevator door opened and we stepped inside. Or rather, he pulled me inside. Thank God it was empty, because I was about to unleash Hell's wrath on his ass. Who did he think he was, manhandling me that way? My insides trembled with fury.

"Get your hands off me," I shouted, shocked by the strength in my voice.

In a blink, I was pinned in the corner. Held silent by a set of pained and angry eyes. "Why the fuck didn't you tell me?"

I couldn't speak. I'd never seen him so enraged.

"That asshole followed you this morning?" He banged his hands against the wall panels on either side of my head. My stomach rolled and my heart relocated to my nether regions. "Why did I hear about it from that fuck of a detective?" he shouted.

I'm not sure where I found the courage, or what I would gain from violence, but I balled my fist and punched Franklin in the gut. That's one thing I learned from my father. How to punch. I flat out refused to take self-defense and karate classes, mostly because I didn't want to wear the stupid outfits. But Dad had let me play around with his punching bag. We had even sparred occasionally.

So, I punched Franklin. He made an *oof* sound and stepped away. That's all I wanted, for him to back off. I couldn't have hurt him. I had too little room to get a good jab in. Pissed that he'd acted the bully, I threw another punch the second I had ample clearance. I aimed for his face. My fist met his forearm. Damn, the man was fast.

Before I could yelp in shock, he managed to block my strike, twist my arm behind my back and pin me to the wall again.

"You were gonna hit me?" he asked, the gravel in his voice deeper than ever.

I turned my face from his, unable to bear the hurt lurking behind his angry expression. "You're being a bully. What was I supposed to do?"

He released my arm. "Shit." Tension rolled off his body and he backed away.

The elevator bounced to a stop and the doors slid open. Franklin stormed out and made a beeline for my car, fisting and stretching his fingers. He didn't look back. I stayed a few paces behind on purpose. I hit the unlock button on my key fob, slid in, started the car, and tried to pull my door shut. Franklin held it open. I was too angry to look at him. What was that shit in the elevator about? Whatever his explanation, I sure as hell wasn't about to put up with it.

He huffed. "Tate, baby. I'm—"

I raised my hand to stop him. "Not now. Not another word. Close my goddamned door and let me go home."

He did.

As I drove away, I rolled my window down. "And don't you dare think about following me."

* * * *

I tossed my keys on the counter and got busy, and a smidge aggressive, with the coffee pot. My skin burned with anger so I splashed cold water on my face. While coffee brewed, I changed into my favorite new article of clothing—Franklin's Pearl Jam T-shirt. It was long enough to cover my rear so I didn't bother searching for bottoms. It's not like I was going anywhere for the rest of the day. Why not be comfy? I ditched my bra, happy to be free of its binds. My room reeked of Gendarme and sex. Not what I needed to smell at the moment. I hightailed it out of there.

I filled my cup, doused it with extra cream, and nestled into the familiar cushions of my couch. It would've been a good time to call my mom, or a friend, but how could I explain what my life had become? Nobody would understand. Mom would worry herself sick and demand I move. My girlfriends would offer empty condolences and insist I spill the dirt on my new sex life. I'd be the gossip topic for the week, then they'd move on. Pissed as I was at him, I would not throw Franklin to the pack of she-wolves.

I wanted to talk to Lizzie. She seemed to get me. She knew Franklin, was fun, and definitely not a gossip whore. I should've asked for her number the other night. I'd have to remember to do that next time I saw her.

So I sat, alone on my couch, drinking coffee-flavored cream and pouting over Franklin Reed, the mystery man. I'd told him not to follow me, and as far as I could tell, he didn't. Of that, I was pleased.

Okay, that wasn't true. Was I happy? No. Abandoned. Vulnerable. Lonely. Not how I expected to feel in my moment of self-righteous indignation.

I wasn't about to call him. Yes, dammit, I wanted him near me, on top of me, in me, but he needed to apologize. He'd have to make the first move. I clung to my phone like a security blanket. He'd call. He better.

At some point during the day, I dug out the photo album I'd wrangled from Mom after Dad died. Flipping through the pages sparked a case of the heebie-jeebies, and reminded me why Wallace creeped me out as a child. In the majority of photos, he sat or stood off to the side, gaze glued to my father. His smiles insincere. His expression…perverted adoration?

Most of the photos were of Mom, Dad and Wallace together. My parents were always touching. Always happy.

I'd have to call my mother and let her know about Wallace. After all, they'd been friends, too. Better sooner than later. I picked up the phone and dialed.

She answered on the second ring.

"Hi honey. It's so nice to hear from you."

"Hi Mom." My voice crackled.

"Everything okay?" she asked, her tone guarded.

"Yes. I mean, no. I mean. I'm fine. Don't worry." Jeez, what was wrong with my tongue? "I'm afraid I have some bad news."

I heard shuffling on her end then the click of a door closing. "What, darling? You're scaring me."

I needed to say it. No sense beating around the bush. "Wallace was murdered this morning."

What came next was a long, uncomfortable silence, then a sniffle. "Mom?"

Her voice wavered when she asked, "What happened?"

"They found him outside our office this morning." I couldn't give the gory details and left it at that.

"Are you all right, Tatum?" she asked. "I know you didn't love the man, but he was like family."

"Yes. I am. It feels weird, you know?"

"I'll catch the first flight I can get."

"No, Mom. That's not necessary. Let's wait. I'll get back to you with funeral details as soon as I know anything."

"You're right. That will give me time to arrange a caretaker for Grandpa."

"How's he doing?"

"Chugging along. He keeps asking when you're coming to visit."

Well, since I was no longer employed, or at least, didn't have an employer, that might be sooner than later. "Kiss him for me. Maybe I'll plan a trip after the funeral."

"Oh, Tatum," her voice raised an octave. "That would be lovely. I miss you so much."

"Miss you too, Mom. I'll call you when I know more."

"Love you." She made a kissing noise.

"Love you more, bye."

Our conversations were always short and sweet. Mom wasn't much of a talker. She showed her love and affection through actions more than words.

Dad, on the other hand, drowned you with it. A full-blown attack from every possible outlet. Physical, verbal, emotional. Nobody doubted Antonio Wood's feelings for them, whether good or bad.

I pulled the photo that Detective Waters had given me from my purse. The one starring Dad, Jacob, and two beautiful women. Mom wasn't in it. The photo must have been older than their marriage. Dad wouldn't have cheated. He hadn't been that kind of man. They'd celebrated their twenty-first wedding anniversary one month before Dad died. Could this photo be over twenty, twenty-five years old? I flipped it to check the back. No date printed. Damn.

I studied the faded image for answers. The woman snuggling next to my father had light hair. Platinum, from what I could tell. Dad used to joke he liked his ladies buxom and blond. I couldn't help but think she looked familiar somehow. Maybe I'd seen her growing up. Maybe she was a family friend? No. That couldn't be right. She touched my father far too intimately for that to be true.

I slammed the photo down, stretched on the couch and pulled the afghan over myself. Franklin still hadn't called. I sure wasn't going to call him. No way. No how.

But Lordy, I was tempted.

Chapter 11

My heart pounded with the ferocity of a herd of cattle stampeding through a wide ravine. My limbs moved with the grace and agility of a ballerina dancing through waist-high wet cement.

Wallace called out, "Don't run, Tatum. Come back."

I tried to run, needed to hide. My legs ignored the commands to move. Wallace slammed me to the ground and held a knife to my throat. "Where's the file? You're lucky to have this job. I can find a better receptionist on the street corner."

I performed a Jackie Chan, super ninja move and landed on top of my attacker. Straddling his waist, I sunk the blade of the knife in the soft spot at the crook if his neck, just above his collarbone. "You're dead, dip-shit."

A thick bulge rose between my legs, rubbing with perfect pressure. I looked down. It wasn't Wallace Cruise looking up, but Franklin. He licked his lips and thrust his hips. The friction made my thighs clench.

Wallace's shrill voice damaged my auditory system. "Where's the file, Tatum? I don't have all day. Bring more coffee. Not too much sugar. You shouldn't wear your hair like that."

"I have to go." I pushed off Franklin and ran to Wallace's office.

He stood at the window, twirling a rose between his thumb and forefinger. His beady, soulless eyes twinkled. "Get back to work." he cackled.

I dove and tackled him to the ground. "You died. Why won't you stay dead?" I stabbed the weapon into his chest. It sunk and disappeared. I fell forward and groped his chest to catch myself. His wrinkled skin nauseated me.

"Killer. You're so fucking hot." Wallace groaned, his voice suddenly rich and husky. "Do you want me?"

"Hell no." Franklin was beneath me again. He didn't make a peep, but thrust and rubbed against me with glorious skill, drawing me closer and closer to a magnificent release. My hips flexed, seeking more pressure.

"Where's Wallace? We have to make him go away." I wanted to roll off him, but was so close to exploding, I hadn't the wits to move. I arched my back and let Franklin have his way with me.

"Baby. Yeah. Come for me. Shit." Franklin's voice boomed from above. Then he penetrated me. Oh, God.

"Killer."

My eyes snapped open. Franklin claimed my mouth with a kiss so possessive, it wiped the vision of Wallace clean out of my head. He palmed my sex, pressed two fingers inside me and held me steady while I shuddered through the aftershocks of my release.

What a filthy, disturbing dream. What a naughty, glorious way to be woken.

"That was the hottest fucking thing I've ever seen." He wore the cockiest grin I'd ever witnessed. "I let myself in, baby. I'm so goddamned sorry about earlier." He nibbled my ear and trailed his wet fingers under my shirt and up my torso. "Can you forgive me?" he asked in a sensual whisper. He cupped a breast and teased his thumb over my nipple.

I'd already forgiven him. Hours ago. "What took you so long?" I asked.

"I had to pack my things," he mumbled against my lips.

Panic's wretched tentacles wrapped around my heart and squeezed. "Pack? Where are you going?"

"I'm going to bury my cock so deep inside you, it'll take an archeological dig to get me out." Franklin crawled onto the couch, guided my knees farther apart and nestled between my thighs.

I heard the drag of a zipper, my new favorite sound, and then he filled me. My back arched, my heels dug into his buttocks, and I choked back a sob. Shit. Why did people ever leave the house when they could spend their days doing this?

Franklin still wore his suit. The gray brought out flecks of brilliant silver in his irises—and damn if that wasn't more potent than any love potion.

"Where are you going?" I asked, afraid of the answer. Anywhere away from me was too far.

"I'm already there."

I smacked his arm. "Stop being vague."

"Here is where I'm going, Killer."

"Oh." He couldn't be serious. "Franklin, I—"

"Shhh. Don't talk," he interrupted. "Let me finish apologizing first."

"You did already," I reminded him.

"I'm not finished." He pulled out of me and slid down to bury his head in the apex of my thighs. With that skilled tongue of his, he licked, delved, sucked, and brought me to the brink of another release, only to leave me hanging on the edge.

With a wicked smile, he rose, sat back on his heels and pulled me against him, so that my butt rested on his thighs. With one stroke, he stretched and filled me. When fully sheathed, he stared down at me. "You do things to me. I'm out of my fucking mind around you. Have no sense of right or wrong. Only you. I lost my head when that damn detective told me you'd been followed this morning. If anything happened...."

"It didn't." I moaned. Damn, he was deep. I was so full of him, so greedy for more, I could barely speak.

"I know, and it won't happen again. I'm moving in."

"What if I say no?" I asked with zero conviction.

"No isn't an option." He fell forward, caught himself on his hands, brought his nose to mine, and pushed deeper. "Silly girl. Haven't you figured it out?"

"What?" I arched against him, craving the friction.

"You gave yourself to me, remember?" he asked with hitched breaths.

"How could I forget?"

"You're my angel," he groaned, pulled out and slammed back into me. "I protect what's mine. At any cost."

Caged between his arms, captivated by the fierce conviction crackling in his baby blues, something in me shifted, on a metaphysical level, and I knew this man was created for me, and I for him.

Silly as it sounded, he would die for me. His gaze held that promise every time our eyes met. I could see that now.

What a beautiful, terrifying revelation.

* * * *

Franklin's too-expensive suit lay rumpled on my bathroom floor. Instead of picking it up, I marveled at the sight behind my glass shower door. That virile, beautiful man wanted to be with me. Me! What had I done in my short existence on planet earth to deserve his attentions? Did it matter? Hell no.

Over the years, I'd watched my friends fall in and out of love. Sat with them, dabbed tears born of broken hearts, celebrated engagements, listened to endless ramblings about new love interests. I'd never been one to seek it out, though. Romance. Dating. The emotional rollercoaster. It wasn't for me.

I'd given up on that fantasy years ago. It was too painful to get excited over a guy, to enjoy a date, get my hopes up, then sit by the phone for days and days, waiting for the call that would never come.

One-Date Tate.

Nope. Wasn't for me.

Not until Franklin Reed.

Through the foggy glass, I admired his form, watched him lather-up from neck to knees. My cheeks warmed when he reached down to wash his privates. Heat rolled under my skin when he fisted his sex and stroked the full length, then lifted it against his tight belly to clean the boys underneath. Who knew such a common act could be so titillating to witness?

"Are you enjoying the show?" he asked. His words bounced off the tiled walls, vibrating every cell of my body.

Oh shoot. Busted.

I bent to pick up his disheveled shirt. "Um, I'm picking up your clothes. Don't want them to get wrinkled." Jeez. Could I have sounded any more ridiculous?

A deep, throaty laugh boomed inside the glass enclosure.

I jetted out of there and searched for space in my closet to hang his things. Wow. Did I put them in mine or the guest bedroom? How would this work? I'd never had a roommate, let alone a live-in lover.

When he dropped the bomb he'd be here on a permanent basis, I didn't protest for a few reasons. One—because his magic wand cast a seductive spell deep inside my womb, rendering me dependent on his touch. Two—after spending two seconds with Franklin, you want him permanently attached to your side. And three—he was right. It would be safer, at least until the stalker was caught and people stopped kicking the bucket.

Poor Wallace. What had his final moments been like? Was he scared? Did he beg and plead for his life? It wasn't a secret that I despised the man, but despite the fact that I fantasy-killed him on a daily basis, I didn't believe he deserved such a cruel exit from the greedy, selfish world he'd created for himself.

I hung the fine wool suit in my closet and tidied up the bedroom. Franklin came out wearing a towel and toe-curling grin. "You okay?" he asked, dropping the cloth to the floor. "Your cheeks are red."

I threw a pillow at him. "I hate you."

He chuckled and tugged a pair of boxer briefs over his thighs. "No, you don't."

"But I do. I really do." I studied him one more time, from pecs to toes, and bit my lip to keep from grinning. "So much, in fact, that I cleaned out that dresser for you," I teased and pointed to the antique chest of drawers in the corner of my room. I wanted to tear my clothes off and tackle him to the floor. My skin tingled just thinking about it. I'd become a sex fiend. Shaking my head, I drew a mind-clearing breath and headed for the kitchen.

Franklin appeared a few minutes later, buffed and shined. I grabbed his hand and pulled him to the couch. "If you're serious about doing this, we need to talk."

He sat and yanked me into his lap. "You're worried?"

I nodded. Was it that obvious?

"That we won't get along?" he asked, with a cocky smirk and a playful twinkle in his eyes.

"That's one thing."

"What else? Throw it at me."

"This thing we have going." I waved my hand back and forth between us. "It's amazing. I mean, blowing my mind amazing. But what if we're only experiencing that short period of bliss. You know, the excitement people feel when they first meet. We don't know each other."

His playful grin disappeared. "I know you."

"You say that. But do you? What if I drive you insane?"

"You do." His worry wrinkles came out to play.

"Come on, this is a huge step." I let out an exasperated puff of air. "What happens when the lust haze wears off?"

Franklin leaned back and crossed his arms. "Are you afraid I'll bolt?"

Bingo! Although we'd yet to have an official date, he had stuck around longer than anyone else. My luck wouldn't hold forever. "Well, yes. No… I don't know. Nobody moves in together after a couple of weeks. We completely skipped the whole dating phase."

"Killer, have you ever fit in with the crowd? Have you ever conformed?"

"No."

"Right. Neither have I. What I feel for you. This *thing* between us. It's real for me. I've lived without you. I refuse to go back to that. From my end, you've got zilch to worry about."

This guy couldn't be for real. "Aren't you worried I might freak?"

"Hell, no. And listen, if you ever feel the need to run. Don't. I'll catch you. I'll drag you home and give you so many earth-shattering orgasms you'll become a junkie for my cock. Understand?"

I had a mini orgasm listening to his threat. I wiped drool from my lip, then tried and failed to form a lucid response.

Franklin slapped my hip and stood, pulling me with him.

"We're not done talking," I protested.

He rolled his eyes. "We're done."

"Listen, Mr. Bossy Pants. I'm agreeing to this living arrangement for now." I pretended to be in control of the situation. "It's only temporary until things get back to normal, understand? What kind of girl would I be if I shacked up with a guy after two weeks?"

Franklin pretended to concede. "Whatever you say. Get your shoes. There's an irate waitress waiting for me to bring you by. She's convinced I'm an asshole. I think she spat in my beer earlier today." Franklin bent to grab his keys off the coffee table. "Where'd that picture come from?" he asked, reaching for the photo I'd placed there earlier. He reached to pick it up, then shook his head and backed away.

"Detective Waters found it in Jacob's apartment. That's my dad." I retrieved my ballet flats from under the couch and slipped them on.

"Why didn't you show me?" he huffed.

"It slipped my mind. I don't know who the women are, but she looks familiar." I pointed to the blonde sitting on Dad's lap. Franklin's fingers stretched at his sides and curled into tight fists. Oh, good Lord, what had set him off this time? "Is something wrong?" I squeaked.

He shoved his hands in his front pockets and dropped his head. "No. Just tired." When he looked at me again, the tension had disappeared. "Let's go, then."

I snatched the photo, shoved it into my pocket, and followed Franklin out the door.

* * * *

Lizzie plopped our drinks on the table and her ass in the seat, bumping my hip with a playful nudge. "I'm glad you're here. Frankie explained what happened, but I needed to see for myself, make sure he was on the up and up."

I smirked, struggling to hold my sex-charged joy to a low wattage. "Everything's good."

"Good, huh?" She studied my face, then Franklin's, who pretended not to listen to our conversation. His mouth quivered at the corner, then relaxed.

Across the room, three women shared a plate of fries. Each of them threw seductive glances his way. He graced them with a nod, leaned back, and pressed his thigh against mine.

"We've been bonking like lovesick teenagers." I blurted. Loud. On purpose. "So I think it's safe to say, things are amazing."

"TMI. Jeez, Tate." Lizzie grabbed my beer and took a sip.

"Told you she was funny, Liz." Franklin wrapped his arm around my shoulder and kissed my cheek. "I don't think everyone in the bar heard you, Killer. You need to work on your projection," he joked, flashing his million-dollar smile.

Lizzie laughed and scooted off the seat. "Listen, I gotta earn my paycheck"—she yanked the front of her curve-hugging tank down to reveal some impressive cleavage—"and my tips, but don't leave. That fucker from the other night came back. I took a picture with my cell when he wasn't paying attention."

Franklin's leg started to vibrate against me. He shifted, then pulled me closer. "Let's see it."

"It's in my locker. I'll bring it out on my break, 'kay?"

The sexy hunk of male next to me tensed like a lion ready to pounce. "I'd appreciate if we could see that picture sooner rather than later." A threatening undercurrent carried the weight of his tone.

She slapped her palms on our table and leaned toward Franklin. "Listen, buddy. I don't take to bossy, overbearing men. I'll get it when I'm damned good and ready. Speak to me like that again, you'll be out on your ass." Her glare could've made the devil himself rattle in his boots, and she shot me a wink before strutting off. That was when I dubbed Lizzie my new best friend.

Franklin shocked me by laughing. "Damn. She's a tough little shit."

"I think I love her," I replied.

"She's holding us ransom, you know. She can grab that phone anytime she wants. The girl practically runs the damn place. The longer we're here, the more beer we drink."

"I'm ninety-nine percent positive it's you she wants to keep here," I stated, remembering our conversation from the other night. Lizzie still crushed on Franklin. It was evident every time she looked at him. Did it bother me? Nah. Not a woman on earth could resist his charms.

"What the hell is that supposed to mean?" he snarled. "Never mind. I don't wanna know." Franklin drew a deep breath and turned toward me. "I watched the parking garage video surveillance from the night the roses were left in your car."

My stomach lurched.

"There's approximately a thirty-minute window when the feed goes haywire. He must have left them during that time."

"Dare I ask how you got access to the video?"

"Nathan in security owed me a favor. We also checked the number the text was sent from. Prick used a disposable cell."

Hmm. I knew better than to push the issue. Or maybe I just didn't want to see anymore grim on Franklin's lovely face. Especially with his hand resting on my thigh, dangerously close to the pleasure zone.

"What do you think will happen with Cruse Investigations?" I asked, hoping to shift the mood.

His shoulders dropped, but only a tad. "Business as usual, I hope. If Wallace had any silent partners, they'll step in. Although, I doubt that was the case. Fucker was too greedy to bring in partners."

"Aren't you concerned about losing your job?" I slapped my hand over his. If it traveled any higher we ran the risk of being arrested for indecent exposure or lewd acts.

He brushed a finger under my chin and studied my eyes. "No, love. You?"

I leaned in and stole a kiss. "Nah. I'm a rich bitch. Besides, I have a roommate now. I'll raise his rent if the need arises."

I'd never discussed my finances with Franklin, or anyone for that matter. I expected him to query me further on the subject of money, but he didn't. "Maybe now would be a good time for me to consider higher education."

"Yeah?" He brushed a tendril of hair from my face and tucked it behind my ear. Holy cow, why did we have to be in a public place? Every nerve ending in my body tingled with delight.

"Why not? It's time I grow up and get a real job." Unless he wanted me to be his sex slave. Now that was a career choice I could sink my teeth into.

"Doing what?" he asked, killing my brain cells one at a time with the blue electricity powering his gaze.

"That's the problem. I don't have a friggin' clue."

Franklin relaxed against the back of the chair and circled the rim of his beer mug with his index finger. "Buy the company."

"What?" I snorted. "Are you insane?"

"Why not? Your father started it. It'd be fitting for you to take over."

"No. Not gonna happen. I don't have the first clue about running a company." I could barely keep my own finances in order.

"Hear me out." He turned toward me, resting a knee on the seat and his arm over the back. "Nan practically runs the place. Give her a promotion. She'd be thrilled to take over. Everyone there loves the shit out of you. They'd stay, just to watch you succeed."

It took every string of self control I owned to not laugh in his face. "What would *I* do?"

"Get a bigger office. Sit there, look pretty. Dissolve the inter-office dating rule. Then we can fuck like bunnies on your big new desk in your private den." He wiggled his thick eyebrows. "There are special perks to being the boss."

"Jeez, Wallace hasn't been dead twenty-four hours and we're discussing how to take over his empire. What kind of cold-hearted creeps are we?"

"You're right." Franklin held his glass in the air. "To Wallace. I hated the bastard, but he was a…well, he was…."

I jumped in to ease his torture. "To Wallace." I tapped my glass against his, downed the rest of its contents in one long swig, and slammed my mug on the table. "Wench. Another round," I shouted to Lizzie.

She smiled and pointed her middle finger to the sky.

"Maybe I could work here," I teased. "Lizzie and I would make a great team."

"Hell, no. You think I'd let you loose in a bar full of drunk assholes? Over my dead fucking body."

Overbearing? Yes he was. "You know, it's creepy how much like my dad you are."

His grin morphed from playful to woeful. My heart deflated.

"Tell me. How are we alike?" He grabbed my hand and squeezed.

"He'd move mountains to keep Mom and me out of harm's way. I'm pretty sure he beat the daylights out of a boy in class who harassed me."

Franklin blanched. "What do you mean?"

I'd never shared that theory with anyone before. No time like the present. "My bosoms made their debut in seventh grade. Boys in school took notice and razzed me. One guy, Jay Masters, teased me relentlessly. Most of the time, I laughed it off. Boys will be boys, you know?" I quirked an eyebrow. Franklin tensed.

"Jay was a football player and twice my size. One day, he was more aggressive than usual. I came home, broke down in tears, and spilled my guts to Dad. The next day, Jay wasn't at school. When he did come back over a week later, he had a cast on his arm and a mangled face. The dick never looked at me again."

Franklin laughed. "Got what he deserved."

It really hadn't been funny. I had felt bad for the kid. "I knew it was Dad. I never asked, but I knew. I was his only child, so I never gave him too much grief about escorting me to all my school functions, sleepovers, or excursions to the mall."

Franklin lifted his hand from mine and wrapped it around his beer mug.

"On the rare occasion a boy actually asked me on a date, I'd catch Dad sitting in the back row of the movie theater, or parked across the street of the restaurant."

Franklin cleared his throat and shifted in his seat. He seemed to be preoccupied with a water spot on his glass.

"I never saw his face, just the dark figure, following me, hovering in the shadows. He was always there, without fail. I pretended not to notice and I certainly never pointed it out to the boy I was with." Second dates had been as elusive as a curly-horned talking unicorn. I certainly hadn't wanted to cripple my chances.

Franklin smiled and nodded as if in agreement with Dad's actions.

"What?" I asked.

"Tate, baby. A real man does whatever it takes to protect the women in his life." He raised his drink again. "To Antonio Wood. The man who kept my Killer safe."

I tapped my empty mug to his. "To Dad."

Funny, I couldn't remember telling Franklin my dad's name.

Two drinks later, my bladder cried for mercy. I could no longer ignore the call of nature. "I'll be right back."

I started to scoot from my seat but Franklin slapped a tight grip around my arm. "Oh, no you don't."

I looked at his hand first, then his face, hardened with possessive stubbornness. "I need to use the ladies room. So, um, yes I do."

"I'll go with you."

I pulled his hand off me one finger at a time.

"Look." I gestured to the loo. "You can see the door from here. It's about"—I air-walked my fingers from his nose toward the door—"fifteen steps. If anyone sneaks up on me, you can do this." I whistled *The Twilight Zone* tune. "That will be our signal for danger. If I hear it, I'll duck and cover until you come—"

Franklin clamped a hand over my mouth. His eyes sizzled, but not with amusement. "Shut up. Just go to the damn bathroom, funny girl." He let me go and smacked a wet kiss on my cheek.

"Well, jeez. Thanks." I rolled my eyes and sauntered off, counting my steps along the way. When I hit the door I turned and shouted. "Fourteen steps, see?"

He didn't smile.

I shot him a wink, then went inside to take care of business. I took my time and primped in the spotty mirror.

Instead of heading his direction, I followed the sound of Lizzie's angry voice. She stood halfway down the dimly lit hall with her back to the wall, pinned between two beefy arms, holding her own against a drunk horndog trying to cop a feel.

I played coy. "Hey Lizzie. Who's your boyfriend?"

Neither of them looked at me. Lizzie pushed at his chest. "This is the last time I'm going to ask. Back the fuck up."

The man smiled wider. "How about a kiss first, sweetheart."

"Hey asshole. Get off," I shouted, pushing at his shoulder.

With barely a grunt, he swung his arm and pushed me into the wall behind us.

Franklin came out of nowhere. In a blur, the man, who stood at least two inches taller and a hundred pounds heavier, ended up face to the ground. Blood spurted from his nose, his right arm lay twisted the wrong way at his side. Franklin held the shithead's left wrist behind his back. That it happened so fast wasn't what scared me. The gun that appeared out of thin air, pointed at the man's head? Terrifying. Holy shit.

I shot a glance at Lizzie. She'd assumed the same position I had with head, hands, and butt smashed against the wall.

Franklin pressed one knee into the guy's back. "This is what's going to happen." He tucked the gun under his shirt. "I'm going to help you up. We'll walk out the back door, nice and quiet. I know you're in pain. It's gonna get worse. If you make a peep before we're outside, I'll blow your fucking brains out."

The guy mumbled something and Franklin chuckled. Chuckled! What was happening?

He turned to me. "Hey, Killer. Go sit. I'll be right back. Take Lizzie with you." He shot me a reassuring wink, like he'd done nothing more than order a coffee and muffin.

I couldn't trigger the right brainwaves to make my legs move.

Franklin's tone darkened. "Tatum. Now."

Lizzie grabbed me by the elbow and lugged me to our table. Neither one of us spoke a word. We sat. Lizzie finished my drink. I stared at the beer bottle chandelier hanging above the bar. I didn't know if I was turned on or repulsed by what had transpired.

I jumped when my phone buzzed in my back pocket. Franklin's eerily tranquil voice came through the earpiece. "Hey, love. I'm gonna run upstairs and change my clothes. You okay?"

I nodded, sucking my bottom lip between my teeth.

"Baby?" he prodded, his voice smooth as chocolate silk.

God, how could he be so calm after that mind-boggling display? My insides trembled. He moved so fast. Too fast. Took a man down. Broke a nose, an arm. Pulled out a gun. He performed his morbid ballet in a matter of seconds. Nobody moved like that.

"Tatum," he barked through the speaker. "You there?"

"Yeah. I'm here." I didn't want to be there. I wanted to be with him, getting answers. "Can I come up with you?" I asked, unable to hide the quaver in my voice.

"No. I'll be right down. Tell Lizzie to stay with you until I get back." He hung up.

A sharp pain speared the big ugly muscle perched behind my left breast. The room spun like a carnival ride and the beer that'd slid down my throat like greased lightning earlier now threatened to hit reverse and make a swift exit. "Oh Lizzie, what have I gotten myself into?"

She gripped my forearm and squeezed hard. "I know, right. That was so fuckin' hot."

Bless her heart. Silly fool.

"I mean, shit. That was unbelievable. Where did he learn to do that?" she asked with an unusual squeak to her voice.

"Lizzie." I turned and cupped her cheeks. "Are you insane? That was scary, dangerous shit." Okay, maybe it was hot. If I'd been watching it on a big screen and munching on popcorn with extra butter I would've cheered the guy on.

"Are you kidding me?" She laughed. "Your boyfriend just leveled a bulldozer, Jet Li style, because he manhandled you."

"He pulled out a gun," I whispered. "Why the hell is he carrying a gun?"

I sensed his presence like an oncoming thunderstorm. Apprehension tickled my scalp.

"Tate. Time to go." He pulled a wad of cash from his pocket and slapped a Benjamin on the table. "That dick won't bother you again, Lizzie."

Franklin laced his fingers through mine and prodded me to follow.

I think Lizzie said thank you, but I couldn't be sure through the tempest of anger, confusion, and frustration brewing in my head. We didn't use the front door. He led me to the back exit and scanned the dark parking lot before venturing forward.

We reached his SUV and instead of opening the door, Franklin crushed me to the cold vehicle with his hips and chest. He kissed me so hard our teeth clashed. One hand smashed my breast, the other gripped the back of my head, holding me firm so I couldn't pull away. It was brutal, the kiss. Painful, dominating, and damn him, turning me the hell on.

A loud whizz passed my ear and glass shattered behind my head.

Chapter 12

Rocks bit my cheek, my palms, my thighs. I'd gone from being ravished against a car to crushed on the ground by hard, pissed off male. The full weight of his body spread across mine, stifling my ability to breathe. Ping, ping, ping. Three more shots embedded themselves in the car just above my head.

Franklin rolled off, cocked his arms, and shot four rounds. He tossed his keys at me. "Run upstairs. Lock yourself in and don't fucking open that door for anyone. Got it? Nobody but me."

Another ping. I wrapped my arms around my head, smashing my face harder into the gravel.

"Fuck." He fired again. "Move your ass, baby. Go. Go!"

I shot a glance at the stairs and cringed. It seemed an impossible distance to travel. I turned my nose away from the scent of dirt and oil.

Franklin pulled a second pistol from under his shirt. "Go. Now!" he ordered.

Oh shit. I pushed to my feet, then scrambled forward. Franklin ran alongside, shielding me until I reached the first step. My legs became lead weights and my trek to the top passed in excruciating slow motion. More gunshots ripped through the early evening air. The blood whooshing through my ears came in painful waves, drowning out the street noise. My fingers trembled. I dropped the keys, picked them up. Oh God, oh God, oh God. I was dead. I just knew it. Any second, a bullet would turn my brains into splatter art on Franklin's door.

Somehow I managed to insert the key, turn the knob, and drag my trembling ass inside. I slammed it behind me, turned the lock, then snapped the deadbolt. My knees hit the hardwood with a thud.

While Franklin dodged bullets, I cowered inside—the helpless victim. Sirens wailed in the distance. An engine roared. Tires squealed. I stayed on the floor. Unable to move. More gunshots popped and a scream rose from deep in my belly.

I needed to move. First, I needed to breathe. Inhale through the nose, exhale through the mouth. Inhale, exhale, in, out, in, out. I regained control of my lungs and crawled like a baby toward the bathroom. Only when I reached the hall did I find the strength to stand. Franklin's bedroom door hung ajar. A blue glow illuminated the dark space and I walked in, searching for a place to hide. I found the light switch and immediately wished I hadn't.

Although the room contained a bed, it wasn't a bedroom—not by a long shot. The closet doors were open, revealing a floor-to-ceiling safe sporting a keypad as well as a large dial. The opposite wall boasted a long metal desk decorated with computers. Above that hung multiple computer screens, all powered on, three of which appeared to have live feeds of every square inch of my home. That alone should have thrown me into a nuclear tizzy. Not me. Nope. What freaked me out? The wall, illuminated in warm lighting, covered floor-to-ceiling with photographs of me. From my grade school years on, as far as I could tell. Hundreds of images, black-and-whites, colored. It was impossible to distinguish, because in that moment, I saw nothing but red.

The small bed, situated in the center of the room, faced the collage. I plopped my ass down and got a whiff of Franklin. Bile rose in my throat. I pushed to my feet and narrowly made it to the toilet before purging the contents of my stomach.

God, I needed my dad. He'd know what to do. I rinsed my mouth in the sink. When I looked in the mirror at my dirty reflection and frazzled hair, my heart dropped to my toes. My father would be so disappointed in me. And Franklin? He'd be dead. Not a doubt in my mind, Daddy would kill him.

I washed my mouth one more time, retrieved my phone from my pocket, and dialed the special number I'd decided to memorize days ago. Sirens blared outside. I slunk to the living room and peeked out the window. Police cars packed the lot and surrounding streets. The phone rang and rang. No answer. My stomach twisted in volatile spasms. My flesh ached. My soul screamed. Why did this hurt so damn bad? I couldn't be in his space anymore, whoever *he* was—the enigma who'd ruined me for any other man. I unlocked the door, bolted down the stairs, and ran to the nearest person in uniform.

Franklin called my name from behind. "Tate!" He seemed a million miles away. "Baby. You okay?" I turned on instinct, drawn to his voice like a moth to a flame. Franklin stopped dead in his tracks when our eyes met.

Tears fell faster than I could wipe them away. I twisted toward the officer. "I need Detective Waters. I need him right now."

"Baby, don't." Franklin warned, his voice gruff and commanding.

I fisted the officer's sleeves and pulled at him. "Please. Now. I need Detective Waters. Tell him it's Tatum Reed. It's urgent."

I looked over my shoulder. Franklin stormed toward me.

Pushing the officer away, I turned to confront the enemy. "No!" I shouted. "No. Don't come near me. Don't call me baby. I saw it. I saw that room! Who the hell are you? Why me? Why? You son of a bitch."

I ran to the man who'd gutted me and started throwing punches. "How could you?" I slapped his face, scratched, spit, kicked his shins.

Franklin remained stone still, absorbing every strike of my bat-shit crazy assault, he stood his ground, a soulless statue. His lack of emotion only fueled my fire. I drew blood with my nails. He didn't flinch. I punched, aiming for his nose. He didn't block, grunt, or curse, only blinked, never tearing his gaze from me. "You liar," I screamed. "You sick bastard."

Two men grabbed my arms and tore me away, kicking and screaming. They stuffed me into the back of a patrol car and shut me in. Franklin didn't budge, only stood, stretching his fingers then clenching them tight, stretching, clenching, over and over. The raw, tormented expression he wore almost had me fooled. Then he blinked and it was gone, replaced with stone cold fury.

I hated him so, so much.

* * * *

The backseat of the patrol car, although cramped and reeking of oil and musty carpet, became my new safe haven. Leland sat next to me and held my hand until the trembling dulled to a faint shake.

Around the same time the moon disappeared behind daunting clouds, Franklin stopped staring at me and followed a man in a dark suit up to his apartment. Most of the responding officers had left. In the stinky vehicle, I spilled my guts to Detective Waters. Told him everything I hadn't before about Franklin. He listened. Jotted notes on his yellow pad. Asked far too few questions, in my opinion.

"Do you think he was behind any of the murders?" I asked. Leland's chuckle ignited a rage in my gut. Why did he find it humorous? It seemed a logical question. Franklin had been stalking me. Maybe he was jealous of my relationship with Jacob. What about hoodie guy? How did he fit into the twisted puzzle?

The detective shook his head and huffed. "I'm not going to answer that. I will be having a conversation with Mr. Reed shortly." He released my hand and rested his palm on my knee. "Is this your way of staying out of trouble?" He faked a smile that only angered me more. "Is there someone you can stay with tonight?"

I looked toward the bar. Lizzie had poked her head out the back door at least a hundred times. The first few peeks, she'd looked worried. After that, irate. At one point, she had confronted a poor young cop. By the time she'd finished with him and had stormed back inside, he'd appeared completely exasperated. "I can ask my friend." I pointed her out.

Another young officer tapped on the window. "Waters. You're gonna want to hear this."

"What now?" Leland grunted, exited the car, and shut the door behind him.

I buried my face in my hands. Where was Franklin? What would they do to him? What line of bullshit did he feed everyone? Why did I care? He'd lied to me from day one. None of it made any sense.

I surely needed to sell my condo and move far away. Florida might be nice. I could hang with Mom and Grandpa in Panama City, play some old-folks games. People didn't shoot each other during bingo, did they?

Leland opened the door and bent to speak to me. "Miss Wood. Officer Johnson will drive you to the station. I'll meet you there."

Uh, oh. I was Miss Wood again. "What's going on?"

"We'll discuss it in my office." He slammed the door, shouted a few profanities, and stomped across the parking lot. I watched him trot up the stairs. Two men in dark suits stopped him halfway up. Franklin surfaced in the doorway, holding a bloodied towel to his nose.

That stupid, silly organ in my chest pitter-pattered at the sight of him. Didn't my heart know better? Bad heart. Very bad!

The engine roared, the vehicle rolled, taking me away from the man I hated with all my might, or was at least trying to. I couldn't tear my gaze from him. He gestured to the men in suits and Detective Waters continued up the stairs.

Shouldn't he be in handcuffs? He'd shot at people. He had a creepy Wall-O-Tatum in his bedroom along with super-spy computers and an industrial vault.

Fire raged in my gut. Franklin should be on his way to the station, not me.

Why did he appear to be in command of the whole scene?

* * * *

Three hours. Three hours I waited for the detective to return to the station. They could've at least put me in a comfortable room. Not a single one of the jackasses in blue would tell me why I was there.

By the time Leland, I mean, Detective Waters, showed up, I was wound tighter than a caged lioness. "What the hell is going on?" I screamed before he shut the door behind him. Exhaustion had settled in, right next to pissed off and devastated. I couldn't sit. The room was so small, pacing had made me dizzy, but I did it anyway. It took my mind off the garbled noises in my brain and the dull ache that emerged from my heart, seeping into my weary muscles.

The detective plopped his rear into a chair and raked his nails through the stubble on his cheeks. The circles under his eyes were darker than I'd ever seen. "Tell me again where you were this morning before you arrived at the office."

I stood in front of the desk and folded my arms. "I was with Franklin. I told you that already. You can ask him."

Leland stared at me unblinking.

My blood turned to ice. "I'm confused. Why are you asking me these questions again? Didn't you bring me here to talk about what happened this afternoon? The shooting? The shit in Franklin's apartment? What does this morning have to do with it?"

"We viewed the building's security footage at Cruse Investigations. You entered at six-forty-five AM. The video feed went haywire. Wallace Cruse was found dead at approximately seven-thirty."

"No. No, no, no." I shook my head and waved a finger at him. "I was home. In my apartment. With Franklin Reed. Check the security cameras in my building."

"We found blond hair entangled in Wallace's fingers. The color matches yours. Will you agree to a DNA test?"

I nodded yes. I would do anything to put a stop to the absurdity of the situation.

"Good. Can you explain the emails?" Leaning back in his chair, he clasped his hands behind his head.

"What emails?" I fought hard not to scream.

"The emails you sent to Mr. Cruse." His cheeks reddened. "The sexually explicit ones."

This had to be a joke. Except the stone cold expression on his face assured me it was not. "I think I'm gonna be sick." I doubled over.

Detective Waters jumped from the table and scooted the trash can to my feet.

"Were you and Mr. Cruse having an affair?" he asked.

I snapped.

"Are you friggin' crazy? Has everyone gone out of their minds? I hated him. That man made my skin crawl. He was a greedy, narcissistic, immoral fucktard who turned my father's business into a sleaze-fest for shitheads who couldn't keep their dicks or pussies where they belonged. I hated him. Do you hear me? Hated him."

He hit me with a challenging glare. "Enough to kill him?"

Oh, why couldn't I keep my mouth shut? I decided it best to stop talking. I plopped my rear onto the hard metal chair, crossed my arms, and glared my anger and frustration, heartbreak and fear at Detective Waters. I shot it right smack between his eyes.

His brows crinkled, eyes saddened. He pushed from the table, walked to the door, and poked his head out. I couldn't hear what he said to the man standing outside. Before leaving, he turned back to me. "For the record, I believe you. We've got a long night ahead of us, but we'll get to the bottom of this."

Officer Johnson caught the door before it closed. "Miss Reed. I'm taking you down the hall where you'll be more comfortable."

I pressed my lips together. A multitude of colorful words bubbled on the tip of my tongue. Words not appropriate for a lady to speak. I would remain silent. I would.

I followed the officer down a long corridor to another tiny room with a small couch. Thank God. I ached from scalp to toes. My hand, swollen from the right hook to Franklin's nose, throbbed a relentless beat. I hoped his face hurt and my fingernails had dug deep enough to leave scars.

The couch offered no give but was a hell of a lot more comfortable than the cold metal chairs. "Would you like some coffee?" The lanky officer asked.

I pursed my lips together and shook my head no.

"Fine then. I'll check in on you soon." He pulled the door shut. Then locked it.

Was it legal to lock me in? I didn't give a shit anymore. I was relieved to be alone, somewhere safe. No dead bodies, no rose-bearing stalkers, no bullets flying at me. No Franklin. A violent tremor rattled my bones. No Franklin. Why did that terrify me?

Leland would get his facts straightened out. He didn't believe I killed Wallace. I relaxed, knowing he was fighting in my corner, and lay back against the hard cushion. Sexually explicit emails? It was laughable.

The shit I know would blow your mind.

I'm going to burn in hell for this.

Franklin's words spun in my head, round and round, taunting, teasing. *So fucking long. You're finally mine. Jesus, Tate. So goddamn many years. You're mine, finally mine.*

What did that mean? How long had he been watching me?

I've loved you for so long.

The memories sliced me into a thousand pieces.

Chapter 13

Cold gray walls narrowed and stretched ahead of me. An exit sign flashed in the distance. My legs moved impossibly fast, but the doors to freedom remained out of reach. Footsteps echoed around me. I skidded to a stop.

Hot breath blew across my shoulder, sending erotic chills across my skin. A heavy hand pressed against the small of my back, then wandered upward to stroke my hair.

"I protect what's mine, at any cost."

My eyes jerked open. Yellow light from the dingy bulb in the ceiling played tricks with my vision. It took too damn long to focus. A soft blanket covered me from chin to toes and my head rested on a fluffy pillow. The familiar scent of lemon-lime, lavender, and orange pervaded the air. His smell. Had he been here?

Sadness pressed on my chest like a road roller. I couldn't breathe.

Out. I had to get out.

Every muscle protested when I jumped from the couch. I banged on the door, rattled the handle. I needed air.

Keys rattled outside. The door opened and a grumpy, disheveled Detective Waters greeted me. "Have a good sleep?"

I shook my head and drew a deep breath.

"C'mon." He stepped aside and gestured for me to follow. "You look like shit."

So did he, but I refused to respond. I walked behind him through the windowless hallway. When we stepped into the open area of the police station, bright sunlight scorched my retinas and shot minuscule razors straight through my brain.

Ow! I covered my eyes. "How long did I sleep? What time is it?"

A familiar voice called my name from behind. "Tatum, is that you?"

Leland clamped a hand around my arm before I could turn to look.
"Is that her?" I heard Nan shriek. "No. Let me go. Is it true? Tatum. Look at me. Did you murder him?"

I glanced over my shoulder and two officers held her steady. If looks could kill, there'd be nothing left of me but a bloodstain on the tile floor.

"Get her out of here," Leland bellowed and hauled me into his office. "Jesus Christ. This place has turned into a goddamned circus." He slammed the door and pointed at the chair. "Sit."

He plopped a brown paper bag on his desk, shoved it my direction and with a grunt, ordered me to eat.

"Thank you."

A warm breakfast croissant smiled up at me from the bottom of the sack. It smelled of bacon and buttery heaven and my stomach rumbled in agreement. I dove in with manners comparable to a wild animal. "Where's yours?" I asked with a mouthful of greasy goodness.

He smiled as if amused at my lack of social graces. "I ate already. You want coffee?"

I nodded. "I'd blow Bigfoot for a coffee right now."

His lip curled on the left side but he didn't crack. "Sit tight. I'll be right back."

I savored another bite and forced myself to slow down. Why was he being nice? Did something change overnight? Damn, the croissant was delicious.

"Tate?" Lizzie's voice crackled from the doorway. "Oh, thank fuck."

"Lizzie! What are you doing?" I'd never been so happy to see anyone and sprang from my seat. "Are you supposed to be here?"

She looked at the door, then back to me. "No. I had to make sure you were all right. I've been here for hours trying to flirt my way into seeing you. So"—she elbowed me—"last night, huh? Don't get to see action like that every day."

She must be an adrenaline junkie.

"Lizzie, they think I killed my boss."

"Yeah, right," she snorted, smacking my arm in a playful gesture.

I shoved the rest of my breakfast back into the bag. "I'm not joking. They locked me in a room."

Lizzie gave me a once-over then pulled me into a hug. "Motherfuckers. In a cell?"

"Not exactly. I slept on a couch."

She grabbed my hand and turned to peek out the door. "This is ridiculous. Have you been arrested?"

"Well, no."

"Then what the hell are you hanging around for? Come on, I'm taking you home." Lizzie tugged me out of Leland's office.

"I can't just leave. Can I?" I whispered, digging my heels into the floor. She stopped, fists to hips, and quirked an eyebrow. "Did they order you to stay?"

"No."

"Then we can leave." She extended her hand and wiggled her fingers. "Follow my lead."

My skin prickled, my head itched, I needed the little girl's room desperately, and I was sure I had the world's worst case of raccoon eyes. Leaving had to be wrong, but staying wasn't doing me any good.

We snuck down the hall. Everyone went about their business. Leland was nowhere to be seen and nobody paid us any mind. Lizzie and I walked right out of the building and didn't draw so much as a sideways glance. Wow. Who knew?

She led me to a beefy green Jeep parked close to the entrance. I climbed in and buckled up. In no time, we rolled away from the station. Cool and casual. Easy-peasy.

"I can't believe we just did that," I gasped, cupping my cheek and glancing out the rearview.

Her bright green eyes grew larger and she flashed me a million watt smile. "Oh. My. God. It's adorable how sweet and innocent you are. What happened last night?" she asked, pushing the gas pedal harder than necessary.

I slunk in my chair. "Someone shot at us. Real bullets. Franklin threw himself on top of me, then went berserk. He had two guns. Two guns, Lizzie. They came out of nowhere and he looked like a damn assassin. He told me to run upstairs. I don't know how I didn't get shot. I should be dead right now."

Lizzie's jaw couldn't have dropped any lower, but she held her gaze to the road.

I wanted to tell her about Franklin's bedroom and share my agony. For some reason, I couldn't bring myself to divulge his secrets.

"Then I heard sirens. When it was safe, I came out. They put me in a vehicle, questioned me, and took me to the station. I didn't argue because I just wanted to be far away from there."

Lizzie shook her head back and forth and pursed her lips as if processing my words. "Franklin was a mess."

Nervous energy burst through my veins. "What do you mean?"

"His face looked like raw meat." She smirked. "Someone beat the shit out of him, which I find hard to believe. I've seen him in action. I can't imagine anyone getting close enough to do that kind of damage."

I looked down at my bruised knuckles. Why had he let me assault him anyway?

"He nearly ripped my head off after everyone left."

"Why?" I asked.

"He barged in after the parking lot cleared. Said he needed to see the photo. You know, the one I took of your stalker."

Oh, no.

"I showed him and by his reaction, he had to know the guy. He yelled…" Lizzie lowered her voice and scrunched her face, mimicking Franklin. "That motherfucking piece of shit. This time, I kill him." She paused and downshifted to make a sharp right. "He handed my phone back, grabbed a bottle of Jack off the wall and left."

"Where's your phone?" I asked. A flood of urgency burst through me.

"In my purse." She pointed over her shoulder. I reached back and rummaged until I found her cell.

"Do you mind?" I didn't wait for her to answer and pulled up her photos.

"It should be the first one."

I pulled it up and zoomed in. My intestines knotted. I knew the face on the screen, too. Jay Masters. The kid my father had given a beating to in high school because he'd teased me. Jay Masters, who had steered clear of me from my freshman year through graduation.

"What the hell?" I asked, looking at her as if she'd have the answer.

Lizzie shot a nervous glance from her rearview to the road ahead and back again. "Do you know him?"

"Yeah. We went to school together."

"Hey, Tate?" she whispered.

What was with the hush-hush?

"I think we're being followed."

I jerked around in my seat. Sure enough, a man on a black Harley followed two cars behind. The same black Harley I'd seen three times too many.

"What do I do?" she asked, more excited than nervous.

I was so done with the bullshit. "Pull over."

"No!" she barked, pushing on the gas pedal.

"Pull over, Lizzie. Now." I yanked on the door handle. She grabbed my left wrist and pulled me toward her.

"Okay, Jeez. Don't kill yourself." She veered into the dilapidated parking lot of a vacant building. The motorcycle followed and rolled to a stop on the opposite end. I jumped from the car and marched straight for him.

"Jay!" I screamed. "Is that you?"

The man on the bike gripped the handlebars and revved the engine.

"Take off your helmet, you coward." I had no idea what I'd do when I reached him. Hadn't planned that far ahead. A burning ball of tired, pissed, and scared female emotions churned and swelled inside me, and so help me God, I wanted to unleash it on his pathetic ass. "Show me your face," I commanded, waving my hands in the air like a crazy beast.

I was ten feet away when he reached into his pocket and drew out a pistol. He flipped up the visor on his helmet and smiled. "Get on the bike or I'll shoot you dead, right here in front of your friend."

I dug my toes into the pavement and stumbled. The false bravado that'd carried me this far waved bye-bye and flipped me the finger. My knees buckled. Lizzie screamed my name. My field of vision narrowed to only his cocky mug. He wore a pleased grin and gave all appearances of being one hundred-percent calm and in control.

Tires squealed behind me. Jay's glare darted from my face to over my shoulder. A wide smile spread from cheek to cheek. "Well, look who we have here."

A vice clamped around my waist and a deep, throaty voice groaned in my ear. "You're gonna be the death of me."

Franklin lifted me off my feet and twisted to station himself between me and the threat, yet again. "Get in the car," he ordered, then fired a shot.

Jay bellowed in pain. His gun flew out of his hand and slid under a rusted, windowless van.

I stumbled and caught myself on the car door. It was a black, sporty get-up. I dove into the driver's side and climbed over the console.

I peered out the window to Lizzie. She jumped in her Jeep and I motioned for her to drive away. The spunky, little thrill-seeker smiled and tore out of the parking lot.

I turned back to Franklin. He fired two more shots, hitting each of the motorcycle tires. Jay's Harley sunk beneath him and teetered, throwing him off balance. He held a bleeding hand to his chest, swung his leg to clear himself of the bike, tripped and fell hard against the pavement.

Franklin slunk into his seat, shifted gears, and squealed tires down the street, closing his door only after we'd cleared a whole block.

"Jesus fucking Christ! Why the hell aren't you at the police station?" he yelled, spraying spittle across his steering wheel. Wow. Not so pretty when he was pissed off.

My heart pounded triple time. "I wasn't under arrest. I left. What the fuck do you care?" I didn't like using the f-word, it never burst from my lips with enough conviction to make the right impression, but sometimes it was necessary.

Franklin cranked the steering wheel hard to the left, turning onto a side street. My shoulder slammed against the door.

"That dip-shit let you walk out of there?"

"No," I yelled back. "Slow down. I'm getting carsick."

He eased off the gas pedal. I lowered my window for some precious air.

"What do you mean, no?" he asked, darting his eyes back and forth from me to the road.

"I left. I wasn't under arrest. I didn't want to be there anymore."

"Shit." He snagged his cell from its dock and fingered his screen. "Waters. Yeah, I have her. No. How the fuck did she just walk out? I asked one goddamn thing. Fuck no, I'm not bringing her back. I don't give a shit. That's classified." He rambled Jay's location to Leland. "She's my responsibility. I'll be in touch."

Franklin tossed his cell at my feet, rolled down his window, and took a deep breath.

Classified? "Who are you?" I swiveled to face him.

His grim expression softened. Barely. "You know who I am."

"Who are you?" I asked again, more a demand than a question.

"The man who keeps saving your ass." He looked my way, and I got my first glance at his face. The skin surrounding his eye boasted several shades of purple and blue. His nose definitely didn't look right, and three large scratches stretched from his left eye to below his cheekbone. Not bad for my first shot at kicking someone's ass. Instinct urged me to reach over and offer comfort. I tucked my hand under my leg to keep it from such betrayal.

"Why were men shooting at you?" I asked, unable to cloak the seething anger in my tone.

"They weren't."

"Now you're not making sense."

"You have to trust me."

"How in the world can you ask me to do that? Why is there a collage of me on your wall?"

Franklin's lips drew into a tight line. The muscles in his jaw protruded. "Classified?" I asked, fed up with the way the conversation was going. "Yes."

My pressure gage blew. I buried my face in my hands and screamed. "Take me back to the police station. I can't be near you. I'd rather rot in a cell."

"I'm afraid I can't do that." His voice remained calm.

I pulled on the door handle. "I'll jump out if you don't start talking. Why were men shooting at you?"

"They weren't aiming for me, Killer. You were the target."

Franklin pulled a syringe from the pocket of his jacket and jabbed the bugger into my thigh. "I'm sorry, baby. It's for your own good."

A flush of heat spread through my leg. I yelped, searched his eyes in confused shock, and wrapped my hand around his as he pushed the plunger of the needle. He blurred. "I hate you…."

* * * *

It took some effort and time to bring my surroundings into focus. A violent shiver forced my eyes closed. My teeth rattled. Warm hands rubbed my arms and back. "Relax. The anesthetic should be out of your system soon."

What? I tried to push away but my muscles wouldn't cooperate.

"Don't fight me right now, love. Just let me warm you."

A surplus of vehement retorts bubbled at the back of my throat, but my jaw clenched tight with the shudders tearing through me. Heavy blankets cocooned both me and the man holding me with fierce resolve, yet I'd never been so cold, like I'd plunged naked into a tub of ice.

"Why?" I forced the question through chattering teeth.

"To keep you safe."

He lied. It didn't make sense. He knocked me out to keep me safe?

"B-b-b-astard. K-k-kidnapping."

"Jesus, baby. I didn't kidnap you. You shouldn't have left the police station. You were safe there. You left me no choice but to bring you here."

I hadn't been safe since our first weekend together. Through the drug haze clouding my head, one truth sliced through the fog—he'd saved my life. Jay had pointed a gun at my face and Franklin Reed had appeared from nowhere to rescue me. My heart hurt, rage boiled in my guts, but I lay protected and unafraid in this stranger's arms.

Franklin rubbed my skin fast and hard, the friction warming my outsides. His scent, mixed with that heady voice, thawed me from the inside. "I know you're confused." He kissed my forehead. "Let's get you warm, then we'll talk."

Oh, we were going to talk, he could be damn sure—as soon as I could move my mouth again, and force my mind out of the gutter, which wasn't easy considering the large erection tucked against my belly.

I shifted my hips away from him in protest. "M-my d-daddy would-d k-kill you," I managed to sputter.

Franklin sighed and trembled himself. "He would. But not for the reason you think."

What was that supposed to mean? More cryptic mumbo jumbo spurting from his lips. I couldn't take anymore. I'd been spied on, shot at, lied to, accused of murder, witnessed gruesome acts of violence, deflowered, and now kidnapped in the course of two short weeks. How much was a girl supposed to take?

I dug deep and forced my arms and legs to move. Inside our tight blanket burrito, I kicked and shoved and wiggled out of Franklin's embrace. "Get off me," I screamed. "Let go."

I wrestled myself free and shoved the shirtless man off the bed. He landed with a hard thud. "Goddamn, Tate," he shouted and pushed to his feet.

I rolled off the other side and stood on wobbly legs, wrapping the comforter around myself. My throat closed up tight when I noticed a trail of blood oozing down his left arm. He cupped his shoulder with the other hand and slumped against the wall behind him.

"Why are you bleeding?" I asked, not sure if I was happy or worried to see him in pain.

"It's nothing," he grunted.

I looked around the unfamiliar room. "Where are we?"

"Safe house." He nailed me with a murderous glare.

"Why in the hell are we in a safe house? What have you gotten me into?" I struck back with an equally fierce scowl.

Franklin's chest rose and fell in rapid bursts. Face pale, his steely eyes shot daggers straight at my heart. He pushed off the wall and stalked toward me.

"Don't come any closer," I warned as I backed away.

He grabbed a shirt off the bed and pressed it to his arm. "Sit down."

I shook my head no.

Franklin pointed to a chair in the corner of the room. "Sit the fuck down, now."

I jumped at the fierce snap in his tone but stood my ground. The door was only a few feet away. Could I reach it fast enough?

"That wouldn't be a wise move, love." He nodded toward the only exit. "It'd only piss me off, and right now, I'd have no problem tying your ass to this bed."

Franklin reached for the door, slammed it shut, and pressed his back against the dark wood. Then he slid to the floor and draped his arms over his knees. He didn't take his eyes off me for a blink.

I couldn't peel mine from him, either. Shirtless and bleeding. What a sight. Muscles low in my belly warmed. Fire danced across my cheeks. It was unsettling, the power he had over me.

I licked the dryness from my lips. "Why are you bleeding?" I asked with a whisper.

"Bullet grazed my shoulder," he snapped.

"Last night?" I asked, choking down unwanted emotions.

His eyes softened and he nodded. "It's not bad. Didn't even need stitches."

"I'm losing my mind, Franklin. You have to tell me what's going on."

He glanced to the ceiling, then rested his gaze on me again. "There are people after you."

Absurd? Yes. I almost laughed in disgust, but I needed to hear his explanation. "Why?"

"Leverage," he mumbled.

"Leverage for what?"

"To use against a man who held the power to destroy them. A dead man who knew too much."

"That doesn't make any sense."

"Rumors surfaced months ago that this man faked his own death. If the rumors were true, the one sure way to get to him is through those he loves."

"What the hell are you talking about? Are you on crack? Mentally unstable? This isn't an action movie. This is my life, and from the moment I let you in, it's gone to shit. Why are you doing this to me? Why?"

"I'm protecting you." Fury backed his words.

"From you? Because from where I'm standing—"

"From them," he cut me off.

"You're being cryptic."

He dropped his head between his arms. His fist clenched and unclenched, causing a rippling of muscle from wrist to elbow.

I growled in frustration, drew the blanket tighter around my body, and stormed toward him. "Who's the man? Who's the dead bastard, Franklin? Stop dicking around with me." I dropped to my knees in front of him.

I'd remember that moment for as long as I lived. Franklin raised his head. Eyes glistening with raw emotion. He grabbed my chin and captured me with a gaze so full of anguish my heart stopped beating.

"Tony Wood," he rasped. "Your father."

A nauseating swirl of shock and fury churned in my psyche. The room darkened, and my line of sight narrowed to Franklin's eyes. Eyes that burned with fierce resolve.

I hated him. I hated him. I hated him.

"Don't you dare bring my father into this sick perverted game you're playing." I slashed my hand across his face. He grunted, then caught my wrist in his powerful fist. Before I knew it, I was flat on my back, straddled by hard thighs, with my hands pinned above my head.

"Stop hitting me," he warned, lips hovering dangerously close to mine.

I turned, unable to bear the ominous force of his glare, and bucked beneath him.

"Look at me." He pulled both my wrists into one hand and pulled my face back to his with the other. "Look at me. I'm tired of the fucking secrets, too. I'm done hiding from you." He closed his eyes and drew a deep breath. When they opened again, something in me broke. The pain he wore wrapped around my soul and squeezed until it burst into a million minuscule pieces.

"Tony taught me everything I know. Everything I am, is because of him." Jagged breaths warmed my face.

"I'm a killer, Tate. Like your father." He searched my eyes. He'd just ripped my world apart. What did he expect to find other than devastation? I tried to hold the tears at bay. They refused to cooperate.

Franklin continued. "Tony recruited me the day I graduated high school. He said I had a fire that few people possessed. The agency didn't hire people so young, especially with no military background. Tony fought for me. Went over a few heads, promised them I'd be the best. He was right, too."

"You're lying," I cried. "My father didn't kill people. He was a business consultant. He didn't have a secret life…." A memory crashed down on me like a tidal wave. One I'd tucked away and had long forgotten.

When I was ten, I'd walked in on mom and dad having a heated conversation. I'd been sleeping but had gone downstairs for a drink. Mom's face was red. I remembered because she had pale, flawless skin, and I'd never seen it so flush and blotchy before. Her hands had twisted the sides of dad's shirt. "How long have you been seeing her?" Mom's voice had trembled, like she'd been on the verge of tears.

Dad had combed his fingers through Mom's hair. His voice had trembled, too. "It doesn't matter, it's over. But the boy needs me. I can't abandon him"

"You've put us at risk, Antonio. Especially Tatum. How could you?" Then she'd pressed her forehead into his chest and started to cry. I'd slunk back up the stairs and hid under my covers. I hadn't understood what they'd been talking about. When I'd woken the next morning, they had laughed and talked and kissed each other goodbye. I remembered thinking that maybe I'd just had a bad dream.

"You're the boy." The words barely made it through the clog of emotion stuck in my throat. "You're the boy he was talking about."

Streams of salty liquid poured down the sides of my face, catching in my ears. I no longer fought to contain them.

Franklin didn't ease his hold on my wrists. He only stared with sad longing. "I loved your dad. I owe him my life."

"He's the man you told me about? Your mom's boyfriend?"

Franklin nodded.

"You're hurting me." I wiggled my fingers. Franklin let go and sat back on his heels.

"I swore on my life I'd protect you. On his death bed, his sole concern was you."

Jealous rage churned through me. I should've been by Dad's side when he died. I was his flesh and blood. "Death bed? You were with him?"

"Yes."

"I hate you." I sobbed and punched at his chest. "Do you hear me?"

Franklin sighed. He leaned forward, rubbed a hand up my belly and let it rest below my breasts. "Don't say that, baby. You don't hate me."

Oh, no. He was not going to sugar-coat this conversation with sex. I raised to my elbows and tried to scoot away. My brain and body were not on the same page. Instead of fleeing, like any sane person would do, my body flushed and I shuddered for a reason that had nothing to do with temperature.

He nudged a knee between my legs, prompting them to spread. The cursed traitors opened, allowing him a nice cozy spot to nestle. He positioned himself between my thighs, then brushed away my tears with the pad of his thumb.

I focused on the scratches and bruises marring his perfect face, and reminded myself that I was furious. "You're lying to me." I dug my heels into the carpet and pushed away.

He crawled right back over me. "No, I'm not."

"I hate you. This is wrong. Let me go."

"I'll die before letting you go."

"Why? Why are you doing this?" I asked, balling my fist. I wanted to strike him again.

"To protect you and…" Franklin paused. His gaze darted from my face, to my breasts, my throat, then he swallowed hard and found my eyes again. "Because I love you. I've loved you my whole fucking life."

How could those three simple words both disintegrate and make me feel indestructible all in the same breath? Everything about this was wrong. "Don't say that, please."

"You want the truth? That picture in your back pocket? The woman is my mom. I was ten the first time I saw you. Tony pushed you on a swing at the park. He didn't know I was there, watching. You saw me, though. You looked right at me and smiled. God, the way your hair blew in the wind, you looked like an angel."

"Stop talking." I couldn't breathe. His words squeezed my heart like a vise.

"No," he continued. "In grade school there was a boy, a few years older than you. Always dirty, clothes too small, hair too long. Always had a black eye or a cut lip. All the kids stayed away from him."

I knew that boy. The floor spun beneath me, the only thing holding me steady were the set of piercing eyes hovering above.

"Do you remember?"

I nodded. "He always looked so sad."

"He wasn't sad. He was angry. All the kids were afraid of him, except for one. A brave little spitfire with golden pigtails and bright blue eyes."

Oh God, what was he saying?

"You asked me if I wanted to play. I said no—"

"I don't play with girls, I protect them." I finished his sentence. My voice weakened under the weight of memories washing over me. Franklin was that boy who always got kicked out of school for fighting, who one day didn't come back and became a faded memory, like so many others.

I reached up to cup his scruffy jaw. "That was you?"

"You were the only girl who ever spoke a kind word to me." He squeezed his eyes shut. "I wanted to tell you that I knew your dad. I wanted to play. I wanted to push you on the swing...." His voice broke and he dropped his head between his arms.

How did I not recognize him? Then again, I was young and I never saw that broken boy after he left our school.

Franklin lifted his head. A new fire burned in his eyes. "Nothing can make me stop loving you. I didn't stop when your dad threatened to beat the shit out of me for stealing your pictures from his wallet. Not when he caught me spying on you and did beat the shit out of me. I loved you through middle school, high school, my shitty sham of a marriage. You didn't know I existed and it killed me. I hated that I couldn't touch you, hold you, bury myself in you...."

He dropped his lips to mine and pressed his hips against my pelvis. My back arched and I moaned, savoring the pressure between my legs, his heat.

He kissed my chin, my jaw, then nuzzled my neck. "I've stayed away from you for too long." His fingers dug deep into my hips. He spread my legs wider and rubbed harder against me. "I want every inch of your flesh to belong to me. I want you consumed, mind, body, and spirit with want for me, for us." He pressed his forehead to my temple and whispered, "I'm going to spend the rest of my goddamned life making you crave me the way I've craved you."

* * * *

I woke naked, sweaty, and sprawled like a drunk skank on top of Franklin. My head bobbed with the rise and fall of his chest. His heart pulsed a seductive rhythm under my ear. I pressed my nose to his skin and inhaled as much of his scent as my lungs would hold. Sweat, sex and cologne—what a potent combination.

My body ached, especially between my legs. We hadn't made love. We'd fucked. Rough, angry, *I'm gonna pound you until I feel bette*r sex. He'd known what I'd needed. He knew me. I'd matched his pace and ferocity, unleashing my anger and hurt with every thrust and grind, and had, much to my chagrin, started to feel better.

I pushed up from him and the hard floor and went in search of the bathroom. I found it down the hall and had never been happier to see a toilet. I relieved myself and then cranked the shower to just below scalding. It was stocked with expensive soap and shampoo, and I took my time, washing and shaving away the grime from the last twenty-four hours. The steamy water relaxed my sore muscles so I sat and let it rush over my head and back.

Could everything he'd said about Dad be true? Had my whole life been a lie? My father had always been such an overwhelming presence in my life. How could he have possibly carried off such a charade? What about Mom? Did she know? Who was Antonio Wood?

I ruminated until the water ran cold. When I stepped out of the shower, a plush robe hung on the hook right outside the door. The gesture, although sweet, only put a small dent in the cast iron shield protecting my bruised heart. Franklin had so much explaining to do.

His husky voice greeted me from the bottom of the open stairwell. "Hey, Killer." He stood, propped against the banister with no shirt and baggy sweats that hung low on his waist. Even bloodied and bruised, the man was a sight to behold.

The uncertainty in his smile was almost a comfort. This was hard for him, too. Good. That made me feel better.

"Want some coffee?"

Caffeine. Damn, the guy knew how to get to me. I nodded and made my way down to him. "Thanks for the bathrobe." I wrapped it tight around my body and tightened the belt. When I reached the last step, Franklin pulled me into his arms and squeezed hard. Although I didn't have it in me to reciprocate, I let him hold me.

"How are you feeling?" he asked, his tone gruffer than usual. "Was I too rough on you?"

I mumbled "no" against his chest. He dropped his arms and I followed him to the massive, sprawling kitchen. He filled two mugs, added cream to mine and led me to the living area. The moon shone bright through the floor-to-ceiling window and I could see an outline of trees in the distance.

"Where are we?" I asked after I cozied into the corner of the overstuffed sofa.

He sat next to me and handed me a cup. I curled my fingers around the mug and savored its warmth against my cheek.

"We're an hour outside of Seattle. That's all I can tell you."

I rolled my eyes and cut to the chase. Didn't have the patience for small talk. "Talk to me about the wall of photos."

Franklin slunk into the couch, laid his head back and closed his eyes. "Are you sure you want to hear this?" he asked, like he was giving me one last chance to change my mind before diving headfirst into a pool of horse manure.

"I need to hear the truth. Like you said to me, no more lies."

He rolled his head my direction and stared at me long and hard before continuing. "You were my mark."

"Mark," I repeated, because I couldn't have heard him right. "Like target?"

"Yes. Tony was training me, only I didn't know it at the time. We used you as a mark. It was his way of having an extra pair of eyes on you and keeping me out of trouble."

Could things get any more ridiculous? My cheeks heated and I fought the urge to assault him again. "Do you know how absurd that sounds?"

"I was a fucked-up kid. Tony assumed responsibility for me because he…." Franklin's eyes glazed, and he drew a sharp breath as if recalling a painful moment. "My mom was ill. Couldn't take care of me. Your dad stepped in. I'd be dead or in prison if it weren't for him."

I shook my head in disbelief. "That doesn't explain the wall."

Franklin set his coffee down, roughed his hands over his face and sighed in exasperation. "Every day after school, Tony gave me an assignment that involved you. He made it a game. I'd have to follow you home from school and not be seen. I'd have to gather intel about what you did during the day, about your friends. He gave me a camera to take pictures, said it would help me stay focused on my target. I know it's fucked up. But I was a kid and I would've done anything to make your father proud."

"You grew up. You got married. Moved on. Why are they still hanging on your wall?"

He scratched his head and lowered his gaze to the soft beige carpet. "I never moved on. Like I said, I've loved you since the day I watched Tony push you on the swing. He recruited me the day I graduated high school. I fucking loved it. More than I should have. I could've easily lost myself in that world. You kept me grounded. When I struggled to navigate the hell surrounding me, I'd concentrate on you until my mind settled. You kept me sane in a world of chaos. I needed that wall. I needed you. Your face helped me sleep at night. It still does."

I didn't know what to say. I stared, searching his eyes for signs of crazy. Because that's what this was—crazy—and I was loony for considering any of this to be truth.

"Why were you with my father when he died? I was told it was a heart attack. He was found in his car a few blocks from home."

Franklin's body tensed. "It wasn't a heart attack."

Oh, God. Did I want details? My imagination tortured me enough. "Just tell me it wasn't you."

"No." He shook his head and released an agitated breath.

"Who then?"

Franklin shifted uncomfortably next to me. "Your father took down several leaders of a human trafficking cartel in Venezuela. He got his hands on a list of clients. There are powerful people here in the States that would lose more than their fortunes if that list were made public. The Salazar Cartel will do anything to make sure their clients remain anonymous."

"What happened to the list?" I asked, knowing he wouldn't tell me.

"I don't know."

"But now they're after me? Because they think he's alive?"

"The cartel is after the list. Threatening you would force him out of hiding."

"He's not hiding, right? He's dead. Because if he were…." I choked back a sob. Daddy couldn't have done that to me and Mom. That would've been unforgivable.

Franklin pried my mug from my fingers and set it next to his on the ornate side table. He lifted me into his lap and cradled me. "Tony died in my arms, baby. He wasn't alone. He didn't suffer. I held him until the end. He cried for you, made me promise to keep you safe, and died with his head against my chest just like this."

I wanted the truth and I got it. Trouble was, I wasn't emotionally ready for it. As tough as I pretended to be, I couldn't handle the God-awful reality I'd fallen into. I slid off Franklin's lap, went to bed, and mourned for Dad again.

Chapter 14

The evening hours tick-tocked by with the speed of an elderly snail. I stared at the ceiling, out the window, then tried to close my eyes. Sleep refused to grant me a reprieve from the shit-storm of a day I'd had.

It wasn't because the cushy little rug of a life I'd lived had been yanked from under my feet. Truth was, I lay naked in a plush bed, writhing with need, while Franklin was downstairs, a million miles away.

Sick and twisted as it was, I ached. The gnawing throb and pulse under the surface of my skin was my body craving, anticipating his touch, the flavor of his lips, the intoxicating scent of him.

I had just cause to be repulsed by the man. He'd confessed murder as a career choice, for crying out loud. He'd admitted to stalking me most of my life. If what he said were true, much of the blame for his Tatum hobby would fall on my father.

The Antonio Wood I knew would never have taken an impressionable young boy and lead him down such a dark path. However, I could understand Franklin's need to please my father, his desire to follow in Dad's footsteps. My dad had that effect on people, Wallace Cruse a prime example. Why, then, would he put a child in danger, when my whole life he'd been nothing but my great protector?

Lost in thought, I didn't hear Franklin enter the room. The blankets lifted and the mattress sunk behind me. My temperature spiked. Warm breath touched my shoulder. He grabbed my hip to pull me toward him. He pressed his lips to mine, urging them to part. Craving his kiss, I let him in. His tongue slid across mine, shooting currents of pleasure to every nerve ending.

He cupped a breast and rolled the hardened peak, pinching and pulling just to the point of painful. He slid his hand toward my sex and I couldn't stop my hips from curling into him with anticipation, begging for the strong fingers that knew where to touch softly and exactly where to apply perfect, blissful pressure.

I gasped when he pressed his palm against my sensitive nub and slid a finger inside me. My head arched back into the pillow when he pulled it out, scraping sensitive tissue. He released my lips and peppered kisses across my exposed throat.

When he pushed back inside me, I whimpered and clenched around him. Squeezing my thighs together, I rocked against his hand.

Franklin chuckled. "Do you still hate me?"

I couldn't speak. I could barely breathe through the need. He removed his hand from between my thighs, leaving me wanting, and slid his wet fingers up my stomach, over my breast to my neck. He cupped my chin and forced my mouth back to his, taking a taste before pulling away.

His eyes brightened with hunger and a deep certitude that our destinies were entwined. It made my breath catch. He whispered against my lips. "It's always been you."

He sucked my bottom lip between his teeth and nibbled before letting go. "It will always be you," he groaned, pressing a knee between my legs and rolling on top of me. "Love me, hate me. I don't fucking care. Just be with me. As long as you're with me." He laid his weight across my body, slid his hands over my arms, then locked fingers with mine, pressing our fists into the mattress at my shoulders.

I liquefied beneath his hard muscles. Franklin raised his hips and positioned himself between my legs. With soft steady strokes, he rubbed his erection up and down my folds, coating himself in the moisture that'd formed there.

"Do you want me inside you?" he asked, voice strained.

God, I did. I'd never wanted anything more. So many emotions churned through me. Anger and hurt for all the lies, fear for my life and the future, envy because he'd known my father more intimately than I had, but more than anything, lust. I'd never coveted anything or anyone the way I did this man.

The tip of his erection lingered at my opening. "Do you want all of me, Killer?"

I ached, down there where he teased with his cock. I did want him, dammit, the beautiful parts, the dark mysterious parts, the ugly parts—and wanting him seemed wrong. Wanting him meant I was every bit as messed up as he was.

I pondered the battle scars on his face. I'd put them there. He'd marred me, too. My wounds were hidden, but painful nonetheless. I wouldn't let them break me. "I hate you. I hate you with every ounce of my being. I loathe how you make me ache so deep I fear I'm dying. I detest the control you have over my body. I'm repulsed by my need for you. I hate you. But mostly, I hate that despite everything, I can't shake you, and I don't want to. I want you. All of—"

Franklin shut me up with a bruising kiss. Then he pushed inside me with one slow, steady, delicious stroke. I clamped my legs around his thighs and blinked away the stars dancing in my field of vision.

He released my hands and cupped my face. "I love you too, baby. I love you, too."

His words cut as deep as the first time he'd said them. They settled nice and tight in my chest, claiming a permanent home.

I pressed my lips to his and rocked my hips. "Show me, then." I reached down and dug my nails into his firm ass and pulled him tighter against me.

Franklin needed no further prompting. He skipped the slow build-up and got right to the hard pounding, relenting only when my insides tightened around him. With the first spasm, he stopped and rolled to his back, pulling me on top of him.

"Put your hands on my chest," he ordered.

I obliged.

Gripping my hips, he plunged inside me again. "Oh shit," I yelped, arching my back. He'd never been so deep and I stiffened, fearing I couldn't accommodate him.

"You're so fucking perfect." Sliding his hands behind his head, he flashed his killer smile and raked my body with a gaze hot enough to melt a steal beam, and hell if that didn't turn my insides to molten lava.

I'd never been on top before and he must've read the uncertainty on my face. "Lean forward and move your hips," he commanded.

I tilted my body toward his and rocked against him.

"Yeah, like that." He sucked in a sharp breath. "Slow, baby. Oh hell, you're killing me." His hands shot to my ass with a stinging slap.

Slow? Did I have another choice? He filled me so completely I could hardly move. In that position, merely taking a breath caused enough friction to have me on the brink of another orgasm.

I stared down into his sex-glazed eyes and moved with lazy, wanton thrusts. His expression, so hungry and possessive, made my heart hurt, and I wanted nothing more than to give him everything I had both physical and emotional, every last drop of me.

I found a steady rhythm and when my thighs burned from exertion and I slowed, Franklin sat upright, snaked his arms around me and claimed my mouth. I came hard and screamed into his kiss. His body trembled with his own release and he buried his face in my neck and whispered, "Holy fucking shit. Do you feel that? Do you feel how perfect we are? How could I ever let you go?"

* * * *

"What now?" I asked, twisting my fingers through his chest hair.

Franklin rolled to his side and traced figure eights over the curve of my rump. "I kill the fuckers." His words didn't match the playful grin on his face.

I smacked his ass. "C'mon. Be serious."

He flopped onto his back and clasped his hands behind his head. "I'm waiting for the call. Then I'm taking them out."

"Oh." He was serious.

"You know who they are?" I asked, unsuccessfully hiding the panic in my voice.

"Yes. The Salazars sent a handful of their goons. Didn't know how to find them until they shot at you. Idiots left a trail wider than the Grand Canyon."

"You have to kill them?" I knew the answer before the question left my lips.

"Tate. These assholes killed Tony. Now they're after you. They left us with few options."

"Does it have to be you?" I asked, terrified of the answer.

"What do you think?"

I sat up and pulled the sheet around me. "I know you can't tell me things. I get that. I won't be pushy. Honestly, I don't want to know. My brain would pop like a gluttonous tick. But please, to ease my conscience, tell me you're fighting for the good guys? It's not drug lords or mafia or anything like that, right?"

I expected him to laugh at my naivety. He didn't. He turned his head and smiled, eyes dancing with deep adoration. "Fuck, baby. You're as beautiful on the inside as you are on the outside. I do bad things to despicable people for the good guys. We're known as Rogues. Regional Operations Ghost Unit Elite."

"Like black ops or secret service?" I couldn't believe I was having this conversation.

"No. Not quite. We're a private entity, not bound by the laws of the government, but under their protection. We step in when there are no options left and do the ugly work while their hands stay clean."

"If you're so elite, how does the cartel know about my dad? How did they find out about the list?"

"I don't know, love. It kills me to admit, but either someone ratted him out, or he screwed up, which doesn't make sense. He never made mistakes." Franklin shook his head and bit his bottom lip. For a moment, he disappeared, perhaps behind a memory or a thought. The vacant expression on his face unsettled me.

"There's another thing I don't understand," I said and continued before he could respond. "You said they wanted to draw my dad out because they think he's alive, right?"

Franklin mumbled, "Yes".

"So why would they shoot at me? If they killed me, I wouldn't be useful to them anymore."

He cussed under his breath. "To send a message. They missed on purpose." The mood in the room shifted, like a dark force swept in and devoured the positive energy.

A chill crept over me. "This is so messed up." How did my dad keep this from us? Mom would've— Oh shit. Mom.

"Oh my God, my mother? Is she in danger? Does she know? We have to call her. We have to make sure—"

Franklin sat up, cupped my cheeks, and pulled me nose to nose, shooting a reassuring glare right through my peepers. "Your mom and grandpa are safe. They're under twenty-four-seven protection. Always have been."

I clutched his wrists like a lifeline. "Always? Since when?"

"Since the day Tony was murdered."

"And someone's been assigned to me since that day?"

He sighed. "Yeah, baby."

"You?"

Franklin released my cheeks. "No, not until the rumors Tony was alive started to circulate. Two months ago, I was put in charge."

Things were starting to make sense. "Is that why you came to work at Cruse Investigations?"

He nodded.

"Does that mean Wallace knew?"

"He knew. He was one of us. Poor bastard couldn't handle the life. Retired when he took over your dad's company."

"Who was the poor bloke assigned before you?"

"Baby, you weren't going to demand every detail, remember?"

I chewed on my thumbnail. Strangers knew every facet of my life. Kept vigil. Babysat. How could they have been close enough to keep me safe without showing themselves? Was I that dense? Dad taught me to pay attention to my surroundings, especially the people around me. Realization hit me, and it was a bitch slap.

Oh. My. God.

The weight of a falling tree hit my chest. "Jacob Smart," I shouted. "It was him, wasn't it? They tried to kill him, didn't they? Because of me."

Franklin sat up and pulled me into his lap. He slid his hands under my jaw then to the back of my head and held my face inches from his. "Listen, Tatum. He failed you. Got it? None of this is your fault. Don't let thoughts like that in your head, not even a little bit, because they burrow in and grow like a damned cancer."

He knew from experience. It was evident by the shimmer of his eyes and the deep set of his stress wrinkles.

"Hoodie man? Was that you?" I wasn't sure if I could handle the answer. Would I be able to look at Franklin the same way if he'd committed such a gruesome act?

He nodded, his eyes glazed and his voice took a dark tone. "He came back for you. I couldn't just make him disappear. I had to send a message."

No. This was too much. I tried to crawl off him. He held me tight. "Please, Tate. You have to understand, this is personal for me. First Tony, then you...." He shook his head. "Don't be afraid of me. Sometimes, the things I have to do, they're necessary evils."

A real man does whatever it takes to protect the women in his life.

His words from the night before spun in my head. Vile as the act was to me, I couldn't imagine how heavy the burden on his shoulders. The weight of guilt and responsibility had to be unbearable. My heart shattered for him. I forced a smile and raised a hand to his beautiful, sad face, tracing the lines across his furrowed brow. Leaning forward, I dusted my lips against his. "You loved my dad, didn't you?"

He squeezed his lids shut and nodded.

I kissed the tip of his nose. "You're so much like him. He'd be proud."

Franklin's shoulders slumped, his hands falling to his sides.

I kissed the bruise under his eye, then the scratches I'd carved in his cheek. I curled my legs around his waist. "I'm sorry I attacked you."

The corner of his mouth lifted.

"I wanted you to hurt like I did."

"I know." He could've teased or chastised me for the violent outburst. He could've played the victim card. He didn't.

His erection swelled beneath me, tickling my rump. I sighed, squeezed my legs tighter, wrapped my arms around his neck and hugged like my life depended on it. "I hate you so much."

He chuckled. "No you don't."

"I do. I really, really do," I muttered.

Then, I showed him how much.

Chapter 15

My hair flowed around me, silken and shiny, in soft, perfect waves that flapped in sync with the American flag perched high atop the skyscraper behind me. I assumed the victory stance with feet apart, hands fisted at my hips, chin held high, and watched the little people skitter about twenty stories below. Each of them clueless to the perils lurking around every corner.

I knew the dangers all too well. I had an intimate relationship with the dark side and I'd sworn to fight to my death to keep it at bay, away from the hordes of normalcy.

I wiped a tear of pride from my cheek and turned to the man coiled in golden rope, wiggling on the cold cement like an earthworm searching for soil.

"Mr. Cruse. You've been a bad, bad man." I stepped off the ledge and swung my hips with confident strides until I stood over him. "You've lied, cheated, weaseled money from the people who trusted you during their darkest hours. For what?"

I laughed because he couldn't answer me. He tried, but the rag I'd stuffed down his throat made even a mumble impossible.

The rooftop door swung open. Nan burst through, followed by Mrs. Montgomery and Detective Waters. "Nan, Dahlia. You're just in time," I cackled. "Leland. Arrest this sleaze-bag before I throw him over the edge."

"No!" Nan shouted. "I love him. I love him...."

Moist lips tickled my jaw. "Time to get up, baby." God, I loved waking to the sound of Franklin's voice.

I laughed and wiped drool from my cheek. I must've slept hard. Franklin rose from the bed and buttoned his shirt. "What were you laughing about?"

I rubbed a crusty chunk from my eye and sat up. "I had another dream. Hey! I didn't kill him this time, just tied him up with my golden rope."

I expected a laugh or lewd comment. When it didn't come, I knew something was up. "What's going on?" I asked.

Franklin didn't look at me. "I got the call."

My insides clenched liked I'd been punched in the gut. "What does that mean?"

Dropping to his knees on the floor in front of me, he clutched my hands. "It means this ends today. I take them out. We go home." His fingers tightened around mine in a reassuring squeeze.

A heavy blanket of dread suffocated me. "Are you leaving me here alone?"

"I've got two men outside and Detective Waters is on his way. He wanted me to bring you to the station regarding the Wallace shit. I told him if he wanted to talk to you, he'd have to come here. It must be important because he agreed to be blindfolded on the drive in."

Why did that tickle my fancy? I didn't envy the grumbling the driver would endure. "Was that absolutely necessary?"

"To keep you safe? Hell yes, it was." He smirked. "It was mostly to fuck with him, though. God, I love my job." Franklin grinned wider than I'd seen in days.

"Franklin?" What could I say? Everything about this situation made my head spin and my heart twist.

He studied my face. "Don't worry, Killer. I'm the best at what I do. They won't see me coming. I'm in. They're dead. I'm out."

Such confidence. "Wow. Don't sugar-coat it or anything."

"Kiss me," he ordered, leaning closer.

I clapped a hand over my mouth. "I have morning breath," I muttered through my fingers.

He pried them off my lips. "Kiss me."

I did, pouring the full weight of my nervous energy into it. I scooted to the edge of the mattress, wrapped my legs around him and locked my ankles.

He stood, taking me to the dresser where he retrieved his belt.

"Did I ever tell you how much your suit turns me on?" I whispered in his ear, right before pulling the lobe between my teeth.

Franklin smacked my bare bum. "If I remember correctly, you said my ass in my suit pants turns you on."

"I hate you, but I do love your ass."

Strong fingers dug into my rear and he returned me to the bed.

"Where'd the suit come from? You keep your safe houses stocked?"

He laid over me and nuzzled my breasts, then my neck. "Colleagues brought it. I had them get new clothes for you, too." He pointed to the black shopping bag perched on the slipper chair in the corner of the room.

"Thank you." I admired his attire, but it didn't seem fitting for his line of work. "You always work in a suit?"

He nibbled my chin before pushing off and sitting back on his heels. "I do. My girlfriend thinks they're hot."

Yes, she did. I rubbed a foot over his chest, scrunching his shirt with my toes. "I imagined you in combat gear."

He chuckled and leaned back over me, cupping my cheeks. "I'm not going into battle. Most of what I do, I do from a distance. If the situation requires tactical gear, I'll change at headquarters." He looked at me long and hard. Promises of naughty pleasure burned in his eyes. "When I come back, why don't we try that hanging-you-on-the-wall thing we discussed on our first date?"

Holy cow. I blushed. "I don't do kinky shit," I teased, trying to hide my smile.

His lips grazed mine. "Who says it's kinky?"

"I say." I slid my hands up the tensed muscles of his torso, his chest, and around his neck. I laced my fingers and pulled his forehead to mine. "Please don't go. Send somebody else."

His shoulders tensed. "It has to be me."

I wouldn't be needy and clingy. I wouldn't. I pulled him in for one last kiss and pushed him off me.

"Go, I've got important things to do, like get dressed and brush my teeth."

Franklin backed his way to the door. "God, you're gorgeous. Look at you, naked and sprawled on the bed." Behind the playful facade, which was solely for my benefit, lay a deadly conviction. He had work to do. I was a distraction. The last thing I wanted was to be the cause of any internal struggle.

With a tight fist, he pounded the doorframe one, two, three times, as if pumping himself up to leave. "See you soon, Killer."

"Bye, Frankie." I blew him a kiss and held the rising panic at bay until the door closed downstairs. I ran to the window and peeked through the curtain. Three men in equally impressive suits ducked into the car with him. He wasn't alone. The dark shadow of worry brightened to a bearable shade of unease.

I took a quick shower. By the time I headed downstairs, Leland sat at the kitchen table with a pot of coffee.

"Tatum," he grumbled.

"Good morning, Leland. We back to first names?" I grabbed a mug from the counter, then sat across from him and filled my cup.

His brown eyes darkened to black. "Morning," he snapped, hitting me with equal shots of scrutiny and chastisement.

Ouch. "I can see you're still angry with me. I'm sorry."

He sat back and crossed his arms. "I'm not here to discuss that."

"I know." I blew steam from my mug and savored the first yummy sip as it danced across my taste buds and slid down my throat.

"Listen. Franklin has made sure you're untouchable right now, and that's a good thing. It buys me time. But you should know we found more compromising emails on Wallace Cruse's home computer. When we searched his bedroom, there were photos of you in his nightstand. They weren't explicit, but a red flag nonetheless. There were blond hairs in his bed. Also, security footage shows you heading to the roof the morning of his murder, about fifteen minutes before he did."

I'd been to the rooftop garden plenty of times. I ate my lunch up there when the weather would allow. Wallace went first thing every morning. I hadn't a clue what he did up there. Never cared enough to ask. "That's impossible. I was home."

Relief washed over his face. "I believe you. Now help me prove it."

Should be easy. "Franklin can tell you."

"He can't, Tatum. Whatever branch of the government he works for, it's so high up, he doesn't exist. He can't be connected to you or this investigation in any way." Crap. Who in the world had I fallen for? If Franklin couldn't help me, I was screwed.

"Did you check the security cameras at my building?" I rubbed at the sharp pain darting up the back of my neck.

"Yes. They haven't worked for months."

"Shit." My head throbbed. "Somebody is setting me up."

Leland rubbed his thumb up and down the handle of this mug. "I believe so. The pieces are coming together too smoothly."

"Why?" What the hell had I done to anyone? "I don't understand."

His eyes saddened. "Tatum, there's another piece to the puzzle that makes you look guiltier than sin. Wallace Cruse left his earthly belongings to you. Including Cruse Investigations."

* * * *

I wrapped the bandage around my finger and flexed to test the blood flow. Leland dropped the last pieces of the shattered ceramic into the trash.

"Thanks." I dropped my butt into the chair.

He grabbed a new mug from the cupboard and poured me a fresh cup. "Sorry, I should've dropped that bomb when your hands were empty." He shook his head in fatherly disapproval.

I plopped my elbows on the table and my chin into my palms. "Why, in the name of all that's holy, would Wallace leave anything, let alone everything, to me? It doesn't make sense."

Leland's chair creaked when he sat. "I wondered the same thing. Obligation, maybe?"

"Could be. He kissed dad's ass like nobody's business. He has family. A sister somewhere on the east coast. Why not her?"

"I checked into that. They're estranged. Have been for twenty years or so. Listen Tatum, you have any idea who would want Mr. Cruse dead? Angry clients? Jilted lovers?"

I knew zilch about his love life. Yuck. "Nobody I'm aware of. Have you questioned Nan Cummings? She was closer to him than anyone."

He blew a puff of air. "That woman had plenty to say." He didn't elaborate. I didn't push.

"When's the funeral?" I asked.

"This weekend. I'll do my best to keep you out of jail if you want to attend."

"My mother would like to be here. It'd be nice to keep her out of the loop. She's under enough stress taking care of my grandfather. I don't want her to worry about me."

Leland nodded in understanding. "Franklin asked me to look into Jay Masters. I've dug up a bit of information. It's disturbing to say the least."

I wrapped my fingers around the warm mug to chase away the sudden chill. "Okay, spit it out."

"The kid was in and out of psychiatric hospitals from high school on. Claims he's been shadowed by a ghost since he was fifteen. He finished a long stint at Western State nine months ago. There have been several sexual assault charges filed against him, but they never went to court."

Rich kid like him? Mommy and Daddy probably swept his shit under the rug and made it disappear. "His parents are wealthy. I'm sure they persuaded the girls to settle." Crazy house, huh? Jay had always been one of the more aggressive boys at school. I'd assumed it was his football player mentality. "So, why me? I haven't spoken a word to him since ninth grade."

Leland tapped his sugar spoon against his cup. "Not sure. I'll keep digging."

"What happens when Franklin returns and I'm no longer on lock-down?" I already knew the answer. Didn't like it, not one bit.

Leland rose and buttoned his corduroy blazer. "We wait for the DNA results." He looked at me with reassuring eyes. "I don't want you to worry. We'll get to the bottom of this."

I wanted to hug him but it didn't seem appropriate. So, I settled on a handshake. "Thank you, Leland." I believed him. I did, but there wasn't a snowball's chance in hell I would wait around for others to clear my name.

I watched until Leland and his escort disappeared down the long gravel driveway. When they were out of sight, I explored the large house. There wasn't much to it. Three bedrooms, two bathrooms. A simple, yet large kitchen and...ooh! A freezer full of ice cream. Oh, that man of mine was going to get lucky. I performed a happy dance in front of the fridge. Then I got busy hunting down a bowl and spoon. Nothing like chocolate, almonds, and marshmallows to drown your troubles.

My heart dropped to my toes when the doorbell chimed. I scurried to the front door and peered through the little hole. One of the men in suits waited outside. I yanked the door open. "What's wrong? Did something happen?"

"No, ma'am. Mr. Reed asked that we give you this." He handed me a disposable cell phone. The guy was all business. Not a lick of warmth on his face or in his tone.

"Um, thanks." Would it hurt him to smile? "Want to come in for coffee or ice cream?"

"No, ma'am. We'll be right outside if you need us." He returned to his post on the bottom step of the porch.

I barely made it back to the kitchen before the phone buzzed in my hand. "Hello?"

"Hey, Killer."

"Hey," I whispered.

"Do you miss me yet?" he asked in a low gravel.

Oh, yes. I did. "No. Not yet," I teased with a devil-may-care tone. "I've been busy. Did you get the bad guys?"

"I'm about to. I needed to hear your voice."

I swallowed hard and pictured his face. Magical eyes, carved lips, the small bump on his nose. "Franklin."

"Yeah, baby." That voice. Even through the phone it held the power to turn me into a puddle of goo.

"Don't get shot." I wanted to say so much more. I wanted to travel through the phone and kiss him hard. "It'd be a shame to mess up your gorgeous face. I hate you, but I do love your face."

His low chuckle made me miss him even more. "I love you, too, baby. See you soon." The call ended and I exhaled.

He did love me. I could feel it. Even from miles away. The mystery man loved me. He was, at that precise moment, throwing himself into the line of fire to save my ass. With nothing but an afternoon full of waiting ahead of me, I grabbed my bowl of creamy heaven, turned on the Lifetime Channel and curled up on the couch for a chick-fest of cheesy movies.

* * * *

I woke with a start, heart pounding, eyes searching for something familiar in the dark void. Franklin's scent lingered but I didn't feel him near.

I sat up for a good stretch and heard the shower running upstairs. Like a cat on the prowl, I tiptoed up the steps, removing my clothing as I ascended. I entered the bathroom and stopped dead.

Franklin stood under the water, palms pressed to the wall, head hung low between his arms. His torso stretched taught, revealing impossible layers of muscle. I'd never tire of the sight of him. The more I absorbed his beauty, the more I craved.

Water cascaded down his back, drawing my perusal to his rear. The flex and stretch of his butt and legs were the worst kind of temptation, inciting dark and dirty urges that made me blush.

I wiggled free of my panties and stalked toward the man who'd reduced me to a wild animal in heat. I slid the glass open and stepped into the wall of steam.

He didn't look up, but his gravel reached me from between his arms. "Killer. I didn't want to wake you."

"You didn't." I slid my hands up his back, danced my fingers over the dips and curves of his muscles. Working my way around his ribs to his chest, I pressed my breasts against his back, marveling at the heat he radiated.

With a loud sigh, he turned and enveloped me. I raised my chin and nibbled from his neck to his square jawline. He lowered his face, capturing me with a heady gaze before drawing his lips to mine.

I melted into him and submitted to every prod of his tongue, every stroke and suck. Putty in his hands, or lips rather. He kissed me soft and slow, trailed fingers up and down my frame.

Aching to be filled by him, I broke our kiss and bent to my knees, gripping his buttocks on the way down. Before he could react, I licked the length of his erection from base to tip, triggering a groan that set my blood on fire.

I'd never performed oral sex. Hadn't a clue what to do. But something about Franklin and what he did to my body, inside and out, made me want to pleasure him in every way. It just seemed natural and necessary. I kissed the tip of him, wrapped my lips around the shiny crown and, one slow stroke at a time, took him deeper inside me. His length and girth made it nearly impossible to find a rhythm. Or maybe it was my lack of experience.

Franklin slapped a palm against the tile and twisted his fingers through my hair with the other hand. "Goddamn. Yeah, baby," he groaned. His hips rocked with a palpable restraint. He wanted to pound my mouth. Thank God he held back. I wasn't ready. Fingers pressed to the back of my head, he pushed deep, slow and controlled, all the while watching, gauging my response.

When he eased off, I slid a hand between his legs and played with the heavy boys hanging below his sex. My ego bloated with a potent sense of empowerment when I squeezed and his cock jerked in my mouth. I wrapped my other hand around the base of his penis and stroked in sync with the pulls from my mouth.

Franklin stopped me. "I want you in bed, not here."

He helped me off the floor, shut off the water, and wrapped me in a towel. Drying himself in record time, he scooped me over his shoulder and carried me to our room. I disposed of the towel the moment he laid me down. Franklin studied my naked body with a wicked grin, then crawled over me. "Tell me you missed me," he ordered.

"But I didn't," I teased, batting my lashes.

"Not even a little bit?" He prowled up the length of me.

I shook my head no.

On hands and knees, he braced my shoulders and tickled my chin with the head of his penis. "I missed you so fucking bad." He leaned forward and rubbed the silky head on my lips.

Oh, God, what was he doing?

"Open for me, love," he whispered.

I did. I parted my lips and raised my head to envelop him. Salty moisture danced across my taste buds, setting off a chain of fireworks in my belly. I relaxed my jaw and Franklin pushed himself between my lips, never breaching the limit of what I could take. My head was pinned to the mattress and he filled me so full, I couldn't even roll my tongue across his flesh. Helpless to do anything else, I raised my arms and dug my nails into his ass.

"God, baby, your mouth. Fuck," he grunted between thrusts.

I wiggled and writhed beneath him. Blood pumped so fierce between my legs I feared I would explode. I could swear, my pussy was jealous of my mouth, and if given a voice, would've screamed in protest.

Franklin pushed in one last time and rested there for a long moment before pulling out. He scooted down and claimed my lips, in that dominant way that assured me he was mine. Then he slid lower and kissed between my legs. I arched into him. The moment his tongue stroked my nub, I came hard, pinning his head between my legs. He latched on and sucked with heavenly, lethal purpose until my body slumped into the mattress and my knees fell open.

Franklin wasn't finished. He probed my slit with his expert fingers. His other hand slid up my torso and rubbed across my belly. "You're so perfect, baby." He kneaded the flesh just above my pubic area. "Soft, in all the right places." He pulled his finger from between my legs and pushed two back in. "Tight where it counts." He worked me until I writhed with want. "Tell me you missed me," he ordered again.

I playfully shook my head no.

Franklin pushed himself off the bed, taking all the warmth in the room with him. "That's a shame." He strutted to the door, giving me a good view of his backside, and disappeared down the hallway. I heard the patter of bare feet travel down the stairs, then loud static as the television roared to life.

I expected him to return with his devilish grin. He didn't come back.

Oh. Well, I could play that game, too. I slunk down the stairs and sat on the third step from the bottom. "I wasn't finished with you. Are you coming back to bed?"

He sat with arms stretched across the back of the couch, knees spread wide, and a throw blanket draped across his waist. It did nothing to hide his arousal. His eyes remained focused on the television. The smirk he wore reinforced my suspicion that his thoughts remained solely on me. "Did you miss me, Killer?"

I leaned back and rested my elbows on the step behind me, then crossed my legs. "Hmm."

He raised the remote and turned up the volume.

Bastard.

I uncrossed my legs and let them fall open. I shook with nerves, because I'd never done anything so lascivious. What had I become? Slut? Check. Horn dog? Check. Nympho? Check, check, and check.

He didn't look my way. I slid my hand down the length of my body, resting it above the naughty zone, and let my fingers linger in the tuft of hair. Was I brave enough to go through with this?

Franklin's eyes widened but never moved from the screen. I smoothed my index finger down the moist crease between my thighs, then drew it back up. God, it felt so good and so damned risqué. I did it again. Franklin's nostrils flared.

I stroked myself once more, resting on the sensitive nub, then rubbed in slow circles. Oh shit. Yes. That was good.

Franklin slid the blanket off his lap and dropped it to the floor. His gaze darted to mine then back to the screen. He smiled wide then grabbed his erection.

Damn. He did play dirty.

I stroked. He stroked.

I moaned, hoping to make him look my way. He let his head fall back on the couch and fisted himself harder. I was turned on, but the sight of his hand wrapped around his sex nearly had me begging for mercy. Thick veins running up his forearm. The flex of his bicep as he pumped. Truly, a thing of beauty.

I spread my folds and pushed two fingers inside myself. It didn't have near the effect his fingers did, but the knowledge that I behaved so wantonly had me wet and ready for more. With my free hand, I massaged my breast then pinched a pink peak.

Franklin's strokes sped up. I circled my clit harder and faster. This was so not what I'd planned, but damn it was fun. His lips parted and lids lowered. He was going to come. I was dangerously close to orgasm myself.

No. This was not what I wanted. I wanted him in me, not across the room.

I pulled my hand off myself and slapped it on the step. "You asshole. Okay, you win. I missed you," I panted. "I missed you. I missed you."

He stopped pumping his sex and was on me in two strides. I leaned back on my elbows. Franklin grabbed my hips and raised them to meet his. "Say it again."

"I missed you," I whispered, trembling under the force of his touch.

His cock stretched and filled me with perfect, painful bliss. "That's my girl." He pulled out and slammed back into me. "Hell yes, you missed me. No way you can hide it. You're so damn wet, baby."

I gripped his forearms and held on while he pounded into me, again and again, each time driving deeper, grunting with unbridled, feral claims over my body. I whimpered, fighting back the painful surges of my oncoming release. When I could fight no longer, my head fell back and my hips tilted, seeking more. He held me tight against him while I came undone, until my last spasm. Only then did he pump again and let himself go.

He collapsed next to me on the stairs until we caught our breath, then led me to the bathroom to wash up before crawling into bed. I lay on my side and Franklin snuggled behind me, pulling me tight into the folds of his frame.

He twirled a piece of my hair in his fingers. "We can go home tomorrow."

I sighed and my shoulders relaxed. "Can you talk about what happened?"

"No, love. I can't"

"Will they come back?"

"They got the message loud and clear. Tony Wood has not risen from the dead and you are off limits."

"Thank you," I whispered, for lack of anything else to say.

"There's nothing I wouldn't do for you." His body stiffened against mine. "How was your visit with Detective Waters?"

"Someone is setting me up, but at least Leland believes me."

"I didn't leave him much choice. You won't go to jail. I can make the evidence disappear. We can vanish."

"I don't want to disappear. I want to know who's doing this, and why me?" I told Franklin the details of my discussion with Leland. He listened without interruption, although I had a sneaking suspicion he already knew everything. When I finished, he kissed my head and rolled onto his back.

"This is so messed up. I can't wrap my head around it. Dad was a lying adulterer."

"Baby." He turned toward me and spread his fingers over my heart. "Your dad was a good man."

"Good men don't cheat on their wives," I snapped. "Or lie to their daughters."

Franklin huffed. "I understand your hurt. If he had extramarital affairs, aside from my mother, I didn't know about them. He worshipped you. That's the one thing I know for sure. Okay?"

I rolled away from him in protest and curled up on my side of the bed. It was cold, lonely and too far from the skin-to-skin I craved, so I rolled back over and snuggled in.

"When we get past this shit-storm, you better start talking." I couldn't shuffle through the piles of lies that were my life, and I didn't want to try, not yet anyway. I could, however, hold on to Franklin and remain grounded—at least for now.

* * * *

Franklin shoved his cell back into his pocket and stretched his arms over his head, gripping the molding above the kitchen door. "The funeral is on Saturday."

I sat on the couch and admired the view. "Detective Waters told me. He arranged a flight for my mom. She's arriving Friday night. Will you go with me to pick her up?" Mom knew nothing about Franklin yet. There hadn't been time to tell her, or anyone.

Franklin's forehead wrinkle did its stress thingy.

"What's wrong?"

"I don't think that's such a good idea."

Unease swirled through me like an oncoming fog. "Why not?"

He dropped his arms and shoved his hands in his pockets. "Her husband had an affair with my mother. I don't want to rub it in her face, do you?"

"Of course not. Nevertheless, we're together. We can't avoid her forever. Am I not supposed to date you because my dad was a cheating bastard?" My voice raised an octave. "She doesn't even know who you are. Chances are, she'll never make the connection." My heart raced, panic tightened my throat.

"Tate. You're right. Calm down." Franklin closed the distance between us. He gripped my shoulders and tilted his head, scrutinizing me, as if searching for sanity in a sea of crazy.

I sucked in a big gulp of air and released it in slow bursts. Jeez, why was I getting so worked up? It would break my heart if I couldn't share Franklin with my family. Would I have to choose between him and them? Would our relationship, or whatever it was, have to be kept a secret?

"Is it safe to go home then?" I asked, needing a change of subject.

"Yes, baby. The police haven't found Masters yet, but they're following some solid leads."

"Why me?"

Once again, his face filled with stress wrinkles, no doubt carved by the secrets he harbored. "I don't want you to worry. I'll take care of it." He knew something. Damn him. I didn't pry. We were about to go home. I wanted to be in a happy mood when we got there. I also hated to see the strain of conflict mar his handsome features. So I attempted to lighten the mood.

"I'd never had sex on stairs before," I announced.

His wrinkles disappeared. "I'm aware of that."

I dropped my chin and batted my lashes. "I liked it."

A storm brewed in his eyes. "Did you now?"

Warmth rose up my neck and rested on my cheeks. "There aren't any stairs at my house."

He raised a brow. "And?"

"I'm not sure I got it out of my system yet, you know, the sex on the stairs thing."

"Damn, Killer. You say the sweetest things." He undid his belt with super speed. I jumped to my feet and shimmied out of my jeans. My panties followed, then my shirt and bra. I leaned toward him and pressed my palm over his hard-on. "I hate you, but I love this." I squeezed him, excited by the way it swelled in my hand. If I kept that up, we wouldn't make it to the stairs. I let him go, turned and sauntered across the living room.

I ascended a few steps by foot, then crawled on hands and knees a few more, nice and slow.

"Stop right there." His large hand splayed across my left butt cheek.

Oh, my. I leaned on my elbows and looked over my shoulder to see him. For crying out loud, those eyes. Bewitching. They cast a spell from which I could never be disenchanted. Franklin moved in behind and tickled a finger along the length of my womanly place.

Then he lowered his head and licked. Holy shit. Licked me from nub to...to that other hole. The naughty hole. My body quaked. Every cell danced with smutty pleasure. It was dirty and taboo and I loved it. He did it again.

"Oh my god!" I squealed, pushing my rear against him, begging for more. My back arched, my face pressed into the cold, hard step—a perfect contrast to his warm, rough licks.

He stroked and stroked, then pushed his tongue inside me, just a tease. I rocked, unabashedly grinding against his face—starving, begging, crying for more.

"Holy Christ, Tate," he groaned. "You're killing me."

I trembled with the need to come.

"Turn over."

I did as commanded. He still wore his jeans, unbuttoned and pulled halfway off his hips. He laid over me, holding most of his weight on his arms. Comfortable, it was not, but I didn't care. My only thoughts were of how he'd fill me, take me, make me his over and over.

"I can't make this soft and slow baby. I'm dying." The deep tremble in his voice made me quiver.

"Uh, huh," was the only sound I could manage. *Stick your dick so far inside me I can feel it until next week* was what I wanted to say, but that wasn't lady-like and I didn't want to shock him flaccid and ruin the mood.

I grabbed his ass and pulled his hips toward me. He plunged, I arched, banging my head against the unforgiving wood. It was frenzied, painful, and exciting. I wanted to crawl inside him. Pull him inside me. I didn't know. Just be closer, be one with this perfect male.

He cupped the back of my head, buried his face in my neck and pounded me senseless. My legs shook with the strain of trying to hold my hips off the hard corners. It was savagely brutal and beautiful. Pressure built. My face burned with the flow of blood. My insides coiled.

His grunts and heavy breaths in my ear only wound me up more. I craved so desperately his skin, his touch, words and eyes on me. My desire for this man would be my undoing.

Chris Isaak's dreamy, soulful voice blared from his pants with "Wicked Game," the song I used to love but now hated.

"Fuck," he grumbled and reached back to pull the cursed distraction from his pocket, never taking his eyes off mine. He laid it on the step above my head and continued to claim my body with the thrust of his hips.

A woman's slinky voice came from the phone. "Reed. Reed? You there, baby?" He must have swiped his finger across the answer button by mistake.

It couldn't have hurt worse if he'd used tweezers to dig a hole through my chest and pull my heart out piece by piece.

"Mother fucker," he shouted and pushed himself off me.

"Who's calling?" I whispered hoarsely. He didn't answer and scrambled for the phone.

The voice asked, "Baby, is someone with you? Is it her?"

He put the phone to his ear and stumbled to the kitchen. "What?"

Something snapped inside me. I followed, naked, aching and suffering a frustration the likes of which I'd never known. "Who is she, Franklin?"

He turned, flashed me an angry glare, and shook his head—a warning not to interrupt.

"This better be important," he snapped to the sexy phone bitch.

I couldn't seem to catch my breath. My eyes filled with angry, salty tears that burned like acid. I'm pretty sure my heart stopped beating for a moment, or two, or three thousand.

Suddenly, I wore my nudity like a bright red, beaming, blanket of shame. I covered my breasts and stumbled backward. Ouch. Ouch, ouch, ouch. This pain was too much. I turned, scrambled into my clothes and couldn't get out of that house fast enough.

The long, gravel drive made for a great distraction. I couldn't seethe properly because I had to concentrate on not breaking my ankles in a pothole or tripping on a large rock.

Damn phone. Damn song. It was a special ringtone just for her. Who, in the name of all that was holy, was she? Why did he jump to attention whenever she called? Why was he always so angry? Why didn't he block her calls? Why did I care?

Because he's beautiful and mysterious and dangerous. Because I'd fallen and fallen hard. Dammit. I was head over heels for a man so far out of my league I may as well have come from Mars.

I needed to blow off steam. So I walked the dusty, unmaintained terrain of the gravel road. Not sure where I was headed or how long I needed to exert to feel better. Heck. I didn't even know where I was. Eventually, I reached the end of the driveway and stood at a crossroad.

I could travel left or right. To the left, the remnants of a dirt road, overgrown with weeds, tall grass and wildflowers led to a vibrant cluster of trees standing watch over a small pond. To the right, the road wound through a dark stretch of pines and by the sound of it, led to a busy street, perhaps a highway. I fought the urge to turn right and run. Hitch a ride home, or maybe somewhere else. How easy would it be to disappear? Not that I wanted to, but I could understand the temptation.

I stood, contemplating. A car approached from behind, crunching across the rocks and pebbles. It rolled to a stop at my side.

"Where you going, Killer?" Franklin's voice set my heart into a jig.

I stole a quick glance over my shoulder. "I was about to head to the pond down there."

"It's not safe."

I crossed my arms and turned, this time resting my gaze on his. "Neither are you."

"I know, baby." He got out of the car and came to my side. "Being with me won't be easy. I'm asking the world of you. I'm painfully aware of what you'll have to sacrifice. Don't for a second think I won't make it worth your while. Nobody knows you like I do. No one can love you like I can."

His words disarmed me, the way only he could. I turned into him, wrapped my arms around his middle, and rested my head against his chest. His heartbeat pumped loud in my ear, filling me to the brim with a heady dose of serenity. I loved that sound.

"Who is she?" I asked.

"Sasha, my ex," he whispered, combing his fingers through my hair.

The ex? If she was an ex, why was she still present in his life? "Why does she call you all the time?"

He stiffened, pressed a kiss to the top of my head, and mumbled, "She's my boss."

A slap across the face would have shocked me less. Well, that put a new wrench in the grinding gears. "Jesus, Franklin. It just keeps getting better and better." I pulled away from him and tried not to let the pain, jealousy, and insecurity show on my face. I was a big girl. I could handle this little hiccup.

He released a frustrated breath and shoved his hands in his pockets. "We need to head back. Get in the car."

"Yeah, home sounds good."

Franklin escorted me to the passenger side and held the door while I situated myself. He jogged around the car and slid in, suave and calm. He turned the ignition, then switched it back off and roughed his hand over the top of his head. "I have to go out of town for a couple days. Wrap up a few things."

"Sure. Okay." I was pretty sure my teeth ground together loud enough for him to hear.

"Hey." He reached over, brushed a strand of hair from my face and rested his hand on my shoulder. "When I get back, it's just you and me, all right? I'm taking a long overdue vacation."

"Perfect. Sounds lovely." I was happy, but too frustrated to show it.

He slid his hand around the nape of my neck and pulled me forward, resting his forehead against mine. "No drama. No murders. No phone calls. Just us."

I nodded and slunk back in my chair.

"Tatum, are you jealous?" he asked, wearing his aggravation like a second skin.

I shot him a glare. Maybe I was. I definitely was, but I sure as heck wasn't going to admit it.

I watched his fingers tighten around the steering wheel, extend in a long stretch, then clench tight again while he stared out the window. "There's absolutely no reason for you to be jealous. You broke up my fucking marriage."

"What's that supposed to mean?" How dare he blame his failure on me.

"I tried living a normal life. Dating, marriage. I couldn't. It meant nothing without you. As hard as I tried, she wasn't you."

How did I reply to that? Nothing about any of this was normal. "I don't know what to say."

"Don't say anything," he whispered with a catch in his throat. "When I get back, I'm locking you away until you don't hate me anymore." The sincerity in his tone made my heart bleed. I didn't want to fight, argue, or be jealous. I wanted his smile back.

"I'm afraid you can't lock me away. I have to clear my name of murder. Oh, and I have a company to run. I'll be too busy for silly stuff like your sexy muscles and killer blue eyes."

"Hmm." No smile, but he almost smirked.

"By the way, your undercover gig is up. You're fired."

Shaking his head to hide the twitch of his lips, he started the car. "Suits me. Does this mean you want to keep the company?"

Did I? "I think I do."

"I'm happy to hear it."

"I know absolutely nothing about running a business."

"If anyone can make it on spunk alone, it's you." This time he flashed a panty-melting, cocky grin.

"Maybe."

He reached into the glove box and pulled out a black scarf. "I'm going to blindfold you now, only for the next few miles. Need to keep the safe house safe." He wiggled his brows and pulled the fabric tight between his hands.

"You're enjoying this a little too much." I leaned forward and let him tie the silk around my head.

"It's this, or knock you out again. You woke up too cranky for my liking last time. I'd like to avoid a repeat of that scene."

I couldn't see, but Lordy, I could feel his heat, his lips dangerously close to mine. My internal temperature spiked and I started to pant. "How long will you be gone?"

"Not sure yet. A few days, maybe four. I'll miss the funeral. I'll also be out of contact. Listen…" He paused to meld our mouths together for a long, slow kiss. "Masters is still MIA. We don't know what he's up to. Promise me you'll not go anywhere alone. Don't leave the house if you can avoid it. Let us get that fucker first."

"I'll be good, I promise. Besides, Mom will be with me."

I heard the squeak of leather, and emptiness rushed over me when he settled back into his seat. "Good. That's good."

He reached over to cup my cheek and rub his thumb across my lips. "You don't hate me."

I leaned into his touch and kissed his wrist. "I do. But I think I love this blindfold. Can we play with it later?"

Chapter 16

The small, dank chapel seemed quite fitting to have Wallace's funeral. I'd arrived early and found a seat in the front. Everyone from Cruse Investigations had shown up. Each person wore a grim expression and avoided eye contact with me.

No way was I in the mood to face the questioning glares and whispers. Mom scooted close and wrapped an arm around me. I heard Nan's voice before she sat in the pew directly across from me.

Although her eyes were red and swollen, her make-up and hair appeared fresh. The small clutch she carried overflowed with tissues.

She looked my way, then shot from her seat when she made the connection. My heart dropped a few inches then bounced into my throat and stuck there. Oh man, she looked appalled, striding toward us with righteous purpose. I was about to stand to meet her when she stopped and shot a scornful glance over my head.

A heavy hand rested on my shoulder and a low, gruff voice warned Nan to return to her seat. I looked up into the weary eyes of Leland Waters, dressed to the hilt in a black suit and tie.

I relaxed into the warmth of mom's embrace. Uncomfortable scene avoided. Thank goodness. Leland sat next to me and stared straight ahead. I leaned toward him and whispered a "thank you." He only nodded.

"Why are you here?" I asked

Keeping his voice low, he chuckled. "Keeping the peace, obviously."

"Did Franklin ask you to babysit?" Silly question. Of course he did. I'd be a fool to think Mr. Overprotective would leave me to fend for myself.

"What do you think?" Leland tipped his head and winked.

I introduced mom to Detective Waters, then the ceremony started. It was short and sweet. Thank the good Lord above. To my surprise, Nan took the stand and gave a heartfelt eulogy. She glanced at me once and her voice quivered, but she regained composure quickly.

I didn't join in the funeral procession or burial, afraid of facing the wrath of Nan. I understood her rage. She believed I'd killed her boss, whom she obviously had a thing for by her behavior of late, so it was only natural for her to lash out. But jeez, ever heard of innocent until proven guilty? Quite frankly, I was hurt she'd turned on me so fast.

Leland insisted Mom and I join him for lunch. He took us to a quaint little Basque restaurant, owned by his best friend, in the Madison Valley neighborhood. We received royal treatment, especially when Leland mentioned we had come from a funeral. The food knocked my socks off, but the wine was to die for. I indulged in a few glasses too many.

Leland, much to my surprise, opened up about his wife and the cancer that took her life several years ago. He acted the noble gentleman and host, and hung on Mom's every word. I liked him. Too bad he was a grouchy old coot on the job. I'd be cranky, too, if I had to deal with people like me on a daily basis.

He saw us safely to our car, followed us home, and walked us to the door. I'd have to thank Franklin later. Although I hated the idea of a babysitter, it was nice to be followed around by someone with whom I was familiar.

Mom and I settled on the couch. She'd arrived late last night, which meant our catching-up time had been put on hold. I knew she'd inquire about the police escort, so I laid it all on the table.

"Mom. I know about Dad. I know what he was."

Her face paled.

"I don't understand why I was kept in the dark. I don't know how much you know or what you can tell me. I just want you to know I love you, and I forgive both of you for lying to me my entire life."

"Tatum." Her shoulders slumped. Her gaze fell to the floor.

I laid a hand on her thigh. "You don't have to explain if you don't want too. I get it. Well, not really, but I understand if there's things you can't say."

She raised her face to look at me. I wasn't met with her usual demure expression. It was tough and calculating. "No. I was briefed back home. They told me what you were going through here. It's time you know the whole truth."

Briefed? Not the reaction I'd expected. This was going to be good.

She turned to face me, tucking a leg under herself. "I worked with your father. That's how we met. We were undercover, posing as husband and wife." The pink tinge of her cheeks morphed to a red glow. "Your dad, well, he was irresistible. He'd always been a ladies' man and I knew he'd never settle down with one woman."

Ladies' man? Dad?

"He made his advances early on. I fought him off, unwilling to be another notch on his bedpost. He was gorgeous. I was lonely. We had worked so close for so long, eventually I couldn't resist him any longer. We had one night, one night of weakness. I told him we could never act irresponsibly again. He respected that." Her eyes glassed over with tears. "But you came along after that one night and everything changed." She reached out to rub my arm. "Best thing that ever happened to me."

"Mom." I tried to swallow past the thick wad of shock and disbelief that stuck in my throat.

"Let me finish, honey. I retired as soon as the agency learned of the pregnancy. They didn't allow mothers in the field, for obvious reasons. Your father, much to my surprise, was thrilled. He insisted we marry. Promised to take care of us. I'd already fallen in love with him. He didn't love me, not in the way I wanted, but I knew he wouldn't let either of us go, so I married him."

My heart broke for her. To love someone and give your life to him, knowing he didn't love you back, had to be the deepest kind of pain. A loneliness so vast and hopeless it'd be impossible to claw your way from its abyss.

"There were other women. I pretended not to know, but he always came home to us."

"He loved you, Mom. I saw it in his eyes, the way he looked at you, the way he touched you. He loved you."

"Yes, he did. Because I gave him you. You're the only girl he truly gave his heart to."

My broken pieces shattered into a million more.

I'd never look at my mother through the same eyes again. After our long and emotional talk, we headed outside for fresh air. The sun was out, the beach was busy, so I figured it was safe. If Jay were out there, he wouldn't dare make a move.

I longed for Franklin. My body didn't feel right without him near. He hadn't called or texted since the night we left the safe house. I had to trust him, or drive myself bat shit crazy with worry. I didn't need any more crazy, so I sucked it up and tried to keep my mind busy. It helped having Mom with me.

We walked in silence for a few blocks. One more question burned a hole in my gut. "Mom. Do you regret being with Dad?"

Grabbing my shoulder, she stopped and turned. "Never. I never want you to think that. Love doesn't always look or feel the way we think it ought to. And I never want you to look down at your father for his infidelities or feel sorry for me. I knew who I was marrying. I never asked or expected him to be anything other than who he'd always been."

She sucked in a deep breath and grabbed my hand, marching back into a brisk pace. "He was exactly who I needed, when I needed him. He was an amazing father and we did have fun together."

Did amazing fathers use their children to train future killers? I wanted to ask if she knew about Franklin, but deep down, I honestly didn't want to know. Or, maybe I didn't want to see her in the same light as Dad.

"Should we get a coffee?" I asked. We were close to my favorite coffee shop and I needed a caffeine boost.

"I'd love some tea."

We jaywalked and slipped inside. "I'm running to the ladies room. Be right back." She handed me her sweatshirt and I laid it on the chair next to me over my phone. My phone that still hadn't buzzed.

I slipped into the bistro-sized table and perused the small menu. A sharp sting pierced my side. A pungent cologne filled my nostrils. "Come with me. Don't make a sound, don't struggle, and no one gets hurt."

Holy shocker of all shockers. He *did* dare to make a move. "Jay," I grumbled through my teeth without making eye contact. "What the hell are you doing?"

He bent over me and feigned a hug. "Stand the fuck up and come with me." The sharp object dug deeper into my skin.

"Okay, okay." I stood, searching for a fork, a knife, a napkin holder, anything I could use to defend myself, but everything was out of reach. I searched the small room for a pair of eyes I could connect with and plead for help. Everyone's heads hung on their shoulders, worshipping their smart phones or tablets or laptops.

Shit.

Something sharp and cold pierced the skin above my hipbone. I grimaced and he pulled me away from the table. "I've got someone in the bathroom with your mother. You don't cooperate, she's not walking out of there."

I stumbled alongside him to the rear exit. A needle pierced my neck. Everything went fuzzy—the tables, the people, the door. He pulled me outside, shoved me into the backseat of a waiting car, then forced the full weight of his body on top of me.

"Drive," he ordered. The car rolled forward. I looked up to see long blond hair in the front seat. Then a dark tunnel, then nothing.

* * * *

The throbbing rhythm in my head, accompanied by stabbing jolts of pain, coaxed me from my state of unconsciousness. Darkness surrounded me, thank goodness. Light would've made my eyeballs explode. A faint hum carried on its business to my left. To my right, a heavily shaded window did little to drown out the street noise. I was a couple stories up, that much I could deduce.

Panic tore through me when I realized my hands were bound to the chair I sat on. As the dizzying buzz in my brain faded, and memories swooped down on me, blood-boiling anger pushed the terror away.

That son of a bitch swiped me from my favorite cafe. In broad daylight. How in the hell do people not notice somebody being kidnapped? What's wrong with this world?

The creak of the door behind me made me jump. "One-Date." A creepy chuckle hung in the air behind me like bad breath in a small space. "Long time, huh?"

A soft glow illuminated the room, revealing a small office. Jay sauntered into my field of vision then squatted at my feet, placing his hands with surprising tenderness above my knees. The gesture that appeared so natural to him was completely vile to me. "I must say. You've grown up quite nicely." The prick offered a warm smile.

"Where's my mom?" I asked with an embarrassing tremble to my voice. "Did you hurt her?"

He clapped my thighs, then stood. "No, no. You came like a good little girl. We didn't touch her." He walked to the window and propped the shade to look out.

"You lied, didn't you?" My voice shook. "There was nobody in the bathroom with her. You said that to make me go with you."

Leaning a shoulder against the window, he pretended to inspect his nails. "It worked."

Yes, it did. I was such an idiot. "What's going on here, Jay? What's the plan? You've been stalking me for weeks—"

"Months," he interrupted. "Two months to be exact."

Prickles of fear danced across my scalp. "Okay, months. Why?"

Showing way too much of the white between his lips, Jay crossed his hands over his heart. "Tatum. You were the one girl I wanted. The only girl I never had. I couldn't wait a moment longer to be with you."

I laughed. "Oh, my God." I threw my head back and laughed so hard, hot tears ran down my cheeks. Had I gone crazy? Maybe. Laughing was better than screaming or crying. Relieved tension, just the same. "That's the most ridiculous thing I've ever heard."

He stalked toward me. I'd expected to see anger on his face. Instead, he laughed, too, like we shared a private joke or something.

"Every girl in school threw themselves at you. You never looked at me twice."

Jay crossed his arms, tilted his head and pursed his lips. "Not buying it, huh? You're half right. I had my pick of bitches. Didn't want them, though, want to know why?"

"Sure, Jay. Why don't you fill me in?"

"You were the hottest chick in school. The cool thing is, you didn't know it. All the other girls, they wanted me for my money."

"Oh, come on. You're certainly not ugly. I'm sure that aside from Daddy's deep pockets and the creepy stalker thing you've got going on, you have plenty to offer a lady."

He didn't appear to appreciate my wit. His dimples disappeared.

"That's precisely the problem. I had more than enough to offer. Someone stole that from me."

"I don't understand."

"I got the shit beat out of me for teasing a certain girl at school. Broken arm, ribs, cracked cheekbone. Any of this ring a bell?"

Oh. Shit. I nodded my head. "You're blaming that on me? How in the hell was that my fault?"

He shrugged his shoulders. His face beamed crimson with barely contained rage. "Well, you know, grudges and shit."

Oh, God, he wanted to make me pay for what Dad did to him all those years ago. I rocked the chair back and forth, struggling to loosen the binds. "What's your plan here, Einstein?"

A spark of amusement danced in his eyes. "We wait."

"For what?"

"The ghost. He'll come. He always comes."

Ghost? Yup, he was crazy.

The familiar clop, clop, clop of heels echoed from behind the door. It creaked open. A proud, toothy grin spread across Jay's face. "Baby." He sauntered past me. I heard the rustling of clothes and something that sounded like a wet, breathy kiss.

The heel clomp drew closer, then a familiar voice made me cringe. "Have a nice nap?" The woman stepped in front of me.

I noticed her shoes first. Red platforms, adorning a pair of naked, fake-tanned, albeit toned, legs. She wore a springy floral number with a flouncy skirt and fitted bodice that accentuated a pair of obviously fake tits.

Dahlia Montgomery.

"Hmm." She took me in with an amused grin for a long, uncomfortable spell. "I don't get it, Jay. What's so special about this tiny thing?"

I pulled at my binds. "Seriously. Could someone please let me in on the joke?"

"I'd be happy to." Dahlia plopped her perky rear on a desk across from me. "Wallace Cruse."

A dull ache throbbed in the pit of my stomach. "What about him?"

"The man was a miserable, lying, greedy son of a bitch. He ruined my marriage, ruined my life. Took everything from me."

"I'm afraid I don't follow."

"Oh, come on now. You want me to believe you weren't in on his elaborate scheme?"

"This isn't funny anymore. What's going on?" I asked, desperately trying to hold the panic at bay.

"Jay, darling. I get the feeling she's telling the truth. She's clueless. Too bad, huh?"

"Yeah, baby. Too fucking bad." Jay smirked.

"I loved my husband and was loyal to a fault, despite his multiple affairs. I made the mistake of telling him I'd leave if he didn't stop seeing other women. He assumed I'd take him for everything he's worth. Who knows, maybe someday I would have. At the time, I'd had no intention. He hired Wallace to investigate me and dig up dirt. There wasn't any. Like I said, I was faithful. So Cruse Investigations made up dirt. Made sure I got screwed in the divorce settlement."

"You had an affair. There were compromising photos."

"No, dear. I didn't." Dahlia reached into her handbag and pulled out a stack of glossy photos. "Do you recognize any of these people?" One by one, she showed me the pictures and watched my response. She stopped at a handsome man and wiggled it in front of my nose. "Doesn't ring a bell?" Her lips pursed when I shook my head. "This is the bastard your boss hired to pose as my supposed lover. He's an actor. All of these people are actors Mr. Cruse hired at one time or another."

I stared, dumbfounded and pissed off. Of course he would hire phonies to make his cases and earn hefty bonuses. I knew the sleaze-ball was scum, but this was a low I hadn't expected. He'd built his empire on a lie. A lie I just inherited.

After dropping the *Wallace was a bigger dick than I imagined* bomb, Jay and Dahlia left me to stew in my murderous juices. I hated Wallace Cruse. He shit all over my father's company, then handed it to me.

I sat, tied to an office chair, and simmered. It sucked, hearing that my father's business had been turned into a seedy house of lies and deceit. Did these crazy loons kill Wallace? Was I next? My head spun. They still hadn't let me in on why I was there. I suppose, for a kidnapping, things could've gone worse. I was in a comfortable chair, a warm room, and they'd given me a drink of water.

I heard their muffled voices through the thin walls. They started to yell.

"This has gone too far, Jay. We got Wallace. Let her go."

"No, the asshole will come. He's getting what's due."

"Come on, baby, this was supposed to be about Wallace. We took care of him, she'll go to jail. Isn't that punishment enough?"

Glass shattered. "Bitch. You don't understand. This is my only chance to get that fucker. He ruined me."

Clomp, clomp, clomp. "Oh Jesus, you truly are insane. Get over it, it was years ago. It's not her fault you were a bully."

Smack. "Ahh!" Dahlia cried out. I felt the sting, and despite being furious, winced for her. "No, Jay. Stop," she begged.

Grunts. Bangs. The wall behind me rattled.

I had a hard time persuading my heart to stop racing. What asshole might come? Who were they talking about?

The wall-rattling subsided. I heard mumbles, pleading, then a loud thud followed by a louder crash. Glass shattered outside the door. Jay shouted, "Shit! Shit! Stupid bitch."

My heart no longer raced—it exploded with a series of rib-cracking whacks. I struggled to breathe, and my eyes blurred with tears of fear.

"Stupid cunt. Couldn't keep your mouth shut for one goddamned second," Jay cried and burst through the door. "This is your fault. Your fucking fault." Spittle moistened my face as he screamed at me. A splash of something dark dotted his shirt and neck.

"What's my fault? What did I do?" I screamed back, trying to shake my arms loose. "I don't know what I did or why the hell I'm here."

Jay's chest rose and fell in angry heaves. His eyes danced wild and crazed, darting from my face to the door. "You cunts are all the same. Playing dumb. Dear old Dad was right about one thing." He paced back and forth in front of me, one hand on his hip, the other pulling the hair on top of his head. "Tits and ass. Tits and ass. That's all you bitches are good for."

"Where's Dahlia? What did you do?" I whispered. I didn't want the answer but I needed to gauge how much trouble I was in. "Jay. Jay!" He ceased pacing and turned toward me. "What did you do?"

"You were always such a daddy's girl, you know that?" he scoffed. "Such a little prude." He clawed both hands through his hair and laced his fingers at the back of his head. "Couldn't take a fucking joke."

"Goddammit, Jay. What are you talking about?"

"You had big tits! Every boy in school talked about your chest. Why the fuck did I get punished for it? I would've been running the fucking company by now." He squatted at my feet and grabbed my forearms. "Do you know what? I was set for life. Now, I'm the crazy fucking son who's too unstable to work in the goddamned mail room." His fingernails scored my flesh. "That asshole stole my future. Now, I'm stealing his."

Jay stood and took two steps back, dragging his tongue slowly between his lips. Dipping his chin, he raised his eyes to mine, then slowly lifted his hands to his belt buckle. A crooked grin spread across his face. My blood turned to ice when he pulled the leather through the loop. My throat closed. I wanted to scream but I couldn't swallow, couldn't form a word. This wasn't happening. No. The room narrowed to the insane man standing in front of me. The devil danced in his eyes, promising retribution.

I wanted Franklin to burst through the door or smash through the window and rescue me from this nightmare. He was a million miles away, and I would never see him again. The last words I'd spoken to him were "I hate you," right before he kissed the ever-loving shit out of me. Had I known that would be our last kiss, I would've…oh God, no. It wasn't going to be our last goodbye. I had to fight. I had to at least try.

"Please don't do this, please. I'm sorry. I'm sorry my dad hurt you. I didn't know he'd do that. I didn't mean to—"

"Dad?" he interrupted. "You are dumber than you look."

"Jay. I'm sorry. He was overprotective. If I'd known he would hurt you, I wouldn't have told—"

Jay silenced me with a slap across my face. "Pull your shit together. I hate seeing a woman cry." He wiped something wet from the corner of my mouth. "What's this babble about your dad?" He cocked his head to the side. "He had nothing to do with this."

"He broke your arm." I lowered my gaze to the floor.

"No, Tatum. Not your dad, you stupid bitch. The ghost. The fucking ghost. He wouldn't leave me alone."

What? Not my dad? Okay. I was seriously at a loss. "It wasn't my dad?" I asked, biting back tears. "Who beat you?"

"I did." Franklin came from behind me faster than his two words registered in my ears. His fists hit Jay's face at least five times before I realized it was him. Blood sprayed, then Jay was on the floor, face down with a gun pressed to his temple. "I warned you then, you touch her again, I'll kill you. There was no statute of limitations on my promise."

A nervous laugh rose from the floor. "Ever wonder why you didn't have a date to the prom, Tatum? Ever wonder why you never got asked on more than one date?"

"Shut the fuck up," Franklin warned.

"Reed. Put the gun down. You can't shoot the guy for being a dick-wad." I jumped at the deep voice. Leland came from behind, tucked his pistol into his holster and knelt to untie me. "Tatum. I see you're staying out of trouble as usual." He freed my arms and offered a hand to help me up.

"Thank you," I mumbled, paralyzed by the sight of Franklin Reed in full *I'm gonna fuck you up* mode.

"What's he talking about, Franklin?"

Jay laughed again. "You were a damn urban legend at school. Nobody survived a date with Tatum Wood. We had bets going to see who'd get a second date. I was convinced he was a figment of my imagination until I saw the two of you together. The ghost. Nobody but me ever saw his face." Jay spat blood on the floor. "But he was there, and if a guy worked up the courage to ask you out? Well—"

Franklin pressed his face closer to Jay. "Another word, I dare you."

A freight train full of memories barreled straight at me. Days wasted sitting by the phone, waiting for a guy to call. Crying into my pillow at night, wondering why the boys avoided me at school. Convincing myself that Prom and Homecoming were no big deal. Rocky Road ice cream. Gallons and gallons of ice cream. "Was it you? All this time? All those years, it was you?"

He dropped his head between his shoulders, then cocked his chin to meet my glare. "I couldn't let those fucking perverts near you. I swore to Tony I'd protect you, and I did."

"Goddamn you, Franklin! Goddamn you!" I didn't know what else to say. "This is so twisted and sick, and…and…wrong. Shit. All this time?"

Face stoic, he nodded.

"I'm done." I was. I'd been bursting at the seams with crazy and that last bit of information snipped the final string of sanity holding me together. I pointed a finger in his face. "Don't follow me. Don't call me. Leave me the hell alone." I turned, pushed Leland out of my way, and strode through the door.

Leland called behind me. "Wait. Don't go in there—shit."

I walked into a kitchen and tripped over a pretty pair of shoes, decorating a set of long lean legs, attached to a lifeless body. I caught my balance only to slip on the obscene amount of blood oozing from Dahlia's half-smashed head.

The room spun in a nauseating whirl of color just before everything turned black.

Chapter 17

I swallowed the handful of pain relievers Mom laid out for me, pressed the ice pack to my head and leaned back.

"Are you sure you don't want to lie down, honey?" Mom whispered, tucking the afghan around my legs.

"Mom, you don't need to whisper. I just hit my head."

"You knocked yourself unconscious and got five stitches," she scolded with the motherly tone of disapproval she'd perfected years ago.

I rolled my eyes. "Technically, I fainted first."

She sat next to me and cupped my free hand in her own. "Sweetie, I'm so sorry I can't stay longer. Your grandfather needs me and I can't find anyone else to watch him."

I turned my head toward her in super slow motion. Not sure why my neck was so stiff. I guess slipping in a pool of blood and cracking your head open can do crazy things to a body. "Mom, it's okay. I'll be all right." Physically anyway. Emotionally? Well, that was a soap opera I wasn't ready to tune into.

"I know, I know. When will your friend be here?"

"Anytime now. She's going to stay the night."

Mom swallowed hard. Her eyes glistened with welling emotion. "Good. That's good."

"Mom, I promise. I'll be fine," I reassured her.

The doorbell rang and Leland let himself in. His gaze fell immediately on Mom, and he looked twenty years younger every time they shared the same space. He nodded. "Afternoon, Ms. Wood."

Mom offered a shy smile.

He turned to me. "Tatum. How you feeling?"

"Peachy," I grumbled. I don't know why I acted like a moody teenager around that man.

"Can I have a word before we go?" he asked.

"Of course." I handed the ice pack to Mom and she got up to take it to the kitchen.

Leland parked it on the opposite end of the couch, taking care not to jostle me. "Masters confessed to helping Dahlia. Claims he had nothing to do with the murder but did help to set you up." He smirked. "Of course, this happened after I was forced to leave Franklin alone with him for a significant period of time." He paused, shook his head, then continued. "The two met at a charity event after her divorce and hit it off. She'd been obsessed with taking Cruse Investigations down. Masters offered to help. When he discovered you and Franklin worked there it was like winning the payback lottery. He put his own plan into action. They paid off one of your tech guys to manipulate the video feeds and hack the email accounts."

"John?" I asked.

"Yes. John Staples. We arrested him this morning."

"Dahlia came to the office asking for Nan the other day. She tripped into me and her rings caught in my hair. I have a bald spot where she yanked her hand free." I ran my fingers across the back of my head. Brilliant. "That explains the hair, but what about the roses?"

"Sick bastard did that for show. Wanted to scare you, and drive Franklin crazy. Thought he'd punish Reed by going after you." Leland huffed and shook his head. "They'd been planning for quite some time. Needless to say, Jay Masters won't be able to buy his way out of these charges. Murder, kidnapping, and the list keeps growing."

"So, I'm off the hook?" I asked with an unnatural squeak.

With a wide grin, Leland patted my thigh and stood. "Yes, Miss Wood. I think we can safely say, you're off the hook."

I shot him a playful wink. "I'm going to miss your handsome mug, Detective Waters."

"Stay out of trouble, will you?" He winked back then turned to my mother. "Shall we head out, Anna?"

Mom blushed and nodded. Leland grabbed her suitcase and stood in the doorway. "I'll meet you downstairs." He flashed a sweet, mushy, tender smile her way, then looked at me. "Get some rest, Tatum."

When he was out of sight, I couldn't help but tease. "Nice of him to offer you a ride to the airport, huh?" I would've wiggled my eyebrows at her if my head didn't hurt so bad.

She smiled her *none of your business* smile and bent to kiss me.

"Have a safe flight." I grabbed her hand and squeezed.

"I'll call when I get home. Love you, Tatum." Mom shot me a wink, blew a kiss, and slipped out the door.

I heard Lizzie's voice and then a faint knock.

"Come in."

"Tate. Holy shit. Your mom is a bombshell. I see where you get your looks."

"Hey," I squeaked, fighting back an embarrassing surge of female emotion. I hadn't asked Lizzie to come stay with me. She'd called, out of the blue, and offered her friendship services. I wasn't dense. I knew Franklin put her up to it. Heck, he had probably bribed her with an obscene amount of money, or had held a gun to her head while she dialed my number. Most likely, he made her wear a wire so he could spy on our conversation. I hadn't spoken to him since the whole kidnapping incident. Lizzie had, and knowing she had, made my bones ache. I fought the urge to drill her about his mental and emotional state. She was here to help, and it was a comfort knowing I wouldn't be alone to wallow in my misery.

After a gentle hug, she plopped on the couch next to me. "You look like you've been butt-fucked by the grim reaper."

I laughed, then winced. Ouch.

"Would it make you feel better to know your dip-shit boyfriend looks ten times worse? God, I'm so happy he didn't fall victim to my charms. Life with him sucks hairy balls."

"Stop making me laugh," I warned, trying not to crack up.

"What shall we do with ourselves?" she asked, looking around the room. "This is quite a spread. You rich or something?"

"Sure am. Just got richer, too. My lawyer says Wallace Cruse had millions stashed in different accounts. Still not sure why he left it to me, but whatever. I might need it. If word gets out about Wallace's scam, there's going to be a butt load of lawsuits coming our way." I couldn't give Lizzie every detail of what happened, but I did hit the main points.

"That sucks. I'm glad I'm not rich. What's going on with you and Mr. Reed? Why is he at the bar with Miss Leather Mini and not here taking care of you? Do I need to rough him up a bit?" Her eyes glowed with spirited curiosity.

A possessive fire burned in my belly. "Miss Leather Mini?"

"Yeah, the woman you mistook for a whore. They've spent the last two days sitting in your booth drinking themselves stupid." She seemed a little too thrilled to be dumping this information in my wounded lap.

An invisible ice pick jabbed at my heart. "I told him I never wanted to see him again." Why did it hurt? "Why do I want to kill her?" I asked, already knowing the answer. Damn, Lizzie. She knew exactly which buttons in my stupid, stubborn head to push.

"I don't think there's any reason to be jealous. The bitch made a pass at me more than once. Franklin finally made her stop." She laughed, then sucked her lips between her teeth when she noticed I wasn't laughing with her. "Talk to me, baby."

"That's the problem. I can't." I couldn't talk to anyone because of his job. "The only thing I can tell you is that he's not the man I thought he was."

She crossed her arms and raised an eyebrow. "Did he hurt you?"

He mortally wounded my heart and soul. "Yes. I mean, no. Not exactly, I guess."

"So what's the problem?"

"I don't know him. Not the real him." He'd lied to me. His stalking skills put Jay Masters to shame. He'd admitted to being obsessed with me since we were children.

"So get to know him. You've fucked already, and by the look on both of your faces when you're together, the fucking is pretty fucking amazing."

Oh jeez. Brash much? "It's complicated."

"Only if you let it be," she quickly retorted.

"You're starting to piss me off."

"Because I'm right. Right? Don't be an idiot. Whatever it is you're mad about, get over it. Men like Franklin Reed don't come around very often. The guy worships you. He'd kill for you. What woman doesn't want to be wanted like that by someone like him, huh?"

"I think I just need a few days. To process."

"Don't wait too long. You'll kick yourself for letting someone like him slip through your fingers."

God, she had no idea. I couldn't enlighten her, either. I couldn't tell anyone. This was my cross to bear. Alone.

Stalker. Assassin. Sexpot. He'd been a major player in my life story, a character I didn't know existed, lurking in the shadows. My protector. Not Dad, the man who'd become a mystery to me. The whole time, it was Franklin.

Franklin was my hero.

* * * *

Bonnie Tyler's "Total Eclipse of the Heart" played on a continuous loop in my head. I finally pulled out my iPod and played it for real. It used to be Mom's favorite song, and when I was growing up, I'd heard it at least once a day, either blaring from the stereo or from her lips. I finally understood why she'd loved it so much.

I made sure Lizzie was squared away in her room and tucked myself in bed after one too many glasses of wine. I downed an ibuprofen-acetaminophen cocktail and dug out my new favorite sleeping garment: Franklin's Pearl Jam T-shirt. He wasn't getting the shirt back. Ever. It was mine. I'd earned it.

I turned the volume to ear splitting level and found a comfy spot on my pillow. My head throbbed and my heart hurt. Every word, mixed with the soulful, husky edge of her voice, wounded me. My muscles ached deeper than I'd ever thought possible. Was it the wine? Maybe. I sang along, pushing through the lump in my throat, wiping away tears with the corner of my pillowcase.

Sometimes, a girl just needed to find a sappy song and sing and wallow. Things would be better in the morning. A good hard cry did wonders for the female psyche.

When I'd regained consciousness on the floor next to Dahlia's dead body, I lost my shit. Franklin had knelt by my side, holding a bloody towel to my head. Like a maniac, I'd screamed for him to get away. To stop touching me. "I hate you! I hate you!" I don't know how many times I'd said those words before I'd pushed him off and bolted out the door. I couldn't bear to look him in the face. Leland had caught me before I stumbled down a set of stairs and forced me to sit until one of his officers could drive me to the hospital. Franklin hadn't come after me. Nor had he come to the hospital, or the police station when I'd given my statement. He hadn't called. He'd stayed away, like I'd told him to.

I no longer fit in my bed. Without Franklin, I was a flea lost in a giant pile of Egyptian cotton. Lost forever in the vast loneliness surrounding me. I turned the music up louder, cried, and sang.

I woke the next morning feeling like I'd swallowed a chalkboard eraser. A glass of water sparkled under the early morning sun on my nightstand. My iPod and headphones lay on the pillow next to me. It'd been turned off. I assumed Lizzie had checked on me. That was until I noticed a crumpled suit jacket at the foot of my bed.

His musk lingered, adding an unexpected warmth to the room. I sat up nice and slow, grabbed the pillow next to mine, and held it to my nose. It reeked of sweet alcohol. I looked to the bathroom, my heart flittering much faster than it should've been. It was empty. I slunk out of bed and pulled a pair of sweats over my naked legs. Lizzie was still asleep in the guest bedroom.

The rest of the condo was empty.

I hated the way grief made my whole body ache.

By the time I'd brewed an extra strong pot of coffee, Lizzie stumbled into the kitchen, rubbing her eyes. "Morning, sunshine." She gave me a peck on the cheek and a slap on the ass. "Nice T-shirt."

I brushed my hand down the front of it. "Thanks. Hey, did you hear anybody come in last night?" I handed her a cup of black heaven.

"No. I slept like a baby pumped full of Benadryl. God, it's so quiet here at night." She quirked an eyebrow at me. "Why? Who would come in? Who else has a key?" She dumped half my sugar jar into her coffee and didn't bother to stir.

"Franklin." Holy cow, I couldn't even say his name without blushing. It belonged on my tongue. It was mine to speak. And fuck my wounded heart, I'd die before letting another woman own it.

"He didn't wake you?" she asked, eyes wide and smiling.

"No."

"Hey, didn't you say he put cameras in here?"

Cameras. How did I forget about those? "You're brilliant. Yes. I've never used them, though. But I think I can access them through my computer. Or my phone. Maybe both."

We ran like giddy schoolgirls to my computer and turned it on. Franklin left handwritten instructions right next to it when he'd installed my new security system. In a matter of minutes, Lizzie and I examined the video feed from the night before, fast forwarding to the good parts.

We'd called it a night around eleven-thirty. I cried and sang in my room for about an hour and a half. At two thirty-six, Franklin came in. Clearly inebriated by the sway in his step. He came straight to my room and stood in the doorway for a good twenty minutes before removing his jacket and slipping my headphones out of my ears. He put them on and listened. For ten minutes he laid on his back and stared at the ceiling. Then he turned off the iPod, rolled to his side, and stroked my hair. He didn't sleep. He watched me, occasionally brushing his fingers over my arm or my hip until five-thirty. He rose, got me a glass of water, and sat on the floor next to my bed with his elbows on his knees and his head in his hands. At six-fifteen, he pressed a gentle kiss to my forehead and left.

"Oh Tate, look at him. He's so, so…" She scratched her head. "Not the Franklin I know."

"Lizzie. What am I going to do?" How could I crave him so desperately when he'd left me with festering wounds?

Lizzie snapped her fingers in my face. "Snap the fuck out of this funk you're in and go get that man. He loves you. Can't you see that?"

I could see he was miserable. But was it just guilt? "It's not that easy. You don't understand."

"What is there to understand, exactly? The hottest man in Seattle, possibly the entire western hemisphere, is sneaking into your room at night to be with you. He could be in any bed, naked, with any woman he wanted. He's here, with you. Do you need to watch the playback again? He is so in love with you, and distraught, and sad. I don't know what happened between the two of you, but it's tearing him apart. He's been drinking for days, Tate. I've known him for three years. He's never done that before."

"Lizzie, who knew?" I hugged her. "Under your tough exterior, you are a big softie. I bet you have romance novels stuffed under your bed, don't you?"

"Eww. No, thank you. I'm more of a horror fan." She rose and grabbed my empty mug. "More coffee?"

I nodded.

"When are you going back to work?"

Yeah. There was that little matter. I didn't want the company. I didn't want the headache, and I definitely didn't want to inherit the bad rep. Wallace had done a number. I had to wipe my hands clean of the place. There was nothing left of my dad there. And quite frankly, I was kinda pissed at Dad. Or maybe, I couldn't bear the weight of walking into that building every day knowing Franklin wouldn't be sharing my space.

"I meet with the lawyers today. After that, I'll check in at work." I didn't want to face my coworkers. I wanted to let the company crumble. But they had families. Bills to pay. I couldn't do that to them.

"Good. Let's get going then, shall we? I need to get back to the bar. Make sure they haven't burned the place down in my absence."

I pulled my new best friend in for a big bear hug. "Thanks for staying with me. It wasn't necessary, but I appreciate it."

Lizzie snorted. "I had fun, baby. Besides, it's not like Franklin would take no for an answer."

"I knew he put you up to this," I huffed.

She grabbed my shoulders. "Hey, I would've come anyway. Like I said, the guy's head over heels. Borderline obsessive, if you ask me."

I laughed. "You have no idea."

* * * *

I straightened my skirt, lifted my chin and pushed through the door. Nan stood at my desk, looking frazzled and shocked to see me. "Tatum. Hi."

Her forlorn expression cut through the wall of defense I'd constructed in anticipation of our reunion. My heart melted for her. She'd lost a loved one. A secret loved one. Leaving her with no one to share her grief.

I hugged her tight. "How are you holding up?" I asked.

She sniffled. "Plugging along. I'm surprised to see you here." Her embrace lacked any effort or emotion.

"Yeah, well. I guess I have a company to run," I said, releasing her.

"So I hear." Dark shadows clouded her eyes, but her face paled.

"Nan. If you don't mind, I'd like you to take the lead while I figure out what the hell I'm doing. Everybody knows you run this place anyway."

She looked at the floor and shifted her feet. "Tatum. I don't know what to say. I assumed the worst of you and I'm truly sorry."

"Don't. It was no secret I detested the man." I paused and sucked in an encouraging breath. "How long have you been in love with him?"

Her eyes snapped to mine. Wide. Disbelieving. Relieved. Her shoulders slumped in defeat. "Years, Tatum. Years."

"I'm sorry." I was. How she could love a man like him, I'd never understand. But loss was loss. Grieving sucked.

"Thank you."

"Is anyone else here?" I asked, plopping my tired rear into my chair.

"Yes. They came back for you, dear. Everyone except for John. I'm sure you've heard. Oh, and Franklin." She hadn't heard about Franklin. Nobody had. They couldn't. I'd have to tell everyone he quit.

I still couldn't believe John had been in on it. "Nan, I have to ask you something." She stopped in the doorway and turned back toward me. "Did you know about the actors Wallace hired?"

"No. I didn't. And I won't believe it until I see proof." Her voice cracked. God, she had been smitten. And delusional.

"Okay," I conceded. How could she have loved the weasel and known the comings and goings of everyone in the company for the last four years and not have a clue about Wallace's shenanigans? It wasn't the day to push. "I'm not ready to dive in yet, but maybe you can help me get his office in order later this week."

"I've already started. Hope you don't mind. I figured you'd want to move in as soon as possible. You can't run a company from this sad excuse for an office." She offered a pathetic grin.

"I was hoping you'd take it. I'd rather work out of the janitor's closet."

Her face lit up.

"Let's talk about this later. Today, it's business as usual. I'll man the phones, you do what you do. Sound good?" I asked.

"Sounds lovely."

Relief washed some of the sadness from her eyes. She shot me a thankful glance and headed to her office. I got busy with my routine. Or tried, anyway.

My Franklin-sized hole was back. The place was a prison. The sun shone bright, but my office closed in around me, dark and dismal. Or maybe that was my spirit caving in.

I dug my cell from my purse and ran my finger over the screen. I could call him. Maybe the sound of his voice would soothe the ache. My finger itched to push the dial button. What would I even say?

The man had stalked me my whole life. He'd manipulated me from the shadows. Kept me from experiencing relationships or nurturing friendships. I had been an unknowing puppet. He'd been the master. How many boys had he threatened? Assaulted? Did Dad put him up to it or did he develop that skill on his own?

Was he watching me now? I studied the small room. There were few places a camera could hide. I wasn't going to search. Instead, I flipped my middle finger to every corner of the room, scooped up my handbag and keys and headed down the hall.

My phone buzzed, announcing a text. A bomb exploded behind my left breast.

That wasn't nice.

Gah! Bastard was watching me. Fire brewed in my belly and spread to my aching brain. I strode to Nan's office. She sat, staring blankly.

"You got things covered here?" I asked.

"What's wrong? Your face is beet red."

So was hers, but I didn't want to say anything. "I have to go. Something's come up. I hate asking you this, but can you handle things?"

Her eyes crinkled at the corners. "Tatum. I've handled things for years. Go. Do what you have to do. You're the boss now, remember? Oh, by the way, I put an ad out to hire a new receptionist."

Huh. Wise move, considering I'd been promoted to head honcho. "You're the best. You know that?"

She waved me off.

I stormed to the elevator, searching the corners and ceiling for cameras. I wouldn't see them. Wasn't sure why I bothered to look. I flipped my middle finger again. My phone buzzed.

You're hurting my feelings.

God. Did he think this was funny? This needed to stop. Today. I couldn't live my life constantly looking over my shoulder, guarding my every move.

I slid into my car and paused for some deep breathing exercises. My hands trembled with rage. My vision blurred with angry tears. I couldn't drive until I calmed down. Resting my head against the seat, I studied the ceiling of my car. Nothing looked unusual. I flipped my middle finger and waited.

Nothing. When I'd calmed, I started the car and headed toward a confrontation that would either make or break me. Or, gauging by the thunderous roar of blood pounding through my ears, end with Franklin bloody at my feet.

Woman scorned and all.

* * * *

I drudged up the stairwell leading to his apartment, bursting with nervous energy. A rush of dread swept through me when I spied the bullet holes in the door. Bullets meant for me, that by some miracle had missed their mark. Except it wasn't a miracle. It was Franklin Reed.

My first attempt at knocking was more of a tap. Sheesh, why was I so nervous to face him? I hit the door again with my palm and made it loud.

No answer.

I headed downstairs to the bar. Like a super magnet controlled me, my eyes were drawn to him seated in our special corner, hunched over the table, eyes glued to his cell. He didn't look up.

Lizzie grabbed my arm and pulled me to the side. "No trouble, okay?"

Did my fury show? "No trouble, I promise. Is he drunk?"

"No. He just came down. I haven't served him yet. Don't want to. I hate seeing him that way."

Why did it warm my heart knowing she was watching out for him? "God, I love you, Lizzie." I kissed her cheek.

I walked slowly to where he sat, biding time to let my courage build. He glanced up, eyes clouded with remorse. My knees buckled. When he caught my gaze, ten years melted off his face. He immediately stood, grabbed my elbow and led me out the back door.

I was out of breath by the time he pulled me into the apartment, not from exertion, but anticipation. Strong fingers sent pulses of electricity through me, striking my girlie parts. The man commanded my full compliance with the force of his being. I was doomed.

He closed the door and pushed me against it, pinning me with his hips. Oh, God. There wasn't time to state my reason for coming. He tilted his head, searching my eyes, stealing my ability to speak, then took my mouth with fierce, desperate abandon.

He melted me from the inside out. The way that man kissed. Holy hell. It was lust, passion, need. But more than that, desperation. Like goodbye. Like this was the last time we'd share a lover's embrace and he wanted to communicate everything he couldn't put into words. He poured his heartache, remorse, and loneliness into it, expressing his internal struggle. I realized, in the midst of his brutally honest kiss, I didn't want to be the cause of his torment. I wanted to be the cure.

I kissed him back, forcing my anger and hurt at him. My own desperate need. His strong hands slid up my back, then he cupped my head just below the stitches, protecting me from the hard door. Always shielding me.

His lips left mine and made their way down my neck, then over my thin blouse to my breast. Oh no, I was going to come. If he so much as breathed on my nipple, I would explode.

"Franklin, I—"

"Shhh." He silenced me. "No words, not now, please, baby." He worked the buttons of my blouse. "Just feel. Feel what you do to me."

"No," I moaned, unimpressed by my own conviction. I'd come here to put an end to this mad affair, hadn't I?

"Not no. Not today. 'No' doesn't exist." He reached down, hiked up my skirt and hooked his thumbs into the waist of my panties. "Say 'yes,' love. Please. I'm suffocating. Can't breathe without you."

Oh crap. Why did he have to talk like that? "Yes," I moaned. Wait. Shit, what was I doing? "No." I shook my head and slapped my palm to his chest. "No." I pushed, but he didn't budge.

His hands fisted against my hips, and he dropped his forehead to mine.

"No." Each time I said it, I reclaimed a few of my wits.

I'd never been overcome by such a mish-mash of emotion. I didn't know how to sort or where to catalog. This was wrong, right? Franklin murdered people—he spied, lied, and God only knew what else. He said it was for the good guys. Did that make it right?

"Franklin," I whispered. "This has to end. We can't continue like this."

A disgruntled groan vibrated low in his throat. "I'm not a monster."

Oh, shit. "No, you're not. And that's my point. What you're doing, what you've done. It has to stop. I'm not your possession or your responsibility. You can't spy on me, or lie, or control who I see, what I do, where I go."

He dropped his hands and stepped back. "You don't understand."

"Then help me, because I'm trying to make sense of this and I can't. You know everything about me. More than I know. It's my life. Do you know how fucked up that is? I can't live like that."

He lifted his face to the ceiling, rolled his shoulders and pumped his fists. One, two, three deep breaths and he drew me to his chest, fingers curling into my shoulders. For the first time ever, I saw fear in his eyes. I put it there. "You can't run. I'm begging you. You are my everything. Do you understand? I can't let you go." His breaths blew hot and measured in my face.

The panicked, desperate pain behind his words should've wounded me, but only added spice to the brewing pot of frustration boiling inside me. "Don't you understand? I don't want to run, but how can I stay? You've manipulated my life for how long now? You're still spying on me. Don't you see how wrong it is? Don't you get it?" I wanted to scream, kick, punch, and draw blood all over again.

"Being without you is wrong," he whispered hoarsely. "That's what I know. You're all I have left. That's my reality." He grabbed my wrist and pulled me with him. I scrambled to pull my skirt down over my butt as he led me through the hallway and into his bedroom, kicking the door open.

He stopped in front of his wall-o'-weirdness. "I was a freshman in high school when I started this board. Fourteen years old. You were ten. Tony said it would help keep me focused on the target. Was it wrong? Maybe. I'm not going to question his motives. It brought me to you." His hand tightened around my wrist.

"You were only fourteen. You couldn't have loved me." I tried to regain control of my aching appendage. He sighed and released me.

Franklin turned, burning a hole through me with the intensity of his glare. "You don't have a Goddamned clue what I felt."

Oh. It was disgusting the way that look made my insides twitch. "You're right, because I know nothing about you." I stepped back. "You know what doesn't make sense? If Dad loved us both so much, why didn't he introduce us? Wouldn't that have been easier?"

Franklin dropped his arms to his sides in defeat. "He didn't want you to know that side of him. Your Dad lived and breathed the darkest parts of humanity. He didn't want any of that ugly touching you. I didn't either."

I stumbled backward and plopped my rear on the bed. "I don't know what I'm doing here, Franklin."

"Killer." He sat and leaned forward, elbows to knees, hands clasped, head tilted to look at me. His deep blue eyes captivated me, sung to me, worshipped me. "You're here because you can't stay away any more than I can. Because we fit. Crazy as it is, we fit." Franklin leaned in and stole a kiss.

"Don't," I gasped, pulling away.

"Don't now or don't ever?" he asked, the tension in his voice palpable.

I stood, brushed a finger across his lips, then turned toward the wall of photos. If there was any chance of things working between us, that wall needed to go, along with the spyware recording my every move. For the moment, I could do nothing about the surveillance gear, but the pictures? Well….

"I know what you're thinking. Please don't," he pleaded.

I looked over my shoulder to shoot him a glare. Then I started ripping the pictures of me off his wall.

I got a few good chunks torn down before Franklin caged me in his deadly weapons disguised as arms. "Please, stop."

"No. These go, or I do." It was a threat I wasn't sure I could follow through on, but I needed to get my point across.

"You're not going anywhere. Neither are they."

"Let go of me." I wiggled against him, trying to wrench myself free. Damn, the man was strong. And he smelled yummy. Made it difficult to stand my ground and fight. "Don't you see? I'm right here. I'm right here in front of you. You don't need those anymore. Take them down, please." God, why was my voice so weak and shaky?

"I can't."

"Why?"

"It's my history, too." He let me go and grabbed a photo from the top right corner. "See this one?" I studied it. It was taken while I waited for the school bus on my first day of high school. "That's the day I took my mother to the emergency room for the first time. She'd swallowed a bottle of pills." He tossed it on the bed. "You helped me cope."

"And this one." He pulled another picture off the wall, then sat back down on the bed. It was of Mom and me eating lunch at our favorite bistro. "That's the day Tony realized I was in love with you. He tried to beat some sense into me. I'd been training, though, and I held my ground. I didn't strike him back, out of respect." Franklin chuckled. "The bastard broke my nose. Told me that love made us weak."

I hadn't known my father at all. I rubbed the small bump at the bridge of his snout. "Why didn't you ever reach out to me?"

"He would've killed me, Tate. He didn't want you connected to this life any more than I did. I was his recruit. And you have to understand, if I fucked up, especially over a woman, it would've tarnished his reputation."

"He wouldn't have killed you literally."

"Baby, the Antonio you knew wouldn't have. The Tony I knew would've in a heartbeat, to keep you safe."

"Just like you."

He shrugged his shoulders. "I learned from the best."

"Take the pictures down." I pushed myself between his legs and cupped his face, tilting it up to look at me. "Put them in a box." I bent and softly grazed his lips. "Put them in a photo album. I don't care. Just no more of this creepy wall." See? I could compromise. "I'm right here. I'm not going anywhere. You don't need those anymore."

Franklin pulled me in for a hug, snuggling his cheek against my breasts. "You're being awful bossy, Miss Wood." He slid his hands down my back and rested them on my rear.

"A girl has to be the boss once in a while."

"Hmm," he groaned, pulling my skirt back up to expose my ass. My body warmed, from the inside out. A throbbing heat hit my cheeks.

"Franklin, I—"

Before I could finish, I was lifted, twirled and tossed on the bed.

"No—no—no. Not here." I scooted back, away from the beast stalking me. Hungry and dangerous. Oh, shit. I was not about to get naked and sweaty in a room filled with computers and a wall full of—me. No way. I jumped from the bed and sprinted into the bathroom, locking the door behind me.

"Tate, baby," he groaned into the door. "What's going on?"

"I need to clean up a bit." Lie. I needed to pull myself together. The man fried my brain cells just by looking at me the right way. "I'll be right out. And we are not going back in that room."

"Fine, but hurry. I'm taking you home where I can fuck you senseless in every one of your rooms. Oh, and I'm bringing rope."

Why did that make my heart beat so fast? Going home would be good. We'd be alone in the car, where he couldn't distract me with sex, and we could talk. Perfect. I used the toilet, fluffed my hair, righted my clothes.

Then I made him wait.

Chapter 18

I grabbed my red Burberry satchel from the spot it'd been so mindlessly discarded on the floor earlier and trotted down the stairs with Franklin. After he tucked me into my seat and closed the door, I checked my phone to find three missed calls from Leland. I'd return them when I got home. I needed the fifteen-minute, sex-free drive time to talk to my man.

Franklin's phone buzzed as he pulled out of the parking lot. He didn't even check the screen.

"That's the first time I've seen you ignore a call," I teased.

"If there's no ringtone, I don't answer." He tucked it into the cup holder.

Hmm. "Do I have a ringtone?" I better. His stupid ex had a ringtone. A sultry ringtone. Mine better be damned good.

His sexy lips curled at the corners and he stared at the road ahead.

"Do I?"

He shrugged his shoulders.

I grabbed my phone to dial his number, but mine buzzed in my hand first. It was Leland for the fourth time in the past hour. A knotted nest of angry snakes took residence in my stomach. I pushed accept on the screen. "Hey, Leland. Everything okay?"

"Tatum, I've been trying to get a hold of you. Where the hell are you?" He sounded breathless and agitated.

"What's wrong?" I croaked.

"Masters is out. Reed with you?" he asked.

No. This was not happening. "Yes. He's right here."

"Good. Don't leave his side." He released a loud sigh, like he'd been holding air in his lungs for hours.

"Out? How did that happen?" I glanced at Franklin. His brows drew tight, cueing his worry wrinkles. A large, dark form charged the window behind him. The glass shattered. Something hard, brick-wall hard and hot, plowed against the side of my head. My world went black.

* * * *

I tried to open my eyes. Only one worked, and not well. Through blurry vision, I saw glass and blood and Franklin's hand. I heard a terrible creaking noise like metal grinding against metal, then muffled shouting. I tried to reach for him. My arms wouldn't move.

Hands snaked under my shoulders and around my chest. I screamed in pain, then heard mumbled voices outside. "Shit, she's stuck. Can't get her out."

"Grab him. Let's get the fuck out of here. Someone's called it in already."

Everything went dark again.

When the world came back into focus, Leland Waters stared down at me with a grim expression. He held my hand, tight and warm in his own. "Welcome back, sunshine. Damn, child. You're going to force me into early retirement." He sounded far away even though he stood right next to me.

When I tried to speak, stabbing pains shot up the back of my neck and head. I cringed, which only triggered more pain. "Where am I?"

"Harborview." He scooted closer and brushed a chunk of hair off my face. "You were in a car accident. Do you remember?"

I remembered bits and pieces, scattered images. I breathed out a "yes."

"You're going to be fine. Legs are bruised badly, but no breaks. Face got beat up, your ear took most of the damage. Can you hear me okay?"

I couldn't. His voice sounded muffled, distant.

I reached up to feel my right ear. It was bandaged.

"Everything hurts," I said, looking down at myself.

"You'll be aching for a while."

"Where's Franklin?" I'd feel better knowing he was okay.

Leland laid my hand by my side and turned to pull a chair close to the bed, huffing as he sat. "They took him," he said with a bitter snap.

"What do you mean?"

"A witness to the accident stated that two men pulled him from the car and loaded him in the back of a van."

"No."

"I'm sorry, Tatum. We've got everyone working overtime to find him."

That wasn't possible. Tears stung my eyes. Men like Franklin didn't get *taken*. Not my overprotective, gun-toting man of steel.

"They wanted me. They tried to pull me out, but my legs were pinned." I wiggled my toes to make sure they worked. A rush of relief swept over me when rough cotton rubbed against my legs. "Masters?" I asked, already knowing the answer.

"My gut's going with yes." Leland nodded.

"How'd he get out?"

"Daddy's deep pockets, political connections, top-notch lawyers."

"He's going to kill Franklin. We have to find him." I hurt, more than I ever had, but Franklin had to be in a thousand times more pain. He took the whole brunt of the impact. Oh, God. What if he hadn't survived the accident?

"We'll find him."

Panic swooped down, sank vicious claws into my flesh and shred me to pieces. "No, you don't understand. I need to find him, now. I need to tell him something. He can't die. I need to tell him...."

The door opened and a curvaceous blonde walked into the room, sucking the oxygen clean out of the space. Her hair, pulled tight in a slick, smart pony, complimented high, peach-dusted cheekbones. Her impeccable gray suit fit every curve perfectly. Her toned legs didn't teeter a smidge in her mile high spike heels. "Miss Wood, Detective Waters." She nodded to both of us with a confident smile. "I'm Sasha Reed." She handed a card to Leland. He glanced at it and handed it back.

Reed? Oh, perfect. My day hadn't been shitty enough.

"I have a few questions for Miss Wood." She stared at Leland, not asking permission to speak to me, but more cueing him to leave.

He cussed under his breath. "She just woke up, and the doctors haven't come in yet. Can this wait?"

"I'm afraid not." She stepped closer to Leland and crossed her arms. "My agent is missing. Every second counts."

"She's the ex wife." Sasha and Leland's heads snapped to look at me. Oh, did I say that out loud?

For the first time since she entered the room, our gazes met. Damn. She was pretty. Snotty, rich-bitch pretty.

"I'm his boss. I'm here to find him."

I stopped scrutinizing her long enough to look at Leland. He glowered down at me, protective fury burning in his eyes. If I'd been able to move, I would've hugged him. "Leland, it's fine. I can talk to her."

"Detective Waters, how about you get her a coffee?" She looked at me. "You love coffee, don't you?"

I glanced to Leland, whose face changed from pale to brilliant red.

"I'll be down the hall." He stormed out of the room.

The blond bitch sat in his chair and crossed her legs, leaning back and clasping her hands atop her knee. "Just so you know, I don't hold a grudge against you."

Nothing like getting right to the point.

"What do you mean?" I asked, cranking up the coy.

"I loved him. Still do. But I couldn't compete with the great Tatum Wood. The marriage was a joke. When I figured that out, I wanted to kill you. Then I just pitied the both of you. Now, this psychotic obsession has put him in danger."

Sasha's eyes narrowed. If she were psychokinetic, I'd be dead.

"Not acceptable. I want you to know, I will find him. Me." She pounded her index finger against her chest. "I'll be the one to bring him home. Your relationship with Reed is over. Do you understand? He's been compromised because of you. Stop indulging his fantasy. Let him go, or the agency will be forced to take action."

It was in that moment I realized I loved Franklin. Deep. Fierce. Forever. I knew, because the absurd idea of letting him go ignited a possessive fury in my gut. Losing him was not an option. I couldn't imagine living one day without him by my side, whether it jeopardized his career or not. The man was mine. Always had been. Always will be. I wouldn't let him go.

I choked back the anger rising in my throat. "I understand." I said what she wanted to hear because I needed her to leave. I couldn't let her see the emotion welling inside me. The fear that swirled and churned, telling me I'd lost him already. I needed to get out of there. I needed to find my hero.

Sasha Reed, a woman I never wanted to interact with again, stood, nodded at me as if we'd come to a mutual understanding, and sauntered out of my hospital room, cool as a cucumber. I closed my eyes and talked myself out of screaming. It wouldn't be worth the pain.

After twelve long hours spent in the hospital, all of which were mental torture, Leland escorted me home. He searched my condo and stationed an officer outside my door. I'm sure there were more men in blue scattered throughout the building, but I didn't ask.

"I'm going to work tomorrow," I told him before I sent him on his way.

Turning on his heel, he clenched his fists and shook his head. "Not a good idea. You should wait until we find Masters."

"Is that an order?" I raised my chin.

He looked like he wanted to throw me over his knee and beat some sense into me. "No."

"Then I'm going to work tomorrow."

"I'll drive you, and that is an order."

I didn't argue. Quite frankly, I didn't want to be alone or go anywhere. But I had resources at the office I didn't have at home. I had to do something. I'd go completely out of my mind if forced to sit home alone and wait.

If the tables were turned, Franklin would've found me by now.

Chapter 19

Blond hair fell in clumps at my feet. I snipped and laughed, snipped and laughed.

"Is this your natural color?" I asked with a sneer. "Or did Franklin make you dye it to look like me?"

Sasha whimpered and shook her head.

"Stop moving. I might slip and take off an earlobe or something."

She mumbled through the gag in her mouth. I stepped back and pulled the wad of cotton from between her teeth. "What was that? I couldn't quite hear you."

"I'm sorry. I'm sorry. You are prettier than I am. I shouldn't have said that."

I shoved the gag back in. "Too late for sorry." I brushed the last piece of long hair down the front of her face and cut straight across on the top of her forehead, leaving only half-inch bangs.

Yeah, she looked hideous—and it made me happy.

"Now, what should we do next? Do you like ink?" I asked, revving up my tattoo machine.

"No. Please, no," she begged.

"You shouldn't have threatened me." I squatted to meet her face to face, then tweaked her nose. "The first one is going to say 'Franklin loves Killer,' and I think I'll put it right…" I circled the needle around her face and settled it on her left cheek. "Here."

I woke with a start, feeling lighter than I had in days. Sasha Reed had replaced Wallace Cruse as my REM nemesis. Nice. The moment reality settled back in, a black hole opened inside me, sucking air, blood, and life into its abyss.

Franklin.

Not one part of my body wanted to move. Everything hurt. I swallowed some ibuprofen and pushed through the pain. Foregoing makeup, I pulled my hair into a loose pony and slipped on my least binding outfit. Leland waited for me downstairs and as promised, escorted me to work.

"There will be someone outside your door. I'll be back at five to take you home. Don't leave, under any circumstance, without one of the officers. Got it?" Grumpy Leland was back with a vengeance and darn if he wasn't starting to grow on me.

"I shouldn't have any reason to leave. Don't worry," I assured him.

I headed in, trying my best to ignore the throbbing pain stabbing at my head and neck. When I stepped off the elevator, Nan passed in the hall and stopped short, eyes wider than the cup of coffee she held.

"For the love of God, Tatum. What happened to you?"

"Fender bender. No big deal." I waved her off.

She grimaced. "With a Mac truck? You shouldn't be here."

"I can't sit home. Need to keep busy." I stepped past her and headed to my office. Nan followed. "Everything okay?" I asked her.

"Things are fine. Can I get you coffee?" She eyed me up and down, eyebrows pinched tight.

"That would be so nice. I'm exhausted just from the walk through the hall." Talking was even a chore.

"Seriously, what were you thinking, coming to work today? And that was no fender bender. Jesus, Mary, and Joseph. Look at you."

"I couldn't sit home alone, Nan. I'll take it easy. I promise." I raised my hands in defense. Ouch.

"I'll get your coffee. You sit."

I did as told. I sat at my desk and put my purse away. Nan came back with a steamy cup of java thick with cream, then headed to her office. A few of my colleagues came by and stopped dead when they caught sight of my face.

By eleven o'clock, I'd had to explain the car accident to ten people, leaving out Franklin's role in the tragedy. I didn't have the energy to explain to anyone else why I looked like I'd been pushed through a meat grinder, and got up to close my door.

As I approached the threshold, Nan's voice carried down the hallway. "Are you sure? No. I'm the only one with a key. The security system hasn't worked for a few weeks. It's on my to-do list. No, no, that's fine. I'd rather you didn't. I'll check it out on my lunch hour. Thank you." She slammed the receiver. "What a day."

I closed the door and got busy at my desk. Wasn't sure where to start. Google, Facebook, Twitter. The obvious go-to's led me nowhere. A soft knock made me jump.

Nan peeked her head in. "How are you doing? Can I get you anything?"

"I'm peachy, Nan." I rubbed at the bandage covering my ear. The throbbing amplified when I pressed against it.

She gave me her *I don't believe you* eyebrow raise. "Can I take you to lunch?"

"I would love to go, but I have too much to do," I lied. "Can I ask you something personal?"

Nan crossed her arms and tilted her head. "Of course."

"Were you dating Wallace secretly?"

Sorrow dulled her eyes. "Yes, and no."

"What does that mean?"

"I wanted to be exclusive. He didn't. I chose to accept sharing rather than lose him altogether."

Another reason for me to hate the man. He probably used her emotionally more than physically. Ew. Naked with Wallace? I wanted to hurl.

"I'm sorry. That had to suck."

She sighed and pulled at a string on her cardigan. "We do crazy things for love."

We? No, just her. And Franklin. I wanted to laugh but that would've hurt too much. So instead, I agreed, "Yes, we do."

"You sure you don't want to do lunch? You need to eat something. You certainly shouldn't drive anywhere. Can I bring you anything? Maybe something from the Mexican truck up the street?"

Oh, Nan was bringing out the big guns. I couldn't resist Mexican food. Damn, it was tempting. "No thanks."

"I might be gone longer than usual. Wallace's neighbor called. She thought she'd seen people in his window. I told her I'd check it out. Nosy old coot. Always in people's business."

"You have a key?"

She blushed. "I do."

"Did you live with him?" Wow. Nan was full of secrets, too.

"No. He flat out refused to live together. Didn't want to cramp his style." She sighed and rubbed her chest, above her heart. "I haven't been there since…well, you know. It's your house now. I do have some personal items there that I'd like to collect, if that's all right. Before you do whatever you're going to do with it."

Oh, poor Nan. I wanted to hug her. "No problem. See you when you get back. And Nan, thanks for everything you've done around here. This place would be nothing without you."

"Thank you, dear." Her eyes brightened. "I'll see you soon." She headed down the hall, heels clomping against the hardwood.

A tall brunette walked through the door and closed it behind her. "Tatum?" she asked, with an accent I couldn't place. Holy cow, she was gorgeous. Long and lean, thick, dark brown hair. Dark eyes. "I'm Annalise, a friend of Franklin's." The woman I'd mistaken for a whore had a name. The woman who'd been drinking with my man after I gave him the boot. The gal who rocked leather pants like nobody's business.

Awkward. "Hi."

She didn't waste any time getting down to business. "I want to help find him."

"How did you know he was missing?" I asked.

I noticed a scar stretching from her left ear to between her breasts and disappearing underneath her shirt. "I can't tell you that."

"Let me guess," I whispered, glancing toward the door. "It's classified."

She leaned a hip on my desk. "You can say that."

I glared at her. More secrets. "You work together, for the agency?"

"We did. A long time ago. Couldn't stand the new boss. What a bitch. I'm a private contractor now."

I huffed. I couldn't stand the boss, either.

"Listen. I'm not a threat. I love Franklin like a brother. Nothing more. He saved my life once. I need to return the favor." Amber eyes stared at me, unblinking, and reminded me of the Irish whiskey Dad favored. Franklin trusted this woman. Maybe I should, too.

I sat back in my chair and crossed my arms. Ouch. Okay, trying to look tough wasn't going to work, not today. I lowered my hands to my thighs. That was a little more comfortable. "You want me to trust you? Then give me something. What do you do for Franklin? What does he pay you for?"

Chewing on her bottom lip, she studied me. Then she smiled. "Let's just say if there's any hacking to be done, I'm the one to call."

Okay. I could accept that.

I nodded. "We need to find Jay Masters. Can you help with that?"

She smirked. "I'm the best, Tatum. That's why Franklin uses me. He'd never settle for less."

Well, Annalise didn't lack confidence, which was admirable. I couldn't imagine she lacked much of anything.

She leaned a hip on my desk and spun my stapler. "So, tell me what you know, from the beginning."

I filled her in on the gory details. From the first rose, to the car accident. She listened. Nodded. Waited patiently for me to finish.

"So they planted evidence to make you look guilty." She crossed her arms.

"Yes. Here and in Wallace's house." A tidal wave of *oh shit* washed over me. "Wallace's house!" I yelled. Ow! Holy hell that hurt. I cupped my ear. "His neighbor just called to say she saw someone through the window. Nan left to check it out."

Annalise stood and crossed her arms. "Well, then. We better be on our way."

I picked up the phone to dial Leland. He answered on the first ring. "Leland. Hi, it's me. I know where—" The phone went dead, because Annalise yanked the wire from the socket.

"You can't tell him about me." The cord dangled from her hand, the glower she wore made the skin on the back of my neck tingle.

"Oh." Classified. "You have a car?"

"I do."

"Good. Can you help me sneak out?"

She laughed. "Do you know how to use a gun?" Like shooting were a natural talent every able-bodied female possessed.

"No." Why did that make me feel inadequate?

"Good thing you have me then. Grab your things. Let's go," she ordered.

I snatched my purse and followed her to the elevator. When we reached the bottom floor of the parking garage, she held up her hand to hold me back, then peaked through the opening.

"Hello again, officer." She lowered her voice and her lashes.

He placed a hand on his belt, shot me a glance and nodded. "Afternoon."

Annalise struck him once in the throat and he fell to the ground. "Let's go." She grabbed my hand and pulled me toward an inconspicuous minivan. I wasn't surprised to see computers and weird-looking equipment where the back seats should've been.

"Did you knock him out?"

"No. Just down, long enough for us to get out."

Gritting my teeth to absorb the pain, I buckled myself in. "I can't believe he'd take Franklin to Wallace's house."

She pulled out of the garage and into traffic, cutting off a taxi. "It's brilliant, actually. The perfect place to hide."

We drove in silence for a few more blocks. I white-knuckled the edge of my seat while she weaved through traffic. "Franklin believed you were safe. That's why, when you told him you never wanted to see him again, he didn't come after you right away. He told me he'd give you one week to come to your senses. That's why he drank and wallowed. He believed you were out of danger. Otherwise, he would've taken you back to one of the safe houses."

I rolled my eyes. What I wanted to do was spin in joyous, girlie glee. I should've known he had a plan. "I'm surprised he gave me a week."

"Me too," she huffed.

Twenty minutes and twelve broken traffic laws later, we pulled over a block from Wallace's house. Nan's car sat crooked in the brick driveway.

"Is this house for real?" she asked, craning her neck to get a good view. "Is that a parapet?"

"Sure is," I said, rolling my eyes.

"You're shitting me. And a turret? Who was this guy?"

I chewed the inside corner of my mouth. I remembered sitting in the turret with Dad as a child. He used to let me look across the sound with Wallace's binoculars. Well, until I witnessed an indecent act on a yacht drifting on the water. I wasn't allowed back up after that incident. The salmon paint and mint green trim would have to go bye-bye. I was sure the neighbors wouldn't complain.

"What do we do now?" I asked, trembling with nervous energy. At least the adrenaline negated some of the pain.

She shut off the engine and slipped into the back of the van. Raising a finger to her lips to keep me quiet, she slid large headphones over her ears. I watched her shoulders relax as she released a long puff of air. "He's in there. He's talking. Sounds like two men and a woman are with him."

For the first time since I woke in the hospital, I could breathe properly. I hadn't realized the weight of worry crushing my sanity until it lifted off me and dissipated into the air. He was alive. "Now what?"

"You wait here. I get Franklin."

Over my dead body. I couldn't sit still while he fought for his life. "No. I want—"

"Can you shoot?" she interrupted.

"No."

Annalise reached into a metal box, pulled out three intimidating weapons and tucked them into the belt of her pants. "Use a knife?" she asked, piercing my resolve with an ice cold, steely glare.

"No." Damn.

"Dodge bullets?"

Bingo. "I've been doing some of that lately." Sure, I wasn't much good at it. But at least it was experience.

Her eyes softened and she laid a hand on my shoulder. "I'll get him. I promise."

"If Jay is in there, he's big and he can fight."

The dark-haired beauty laughed at me. "I appreciate your concern. It's cute. Are you a good driver?"

"Sure." Even better when I can move muscles without them screaming in protest.

"Get in the driver's seat. When you see me come out with him, get your butt up there and be ready to roll."

I nodded yes.

Annalise walked casually up the sidewalk. Her ability to hide guns in her tight pants and black T-shirt boggled my mind. Was that part of secret agent training? I'd have to ask Franklin. When she disappeared around the back of the house, I glanced around the neighborhood. Aside from a yapping dog two houses down, it was quiet.

My phone buzzed and I dug it out of my handbag. "Hi, Leland. I'm sorry we got cut off earlier."

"What's going on, Tatum? Please tell me why your friend took down one of my men."

"It's classified. That was pretty cool though, huh?"

"Why don't you ask him how cool it was?" It's too bad Leland never had kids, because he killed the chastising parent vibe.

"Sorry."

"No, you're not. What's going on? Who's the woman?" he asked, demanding my compliance.

"Never mind her. Jay has Franklin at Wallace's house. Nan is there, too."

"How exactly do you know this?" I could tell he was walking by the way his breaths blew into the phone.

"There's another man here. Don't know who he is."

"Goddamn, Tatum," he yelled. "Tell me you aren't there."

I cringed. "I'm not there. Technically, I'm a block away."

"Get out of there, now. Leave. I mean it. If you step one inch closer to that house I'll lock you up and throw away the key."

"I can't leave. I have to drive the getaway car."

"Getaway…what…I don't even want to know. I'm on my way." He ended the call, but not before I heard a few unpleasantries.

I stared at the house. Minutes ticked by. Soon, I heard sirens in the distance. The closer they came, the harder my heart knocked against my breast.

He had to be okay. Had to be.

I tapped on the steering wheel, bounced my leg up and down. Fidgeted in my seat.

A pop, pop, pop came from the house. I never wanted to hear that sound again. My adrenaline spiked into overdrive. I started the engine and peeled away from the curb. I lurched to a stop in the grass a few feet off the driveway and limped toward the front door.

He had to be okay.

As I stepped onto the front stoop, the door swung open and Jay stumbled out. Face pale, eyes wide, he wrapped an arm around his midsection. "Ah, Tatum. I'm afraid you're too late. You missed the fun."

The sirens were deafening behind me and red lights bounced off the windows of the house.

"You're the worst thing that's ever happened to me," Jay sputtered and lunged toward me. I jumped back and he fell at my feet, landing on his back. Blood spread across his torso and stained the Italian tile of the front stoop.

I stepped over him and stumbled inside. Annalise crouched over Nan, who lay with her face to the floor. Over her shoulder, Franklin slumped in a chair, arms tied to the sides, head hung forward with the handle of a knife sticking out of his right pectoral. Another man lay motionless at his feet.

I called his name and hobbled to him. He didn't move. My heart seized. My lungs deflated. So much blood. Everywhere.

I cupped Franklin's cheeks, his skin ice against my fingers. I lifted his face to see me. There was no life in his eyes.

Behind me, I heard shouting and footsteps barreling through the door. I looked up, Annalise was gone.

And I was losing Franklin.

"No!" I shouted, pulling his face closer to mine. "No." My hands trembled against cold skin. "You aren't going anywhere, you hear me?" I slapped at his cheeks as if that would wake him. A thick arm ensnared my waist and tried to pull me back. I kicked, punched, and pinched until I was free. Franklin needed to know what he meant to me. Maybe he'd fight harder. "You can't leave me, Franklin. I love you. Do you hear me? You can't go away." I wrapped my arms around his head and held him to my chest. "Wake up, please. I need you. I love you so much, don't leave me. You can't—"

"Tatum." Leland placed a hand on my shoulder. "Let me have a look."

Tears poured down my cheeks, burning my skin. I knelt and held his face in my hands again. "Don't leave me, please. Wake up, please. Wake up," I pleaded, stroking the sides of his bloodied face.

Leland called over his shoulder, "Where's that fucking ambulance?"

Someone answered, "ETA three minutes."

"Tatum. You need to let me do my job." He placed his hands over mine and pulled them away from the lifeless body of the man I loved.

I wanted to die. I wanted to pull the knife from his chest and plunge it into my own. Oh, God, it was the worst kind of pain, seeping through flesh and bone, suffocating any hope. I fought to stay close to Franklin, to breath him in for as long as I still had him here on earth. Leland used his muscle and forced me away. "Hold her!" he shouted.

Somebody grabbed my shoulders from behind, squeezed tight and pulled me back. I fell to the floor and gasped for air.

Leland blocked my view of Franklin. "He's breathing, but barely."

Nan lay on her stomach, arms wrapped around her head in a protective lock. I crawled to her side. "Oh my God, are you okay? Did they hurt you?" I lifted her arm. Purple and blue covered the left side of her face and her eye was swollen shut.

Nan's tears flowed almost as heavy as mine. "Is he dead? Oh, Tatum. I tried to help, I tried."

I wrapped an arm around her. "Shhh. It's okay. He's fine. He'll be just fine." If I said it enough, it'd have to be true.

Paramedics burst into the kitchen. Leland pulled a utility knife from his back pocket and cut the binds off Franklin's wrists. His arms fell to the sides. They laid him on a stretcher, and a man lifted me to my feet and walked me outside. "We need to clear the scene, Miss Wood. I'm sorry."

I buried my face in my palms and released a flood of tears. My face, my head, everything hurt so damn bad, but I couldn't stop. Franklin couldn't be gone. I'd just found him.

We reached the ambulance and paused. "Detective Waters wants you to ride with Reed to the hospital. Can you climb up?"

I didn't answer but crawled into the back of the vehicle. A few short breaths later, Franklin, motionless and pale, was lifted in.

The ride took eons. I held his hand, tried to breathe, and willed my heart to continue beating.

The waiting room walls closed in around me. After four hours, I called Lizzie. She brought me clean clothes and greasy bar food that I couldn't eat. We didn't talk. Lizzie held my hand and let me cry. Leland checked in a few times, promising he'd be there as soon as he finished at the scene. Jay Masters and the other man were dead. Gunshot wounds. Nan was recovering from a nasty blow to the head. She'd already been released from the hospital.

Seven hours after our arrival, a nurse came in and asked me to come with her. "He's asking for you."

My heart compressed, pumping the black, oily sludge from its chambers, then filled again with bright red, energizing blood. "He's okay?" I jumped out of the seat so fast, my head buzzed and the room spun. I had to grab the nurse for balance.

"He's going to be fine."

I kissed Lizzie and told her to go home. "I'll check in with you later." She waved as I strode through the swinging door, feeling the weight of a thousand lifetimes lifting from my shoulders.

"Killer," he breathed as I walked through the door. His playful smile gutted me.

"I hate you," I cried and buried my face in his uninjured shoulder. I didn't want to break down in front of him. I wanted to be strong, show him I could handle whatever shit came my way, but the sight of him blew the false composure I'd mustered to bits.

He pressed his face to the top of my head. "Shush, baby. I'm here. I'm not going anywhere."

"I thought you were dead," I mumbled into his chest.

"Silly girl. You think I'd let death take me away from you?"

"No," I snorted. "You wouldn't."

"See? You worried for nothing." Soft lips pressed into me. "Besides, you hate me, remember? You should be throwing a party."

I lifted my head and looked long and hard at his gorgeous, battered mug. I reached out to stroke his face, and he closed his eyes, a low groan rising in his throat. "Say it. Please. I need to hear you say it. Just once."

I leaned over and kissed the corner of his mouth that wasn't bruised and swollen. "I love you."

He kissed me back and his lips slackened against mine.

"Sleep, Frankie, I'll be right here," I whispered. And I would be. Every day. Like he'd always been there for me, waiting in the shadows.

"Isn't this the sweetest thing I've ever seen?" Sasha leaned over my shoulder, blowing her minty breath across my cheek.

My fists clenched. I wanted to punch her. Lucky for her, my body wasn't up for a game of Rock 'em Sock 'em Robots.

"What are you doing here?" I asked, not giving her the satisfaction of looking her way.

"It's time to let him go. You're only going to hurt him if you stay. His career will be over." Sasha splayed her hand across my back and rubbed with comforting strokes. "He's nothing without his job."

"I'm nothing without him." I shrugged her hand off me and turned to meet her square on. "I'm sure you know how that feels."

Her composure faded for the briefest moment, and she stepped back before she forced a challenging smile. "You almost got him killed."

Protective, possessive rage swirled in my abdomen and rose to settle in my cheeks. The throbbing heat made my eyes water. I straightened my shoulders and stepped closer to the woman who'd pushed my last button. Wrong day to challenge me. "Maybe. But I found him." I pressed my index finger into my own chest. "I brought him home. Me." I raised my other hand and pointed at her, then toward the door. "You failed. I win. Now, get the fuck out of here." My chest rose and fell in rapid bursts.

Her peachy cheeks darkened to red. "I'm not a woman you want to piss off. You don't want me as an enemy." Sasha's gaze drifted to Franklin, drew up and down the length of his body and rested on his face, then she turned to leave. I had a feeling it wasn't the last I'd see of Sasha Reed.

Chapter 20

His rough tongue brushed the length of my sex. "Franklin, you're still recovering. We shouldn't do this. It's too soon." I hoped he didn't take me seriously because holy, horny heck, I needed it.

"It's been too long, baby. I'll make it quick, I promise." His finger penetrated me and I arched into him, grinding against his mouth. He was a man of many, many talents and I'd become a slave to each and every one of them. I came hard, digging my nails into the sheets.

Before the tremors subsided, he prowled over me until his erection rested against my tummy, kissed me silly, then pushed inside, slow and steady. We hadn't made love since the accident, three weeks ago. Doctor's orders. It hadn't stopped him from trying. Today, I let him win.

"Does it hurt, baby?" he asked, voice husky with lust.

"No," I moaned, cupping his ass and pulling him against me.

"God, I love you," he whispered as he stretched and filled me one delicious stroke at a time. When fully sheathed, he paused and lifted his head to meet my gaze. "Say it. Tell me again."

"I hate you," I teased. He shoved a hand between our bodies and pinched a nipple. "Ouch!" I squealed. "Okay, okay." I pulled his face to mine and bit his bottom lip, then stroked my tongue across the surface. "I love you, Franklin Reed." I paused to make sure he was looking. "So *fucking* much."

Franklin punished me for the profanity with another tweak to my nipple. "Stop. Stop." I laughed and smacked his hand away. "I love you. I love you. I love you."

"I love your laugh." He thrust his hips against mine, then groaned. "You're my heaven, Killer. Swear to God, my heaven."

"Mmm." I moaned into his neck, nibbled and sucked. He tasted so good.

He pumped into me again and again. Sweat beaded across his brow. The exertion was too much for him. Legs locked around his waist, I arched my back and pulled him closer, knowing it would set him off faster. Franklin came, face buried in my hair, proclamations of love murmured in my ear, then collapsed at my side with a tremble.

"Shit. I could sleep the day away." He yawned and dazzled me with a lazy grin.

I stroked the spot between his eyes, tracing one of the wrinkles. "You sleep. I'm going to shower." I kissed his luscious lips one last time and rolled out of bed.

When I came out of the bathroom, feeling drained, I wasn't surprised to see my sexy man up and at 'em. Franklin stood by the kitchen counter, wearing his ass-enhancing jeans, one of his skintight, long sleeved jerseys, and looked downright yummy. He held a coffee mug to his lips. I'd died and gone to heaven. Franklin and coffee. What more could a girl ask for?

I rifled through my handbag to find my phone and pushed number one on my speed dial. Eddie Vedder's haunting voice rose from Franklin's derrière.

Franklin shook his head. "It's just getting old now. The first twenty times, it was funny. Now? Not so much."

I sauntered across the cherry wood floor humming the tune to my new favorite song, Pearl Jam's "You Are," and locked my arms around his waist. "You have got to be the hottest barista, ever. It's gonna suck for me when you go back to work." My babies roared to life against the hard muscle of his back. This man of mine was deadly sexy and the ultimate aphrodisiac.

He set his cup down, turned, and hooked a finger under my chin. "I don't have to go back, you know. We could leave, travel the world until we find some place to call home."

Oh, my. Talk about tempting. "But you love your job."

Franklin gripped the sides of my head and tilted my face up to meet his. "I do. But you're my life. You come first."

I closed my eyes to absorb his words. They nourished me. "I won't lie. Your profession scares the shit out of me, but I could never ask you to quit."

He released me and walked around the counter to pull three coffee mugs from the cupboard. "Killer, you don't know how happy I am to hear that."

"Are we expecting company?"

"We are." He poured cream and coffee into my favorite mug. "They'll be here any minute." His smile could've powered the entire city of Seattle for a week.

I quirked my brow at him. "What're you up to?"

"Business." He scooted the cup my way.

"Have you been wheeling and dealing behind my back?" I asked, wondering when he'd found time to talk to anyone. We'd been inseparable since he left the hospital.

"I had a feeling you'd want to distance yourself from Cruse Investigations. I wanted to make the decision a little easier for you. If you want to sell, it's a done deal. If you decide to stay, no hard feelings."

I looked up to find his eyes burning bright with amusement. "You do know me better than I know myself."

He shrugged his shoulders. "Well...."

The doorbell chimed. "They're here." Franklin slapped my ass and jogged to the panel to buzz the mystery guests in. He opened the door and waited, leaning against the jam. I stole that moment to admire him and enjoy a few sips of caffeine bliss.

A couple of minutes later, Lizzie burst into the room, all sunshine and positive energy. She engulfed me in her skinny arms, then leaned back to study my face. "Hi, Beautiful. You look so much better. The bruises have faded."

I didn't realize how much I had missed her until she stood before me, bright smile, eyes gleaming. Leland followed her through the door, stopping to chat with Franklin. He smiled bigger than I'd ever seen. Except for when he talked about, or to, my mother, which happened quite frequently.

Leland came my way and I jumped in for a bear hug. I could do that now. I was no longer under investigation. He didn't seem to mind too much. Everybody needed hugs. Even rough, gruff detectives.

"Shall we get to it?" Franklin clapped his hands together and rubbed.

Lizzie squealed and bounced up and down on her toes. "Yes. I can't wait to see the look on her face."

"What's going on?" I asked.

Franklin hooked my waist and pulled me to the counter. "Come here." He lifted me onto the barstool, planted a kiss on my cheek, then poured coffee for our guests.

Lizzie claimed the stool next to mine. "Let me go first." She turned to face me. "The Malted Maven is up for sale. Well, the whole building, actually. The owners want to retire and move to a drier climate." She reached over and squeezed my arm. "I want to buy it."

"That's great Lizzie! You should."

"I want you to be my partner."

"Me? I don't know."

"Oh, shush. Listen, I have a business degree but no cash. That's where you come in. You've got it coming out your ears and don't know what to do with it. And get this, the vacant space next to the bar is perfect for a coffee shop. You could be surrounded by coffee all day long. Imagine that!"

I was speechless. But damn, she was right. I would love to run a small cafe. Why had I never thought of that before? "What about Cruse Investigations?" I glanced at Franklin like he would have the answer.

"I want to take that off your hands," Leland chimed in.

"But, your job?" I squeaked.

He chuckled. "I retire in two years. Nan's settled in as CEO. She can run the place, and I'll learn the ropes in my spare time. I'm old, but not dead. Need something to fall back on."

Wow. Just. Holy crap. "How can I say no?" I threw my hands in the air.

Lizzie jumped from her chair and hugged me hard. "You can't say no. You love me too much. Oh, my God, Tate. We're going to be kick-ass partners. Watch out Seattle! Wine, where's the wine, or hard alcohol. Where you hiding it? We need to celebrate."

Franklin showed her to the liquor cabinet and pulled down the glasses. Leland sat next to me. "How you holding up?"

I glanced to Franklin. He stood by the sink, hip against the counter, opening a bottle of Chopin Vodka. "I've never been better."

"You're a damn lucky woman, Miss Wood. Things could've ended on a very unpleasant note."

I shook my head. "Nah, not lucky. I have a Franklin and a Leland fighting for me." I winked at him. "I hear you're going on vacation."

"Yeah, I've never been to Florida. Thought I'd give it a whirl." He smiled and patted my shoulder. "There's a pretty lady down there I'd like to see."

Oh jeez. Sappy. But it made me happy to think my mom might have a chance to experience mutual love. I couldn't think of a better man for her.

As for me? I'd fallen and fallen hard. No going back to where I came from. No room for confusion or doubts about Franklin, and that was the one sure thing in my life. My job, my future—it was all up in the air. Franklin? He was for sure. He'd always be my home.

He always had been.

* * * *

After a week full of meetings with lawyers, bankers, and realtors, I was ecstatic to have a weekend alone. With Franklin. Who was soon to be my tenant.

He'd insisted I come to his place to help him with some things. On my way to meet him, I was shocked to find movers carting boxes into Jacob's apartment. New neighbors. That was good. Maybe I'd bake some muffins for them when I got back. I couldn't pass Jacob's door without tearing up because I missed him, or fighting bouts of anger because I was still angry that he'd been forced into retirement and sent away somewhere top secret. I didn't get to see him or say goodbye. Franklin assured me he was healing well and happy as a clam.

Although he'd stayed with me while recovering, I didn't let Franklin move in. He'd put up one hell of a fight, but I held my ground. It was perfect. The man was still bossy and overprotective, it was his nature, but when it was too much, I merely had to show him to the door. And boy, was that fun.

"Thank you for letting me do this." I hugged him for the third time and reached for the one remaining photo on the wall. He'd made me save that one for last. It was a photo of Mom, Dad and me on Easter Sunday when I was still in grade school. We were standing outside the church talking to some of their friends.

I brushed my fingers over the glossy five-by-seven. "That one has always been my favorite," Franklin whispered. "You're so sweet and innocent with your pigtails and frilly socks. I often pictured myself standing between you and Tony, like I was one of the family."

His words tore a fissure through my heart. We had been his family, hadn't we? From afar. I wanted to hate my father for what he'd introduced Franklin to at such a young, impressionable age. I couldn't, though, because if he hadn't, I wouldn't know this beautiful, intense man.

Franklin cleared his throat. "Tate."

I paused and glanced over my shoulder. Expectant delight danced through me at the sight of him rising from the bed and drawing close.

"I need to tell you one thing before you take that picture down."

I turned and pulled his hips to mine. "Yeah?"

"The job can take me away at any time, for extended periods. I need you to know no matter what, I'll always have your back. You'll never be alone. Even when you can't see or touch me. I'll be there, keeping you safe."

His words, the tone in which he spoke them, the penetrating gaze, made my heart palpitate. "You're doing the creepy stalker thing again. Lighten up, will you?"

He smiled as he brushed his lips across mine. When I pulled the last picture off, there was a hole carved in the wall behind it. In the gap sat a crystal box.

"What is this?" I asked.

"Open it." He wrapped his arms around my waist and rested his chin on my shoulder.

"Franklin."

"Open it."

I lifted the lid. The ring, perched in champagne silk, twinkled even under the dull light of the room. The delicate band, lined in two tiny rows of diamonds, met at each end to frame an octagon shaped, dark purple stone.

"What is it?" I asked with barely a whisper. I stroked the large rock.

"A purple diamond." Franklin reached around me and pulled the ring from the box. "It's incredibly rare. Like you."

I turned to face him. My heart leapt through the roof when he lowered himself to one knee and captured my left hand. Tears blurred my vision. Emotion clogged my throat.

"Tatum Elizabeth Wood, I lived my whole life loving you from the shadows, never believing you'd be mine. By some miracle, you're here with me. I hope you know I will never let you go. I'll never leave you. Every day that passes, you'll feel how much I love you. Will you please make my life complete and marry me?"

I dropped to my knees, because they were weak, because I needed to be closer to him. Just because.

I drew a long, deep breath. "Before I can even consider your proposal, there's something I need. It's something you stole from me, over and over. I want it back."

"What, Killer?" he asked, fear settling across his face.

"A second date."

His smile stretched from ear to ear. "I'll give you a million second dates. Take you to the fucking moon if that's what you want. Just say yes."

"And a very long engagement. You've had years to get to know me. I need time to catch up."

He blew out a nervous breath. "I can live with that."

Krissy Daniels

I wiggled my fingers, eager to feel the weight of his gift on my hand. He slipped it on, sealing my future. "I hate you Franklin Reed, with all my heart. I will continue to hate you with every breath I have until my dying day. Yes. Yes. Oh my God, yes."

He kissed a tear from my face, groaned, and snuggled me tight between his arms.

"You don't hate me," he chuckled.

"I do. I really, really do."

Meet the Author

Krissy is a full time writer, reader and lover of all things romance.

Growing up surrounded by the great outdoors, life was full of adventure that fueled an overactive imagination and ignited a passion for storytelling. Whether it be dolls, or running free through the wooded areas surrounding her home, playtime always included a tormented villain, a damsel in distress and a larger than life hero.

After relentless encouragement from friends and family, she finally put the characters in her head to pen and paper. The only thing she loves more than curling up with a steamy romance novel, is cozying up to her desk and writing her own sexy adventures to share with others.

Turn the page for a special excerpt of Krissy Daniels's

Aflame

To save her soul, he'll let her burn.

Grayce has been on the run for years. Having escaped an abusive relationship with a violent psychopath, she is trying to rebuild her life one small step at a time. Things are going well until Zander crosses her path, badass and sexy as hell. His presence awakens heated desires she long ago buried. Last thing Grayce wants is a man, and the way her body reacts to Zander scares her more than the threat of being found.

Tyr will do anything to get his little dove back. She is a Beacon, and her raw, burning energy gives him power and strength. More than the evil that already compels him. But a blond giant of a man hovers protectively around her. No matter. He'll play with him too.

When Zander rescues Grayce from Tyr's first attempt to reclaim her, he reveals his superhuman abilities. Power that Grayce also has, but is yet to understand. As predestined soul mates in a race of fallen angels, Zander must help Grace control her rage before her fire threatens to destroy everyone and everything in her path. But his true challenge is more than that—to show her it's possible to trust and love again.

On sale now!

Chapter 1

Two more minutes. Two more minutes of torture, then *adios amigos.* Grayce out. Tired? Not a chance.

Grayce hopped off the elliptical before it stopped, grabbed her bottled water and glanced around the massive room.

No sign of him anywhere. Thank God.

On shaky legs, she forced herself to head to the weight machines. If luck was on her side, she'd get through an entire workout without running into the obscenely attractive, gargantuan blond who tracked her every move. The beast was a sight to behold. She pretended not to notice. She'd die before ogling him like the other women. Problem was, he ignored everyone. Except her.

He was the only man who could make her blush and that pissed her off beyond measure. Rounding the corner, a familiar, heated flush pulsed through her body. The warning, however, did not come soon enough. It didn't allow her enough time to run the opposite direction before her face acquainted itself with a brick wall disguised as a chest.

"Ouch, shit." Her ass narrowly avoided a painful introduction to the floor when a pair of strong hands caught her mid-fall and set her upright. Tears threatened to surface. No need to look up. Grayce cupped her nose and forced her gaze to the far wall, painfully aware of who she freight-trained into.

"You all right?" His deep silky voice cut right through the heavily guarded walls she'd built around herself, and melted a layer, possibly two, of the hardened steel protecting her most vital organ. And that was precisely why she needed to get as far away from him as possible.

Without a word, Grayce turned on her heel and jetted the hell out of there.

* * * *

Heart in his throat, Zander watched her walk away. She hadn't uttered a word. As per her norm, she looked at the wall, his shoes, the old lady riding the recumbent bike. Everything but him.

Stunned by the energy burst searing his veins, unsteady legs refused their command to follow her. Instead, he enjoyed the view. As she huffed away, blood rushed to his cock. A baggy cotton ensemble hid her form, which made her all the more tantalizing. Large breasts, curvy hips? Small waist with a firm tight ass? Made no difference to him. When he finally had her good and naked, she'd be perfect, because she belonged to him.

Full of hellfire and fury, she marched her petite frame toward the exit, shouted an obscenity, then backtracked to the locker room. He couldn't help but chuckle. Saucy little lady.

They'd get along just fine.

Being a descendent of an ancient warrior race planted on earth by fallen angels had its perks; superhuman abilities, immunity from illness and extended life spans to name a few. But there was a downside. Males of his heritage could never reach their full potential until they'd found and bonded with their other half, or soul mate as he preferred to call it.

Zander's search spanned almost twenty years. He was one of the lucky ones, knowing his one true mate existed. Most of his kind hadn't a clue. Finding their better halves was the hard part. He'd done it. Yet, there he stood, watching her walk away again.

Moments passed before Zander realized he hadn't moved an inch. As he glanced around the gym, it was no shock that everyone stared in his direction. Ladies flashed him their brightest smiles, men straightened their backs in attempt to make themselves taller and boys simply scurried to clear a path. Common reactions. None of it mattered. What was important? After years of tireless searching, his future was within reach.

Shit. He didn't even know her name.

Fuck the taking-it-slow approach. It was time to get the girl. He forced uncooperative legs to move. At the same moment, she stormed from the locker room rubbing her nose. An impressive combination of profanities followed her through the exit, drawing gasps and sneers from anyone within earshot. With a deep breath, he straightened his shoulders and trailed a few paces behind.

"Hi, Mr. Vascos," Carrie shouted from behind the counter.

"Yeah, yeah, whatever. Leave me alone. I have a lady to claim," he grumbled under his breath, waving her off as he passed.

Carrie's deflated sigh pulled at his heart strings. He was such a sappy bastard. Abruptly, he turned toward her, forced the biggest smile he could muster and took a moment to be kind to the only other person in the gym he gave two fucks about. "Carrie. How are you today?"

Blushing violet, Carrie leaned toward him. "I'm wonderful, Mr. Vascos. I met someone." Sunshine poured from her smile. "He's tall, dark and handsome and drives a Porsche. My first time in a Porsche. Absolutely amazing." Her grin grew even wider as she stared glossy-eyed at the ceiling.

"That's great." He didn't roll his eyes, but damn it was tempting. Porsches were for pussies, or men who needed help getting pussy. "He better be good to you or he'll have me to deal with." Zander winked, jogged toward the exit, and left Carrie in her state of bliss.

* * * *

Tyr Collins leaned back, rested the heels of his A. Testoni shoes on the windowsill and plucked lint from his slacks. It became impossible to hold back a smile. Worried that the stretch of his cheeks might add wrinkles to his near flawless skin, he concentrated on relaxing the major muscles in his face.

Grayce, his little dove, was finally coming back to him. The wait had been torture, but he'd set the wheels in motion, and soon her addictive energy would be his again. Unable to ignore the annoying erection that strained painfully against his trousers, he reached down for a quick rub and adjust.

Three years had passed. Slippery little slut. His spine tingled with anticipation at the imagined look of horror on her face when she'd realize he'd claimed her once again.

God, she was going to pay. Dearly.

Binoculars raised and focused, he scanned the gym parking lot to make sure his latest game piece was in place. This was going to be fun. It would've been much easier to grab her himself. But why? There was much more pleasure to be gained in toying with prey before you strike. And the fear, oh yes, the fear made it so much more satisfying in the end.

* * * *

Certain the steam screaming from her ears was visible to everyone, Grayce stormed toward the exit doors. Distance is what she needed, and mere miles wouldn't be enough. The familiar ache ignited by his presence consumed every inch of flesh. Intense attraction, need, lust. Emotions not welcome in her world forced their way through an obsessively guarded wall.

Her long lost libido had come back with vengeance and completely betrayed the memory of the hell she'd lived through at the hands of men.

With temper rising to near nuclear proportions, she struggled against shaky fingers to unlock the door to her rundown VW Rabbit.

"Don't turn around." A sour stench filled her nostrils before the words registered. Tobacco and skunk. A heavy hand weighted her shoulder. "Get in the car and slide over." The raspy voice and wheeze with each breath were a dead giveaway the man had held a thousand too many coffin nails between his lips over the course of his lifetime.

Oh hell no. Bravery, fueled by intense anger, filled Grayce with an unexpected sense of power. With a quick turn she swung her right arm at the man. Damn gym bag. Its weight slowed her momentum, and the strike barely fazed him. No way in hell was she going to allow the fat bastard to bully her into the car.

Before her bag hit the ground, her foot met his shin with force enough to evoke profanities. Freak may as well have been Superman and she a toddler for all the good it did. Putrid stench brought the sting of tears to her eyes as he grabbed both shoulders and shoved her into the front seat.

Scream damn you, scream. "You fucking bastard, get off me!" The strength in her voice came as a surprise, as did the new wave of adrenaline that pumped through her veins. Desperation guided her movements as she batted, kicked and successfully thwarted his efforts at getting a solid hold on anything other than her clothing. What had the self-defense class taught her? Crap, who could remember? Should've paid better attention.

Frenzied attempts at kneeing his groin had her awkwardly positioned, half in, half out of the car. Four kicks in, she found her target. The man wore a fearsome grimace as he doubled over, spit, and stumbled backwards in pain.

Pure evil flooded his bloodshot eyes.

Seizing the opportunity, Grayce lifted her legs at a feeble attempt to strike again. Her butt slid down the edge of the car seat and landed with a thud on unforgiving pavement, knocking the wind clean out of her lungs. Stunned and struggling to regain her bearings, she looked up in time to see a dirty, hairy-knuckled fist shoot straight for her nose. Except, it didn't make contact.

Playing out like a slow motion scene from an action movie, the perp was violently jerked back by the nape of his neck. Arms and legs flailed in front of him as he was lifted off the ground, eyes wide with disbelief. Tossed like a rag doll across the parking lot, he bounced off the chain link fence, wrapped around a street lamp and landed with a thud. His body twitched, then lay ragged and motionless, slumped in a heap on the cement.

Grayce fought to draw breath as her gaze traced the length of the figure towering with protective intent. Hmm, muscles and more muscles. Horrified and dazzled simultaneously, she stared into the face of the man she'd tried so hard to avoid.